SCOT OF PASSION

She set out to ruin the courtship, but the only one in danger of falling... is her.

THE MACKINTOSH CLAN
BOOK 8

SHONA THOMPSON

ABOUT THE BOOK

He was meant to be no match for her. Still, she never expected to meet her equal.

Lady Diana Macgillivray has mastered the art of evading suitors. Yet, if enduring a courtship means securing her sister's happiness, she'll do what she must.

Regardless of how infuriating... and tempting her indented is.

Forced by a lie, Lorne Davidson reluctantly goes to meet a possible bride. A quiet, agreeable lady he imagines. Instead, he gets Diana—stubborn, unpredictable, and impossible to ignore. But his family's future depends on the match... and this one lie never getting out.

All he has to do is convince Diana to accept him.

But games become dangerous when real feelings slip in. And when secrets come to light, desire may not be enough to hold them together, when trust is already broken.

AUTHOR'S NOTE

My lovely Reader,

Welcome to the captivating world of *The Mackintosh Clan series*, where each book unveils the journey of a different person in the Mackintosh family navigating life's challenges, both on the battlefield and in matters of the heart.

What makes this series truly special is that each book is crafted by a different author, bringing a unique perspective and voice to the captivating saga. I am deeply thankful to my esteemed colleagues and dear friends in the Scottish romance genre—*Fiona Faris, Lyla Rosewood, Juliana Wight, and Kenna Kendrick*—for embarking on this thrilling adventure with me.

This could never happen without them!

Join us as we journey through the enchanting landscapes of Scotland, where passion and danger collide, and love conquers all.

Get ready for an unforgettable adventure!

Warmest regards,

Shona

FAMILY TREE

My lovely Reader,

Before we delve into the tales of the Mackintosh siblings, take a moment to explore their family tree and to familiarize yourself with the role each character plays in the fictional world we've crafted for them.

Happy reading,

Shona

FAMILY TREE

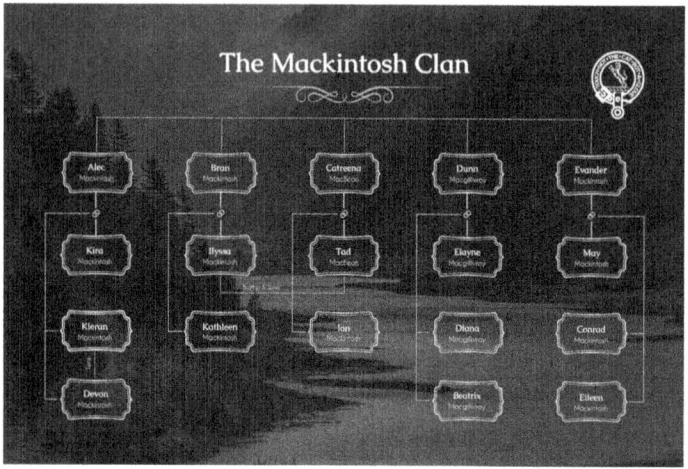

BONUS PROLOGUE

Two Months Before...

"I dinnae ken why I let ye talk me intae these bleedin' things," Lorne muttered. "Ye ken how much I hate it."

Gavin laughed. "Think of this as a way tae broaden yer horizons."

"Me horizons are broadened enough."

"Yer horizons dinnae extend past the lands of our clan."

"'Tis far enough fer me."

His cousin sighed. "One of these days, when ye are laird—if nae before—ye will need tae take a bride," he said. "Where are ye goin' tae meet a bride if ye dinnae look past our borders."

"There are plenty of suitable women within our clan."

Gavin scoffed. "Perhaps ye'd like tae be matched with Isla?"

Lorne pulled a face. "Isla? She's manlier than I am."

"Well, 'tis nae sayin' much really, but I think ye're startin' tae see me point."

Laughing, Lorne punched Gavin in the shoulder. "Bleedin' donkey."

They dismounted in the yard of Castle Magillivray and took it in for a moment. Music and laughter drifted out of the open doorway of the keep. The party was already in full swing. A pair of stable boys appeared and took their horses from them, leading them away to be watered and fed. Lorne shifted on his feet, pulling his breeches down, then tugging his black velvet doublet. He looked down at himself and frowned.

"I look like a fool," he muttered.

"Aye. But nae any more so than any other day."

Lorne grinned. "Dae ye take anythin' seriously?"

"I try tae avoid it if I can."

"Ye dae a good job of it."

"Thank ye," Gavin chirped. "I'm glad tae see me efforts dinnae go unnoticed."

His cousin was dressed in blue and red velvet and looked every bit as foolish as Lorne felt. Just when he thought it couldn't get worse though, it did. Gavin produced a pair of white masks and handed one over to him with a smile.

"Put this on," he said.

"I'm nae puttin' this on."

"'Tis a masked ball," Gavin said. "Ye have tae."

With a loud sigh, Lorne did as Gavin asked and tied the mask on. It covered the top half of his face, leaving nothing but his mouth exposed. If nothing else, at least nobody would be able to recognize him. That was the only positive Lorne could find in this. He did not know how he'd let his cousin talk him into this in the first place.

"Come," Gavin said.

Feeling as if he was on a death march, Lorne walked alongside Gavin. They mounted the steps and marched through the front doors of the castle. They passed masked men and women, laughing and acting like children as they ran up and down the corridors. Following the sound of the music, they passed a group of women, young and comely with tight fitting velvet gowns, who eyed them closely and approvingly as they passed.

"Ye see?" Gavin said. "Even ye should be able tae find a woman in a place like this. Maybe even a woman who can put up with ye're broodin' self."

Lorne huffed but said nothing. He was not looking for a woman of any kind. Marriage was not something he had given any thought to or had any desire for. He knew that eventually he would have to wed, it was inevitable. A laird was expected to marry and produce an heir. But Lorne would cross that bridge whenever he came to it. He certainly didn't expect he to cross that bridge while wearing velvet and a mask.

Gavin turned to him and grinned. "In a place like this, with women as fine as these roaming the corridors, I'd reckon ye can find a woman even yer faither would approve of."

Lorne scoffed. "I doubt it."

His father did not approve of anything Lorne did. He had been chasing his approval since he was a young boy, but nothing he did ever seemed good enough for the man. Lorne longed for his approval, wanted nothing more than to see respect in his father's eyes when he looked at him. But it never happened. It was not that his father was unkind or did not engage with him at all, but he was always somewhat aloof and cold, with an air of slight impatience when he was around him.

Gavin stopped walking, forcing Lorne to stop short as well. He put his hand on his shoulder and gave it a squeeze.

"Yer faither wants the best fer ye. And he believes in ye," Gavin said.

"He's got a funny way of showin' it."

"Uncle Tiernan is tough. Hard. He rides ye only because he's tryin' tae get the best out of ye because he ken it's in there," Gavin said, tapping on Lorne's chest. "Maybe ye dinnae find the woman of yer dreams here. 'Tis all right. But if naethin' else, cousin, then ye should have some fun tonight."

"Fun," Lorne muttered. "I couldnae tell ye what that is."

The word was as foreign on his tongue as the concept was. His father had never approved of fun. He did not believe in being frivolous or acting like children. He would most definitely not approve of dancing and wearing velvet and masks. That was not his way. Which was why it was not Lorne's way either, as he had been brought up that way and was trying so hard to mold himself into his father's image. He thought—hoped—that if he was more like him, the man would come to approve of him.

Gavin knew everything going through Lorne's heart and mind right then and nodded solemnly. They had talked about it endlessly and an expression of compassion momentarily showed in his features, but he swallowed it down and put a mischievous grin on his face.

"I'm sorry, lad," Gavin said. "But tonight is nae fer lamentin' those things we dinnae have. Taenight is fer drinkin', dancin', and behavin' like a fool."

"I'll have tae take lessons from ye on that last point."

Gavin laughed. "Then prepare tae study the master."

He let his cousin lead him to the castle's great hall. They stepped through the doors and into an entirely different world. The hall was brightly lit and music echoed off the stone walls. A group of musicians sat off in a corner, playing a lively tune as throngs of people danced and laughed. The air around them was redolent with the aroma of delicious foods and household servants bustled around carrying trays bearing cups of wine.

Gavin stopped one of the servants and plucked a pair of cups off her tray, then handed one of them to Lorne.

"Thank ye," Lorne said.

"'Tis only the beginnin'."

He plucked a pair of roasted meat pastries off a table and popped one into his mouth. His eyes rolled to the back of his head, and he made a sound that bordered on the indecent.

"That was amazin'," he said. "We need tae teach the kitchen staff back home tae make those things."

"I'll be sure tae get the recipe," Lorne muttered dryly.

"Come, cousin. Let us mingle."

Lorne sighed thought about running out, fetching his horse, and riding home. The only thing that kept him there was fearing what shame Gavin might bring down on their clan if he was left alone and unsupervised.

"Fine," Lorne said. "Let's go… mingle."

"Ye need tae loosen up," he said. "And just try tae pretend ye are having fun. If ye dae, who kens? Ye might have some by accident."

They skirted the edge of the hall, ducking and dodging the people dancing and running about. Lorne offered a smile to those he passed, but it felt false on his face. He was trying, pretending, but he wasn't having any fun. His cousin on the other hand, laughed and talked with everybody he met like they were old friends. People genuinely seemed to like Gavin, they gravitated toward him.

It was something Lorne had always envied about his cousin. That natural ability to connect with people. It was something he'd never been good at. He tended to keep people at an arm's distance.

Gavin gasped and grabbed Lorne by the shoulder. He stood close, but his eyes were elsewhere. Lorne tried to follow his cousin's gaze but couldn't see who or what he was looking at. He turned to look at him.

"What in the bleedin' hell has yer attention?" Lorne asked.

"Me future bride."

He laughed. "Yer future bride, eh?"

"Aye. Small, auburn hair, fair, creamy skin," he said. "She's the most exquisite creature I've ever seen and I must go speak with her."

"Then go and speak with her."

Gavin turned to a man standing next tae him. "Excuse me, good sir. The young woman with auburn hair in the green gown with the white mask runnin' about, dancin', with the most captivatin' smile. Ye wouldnae happen tae ken her name, would ye?"

The man chuckled. "Sounds like ye're describin' Beatrix Magillivray. Daughter of Laird Dunn Magillivray."

"Beatrix Magillivray," Gavin said with a note of wonder in his voice.

Lorne watched his cousin and saw the gleam in his eye he got when he was about to suggest they do something he knew would not end well. Gavin turned to him.

"Come, cousin," Gavin said. "We must go and meet me future bride."

Against his better judgment, Lorne let Gavin lead him through the crowd, seeking out the auburn-haired beauty that had captured his attention. Lorne shook his head.

"Naethin' good will come of this," he said.

"Think positive, lad. Think positive."

Lorne grimaced. He was positive nothing good would come of this.

CHAPTER ONE

March, 1715
Macgillivray Castle, Dunmaglass

Diana Macgillivray wanted to be anywhere but where she was. The grand ballroom was brightly lit, filled with music, and teeming with people, most of whom she didn't know, in elegant attire and masks. The tables against the far wall were laden with food, the aroma of a thousand different delicacies filling the air, and the mood in the room was fun and festive. Laughter and conversation filled the hall as people made merry, but to Diana it sounded like the buzz of a swarm of flies on a carcass.

She adjusted the mask on her face, grumbling under her breath. Her mother had forced her to wear the heavy black gown and a black and white mask. It was uncomfortable, warm, itchy, and she wanted nothing more than to go back to her bedchamber. She had no interest and even less use for frivolous balls. She would never understand why people seemed to love those kinds of festivities as much as they did.

"Ye dinnae look tae be havin' a good time."

The tall, lean man her mother had introduced her to, Laird Finley Munro, sauntered over to where she stood. He moved with a casual grace, the swagger of a man who was well-trained with a sword, and the arrogance of one who knew he was handsome and drew the eyes of every woman in the hall. His dark-blond hair was wavy and perfectly cut, but his green eyes were flat.

She watched as clusters of gown and mask-clad women huddled together, stealing glances at him. Finley leaned against the wall beside her, making a show of pretending not to notice the attention he was receiving, but Diana could see he was eating it up. He was aware of the stir he was causing and loved it. It was one of the reasons Diana didn't think he was anywhere nearly as handsome as he believed he was.

"Are ye nae havin' fun, me lady?" he pressed. "'Tis a fine ball."

"I'm nae one tae enjoy such frivolities."

"Nay? Then what dae ye enjoy?"

His feigned interest in her was tedious and tiresome. She knew enough about Finley Munro to know his biggest interest in his life was himself.

"I enjoy readin'," she said. "And betterin' me skills as a healer."

"A healer," he said. "I'd heard ye were a healer."

"Aye. People need tae be cared fer."

He shrugged. "I suppose. Nae by a castle lady, however."

Her lips curled downward as a sour expression stole over her face. His casual dismissal of the health and well-being of people lower than him turned her stomach. He took a sip of his wine, then turned to her.

"Dae ye ken who I am?" he asked.

"Aye. I ken who ye are, Laird Munro."

His smile was wide and predatory. "Aye. 'Tis right. And dae ye ken what I'm daein' here?"

"I'd imagine the same as everybody else here," she said. "Ye're here tae eat, drink, dance, and laugh at jests that arenae all that funny."

His chuckled was a deep rumble. "Ye dae have a sharp wit and sharper tongue, lass. I'd heard that about ye. Personally, I like a woman who isnae afraid tae speak her mind."

She turned to him, a cruel smirk playing across her lips. "Is that so?"

"Aye. 'Tis so."

"And if she has a thought or opinion that differs from yers?" she asked. "Would ye still like a woman who spoke her mind then?"

He shrugged and flashed her a smug grin. "Hasnae happened. I've found most women tend tae think much the same way I dae."

"Amazin', that."

"Aye. I thought so too," he replied. "I suppose most women see me as a logical and rational kind of man and that me opinions are sound. 'Tis hard tae disagree with that, eh?"

Hearing her mother's voice in her head, telling her to always be a proper lady, Diana resisted the urge to roll her eyes. The man's arrogance was trying. But despite her distaste, she managed to put a pleasant smile on her face.

"Aye, I suppose so," she said evenly.

As the man's eyes slid up and down her body, lingering on her full breasts, which were accentuated by the abomination of a gown she'd been forced to wear, Diana shuddered. Perhaps mistaking it for a rush of pleasure, Finley flashed her a wolfish smile.

"Ye didnae answer me question," he said.

"And what question was that, me laird?"

"Dae ye ken what I'm daein' here?"

"I assume ye received an invitation from me parents."

"Aye. But then, I receive many invitations tae many events. Most I dinnae go tae. I tend tae find most gatherings borin'."

"And why have ye graced us with yer presence then?"

"I came here thinkin' I might be able tae find somebody tae court," he said. "As laird of me clan, I'm expected tae marry and provide an heir."

Diana made a point of glancing at the knots of women all around the hall, most of whom weren't being particularly subtle about looking Finley's way.

"Well, it looks as if ye have yer choice," she said. "Ye've got quite the selection tae choose from, me laird."

His chuckle was a deep rumble in his chest. He never glanced at the women in the hall though, never taking his gaze off her.

"I'm rather particular about the sort of woman I'd be willin' tae take as me bride."

"I'm certain whoever ye select will be very fortunate tae have yer affection."

"Aye, she will be."

Diana suppressed another shudder but edged a couple of steps away from the laird, searching for a way not just out of this conversation, but out of this tiresome social obligation altogether. She glanced at her parents Dunn and Elayne, who sat upon the dais at the far end of the hall. They were engaged in conversation with a couple of their noble friends and didn't seem to be paying attention to her. As if her thought drew her mother's attention, though, she turned and locked gazes with Diana. She felt pinned to the wall and unable to move.

In a blur of red and white silks, Diana's younger sister, Beatrix, swirled in, laughing and smiling wide. She took hold of Diana's hand then turned to Finley.

"I hope ye dinnae mind me borrowin' me sister, me laird," Beatrix said with a giggle. "I need her help with somethin'."

Annoyance flashed across his features, but he quickly got himself under control and sketched a stiff bow. "Of course, Lady Beatrix."

Diana let her sister pull her through the whirling, dancing crowd, somehow narrowly avoiding crashing into the people. Beatrix pulled her behind the curtain and into a small room to the right of the dais where her parents sat. Diana pulled the curtain aside gently and caught sight of her mother looking this way and that, searching for her. She smiled to herself.

"Ye're welcome," Beatrix said.

She sighed. "Thank ye, Beatrix. Though tae be honest, I thought ye would have rather enjoyed seein' me squirmin' under that man's attention."

"Believe it or nae, sister, I dinnae want tae see ye sufferin'."

Beatrix and Diana were opposites in every meaningful way. Whereas Diana's hair was the color of honey and was usually in a braid, or pulled back like it was now, Beatrix's hair was a deep, rich auburn that she usually let spill free over her shoulders. Her eyes were dark and Beatrix's were a vibrant green. Even their body types were different. Diana was slender and lithe, her sister shorter in stature and lusciously curvy.

Their personalities were as different as their physical traits. Diana was quiet and thoughtful. She was reserved and preferred spending her time at study or plying her knowledge to help heal others. Beatrix was... wild. She was a vivacious girl with a personality larger than her stature. She laughed easily and often and seemed to make friends wherever she went. People genuinely seemed to like her sister while they seemed to see Diana as more of a curiosity.

Diana laughed. "'Twas torture tae be nice tae that man. I appreciate ye pullin' me away."

Beatrix grinned at her. "I cannae lie. I enjoyed seein' ye squirm a little bit. I only stepped in when ye seemed ready tae bolt yerself. Thought it might give ye some cover from Maither's wrath."

Her sister's consideration was surprising to Diana since they didn't have the warmest of relationships. Their differences in personality, as well as the different ways they saw the world around them, led to them frequently butting heads. Diana liked to say they spent more time at each other's throats than they did being sisters to each other. It was a never-ending source of consternation for their parents, who just wanted their daughters to get along. Diana didn't think that wish was going to be fulfilled. Not in this lifetime.

But every once in a while, Beatrix surprised her with a kind thought or gesture. This was one of those times, and like every other time it happened, Diana was taken aback and wasn't quite sure how to react. She cleared her throat and smiled.

"'Twas very kind of ye, Beatrix. Thank ye."

She flashed Diana a toothy grin. "'Twas nae all altruistic."

"Nay?"

Beatrix shook her head. "As the second daughter, I cannae be courted or marry until ye are married. We may nae always get on, but that daesnae mean I want tae see ye trapped in a horrible marriage tae a horrible man. I want ye tae be happy, Diana. And as that man is nae goin' tae make ye happy, which means ye'll only drag yer feet on marryin', the sooner we find somebody that makes ye happy, the sooner we can get ye married, and the sooner I can find a man of me own."

Diana laughed. It was very much Beatrix's logic. She had always been boy crazy and was looking forward to the day she was allowed to be courted. Self-serving or not, Diana appreciated her sister's intervention.

"And is there any particular man ye've got yer eye on?" Diana asked.

Beatrix's cheeks flushed and she smiled. "Aye. Come and see."

Her sister pulled the curtain back a bit and pointed to a man standing to the side of the hall. He was holding a cup of wine and his mask in his hand and was talking with a couple of women who giggled and fawned all over him. The man was tall and lean, athletic and well built. He moved with the same sort of casual grace Finley did, telling Diana he was a swordsman. His hair was sandy brown and tousled, and his light brown eyes sparkled with the same sort of mischief that glinted in her sister's eyes. They seemed like two sides of the same coin.

"He's handsome," Diana said. "What's his name?"

"I dinnae ken," she replied. "Nae yet. But I intend tae."

"Aye, well, ye better nae let Maither and Faither catch ye learnin' his name."

Beatrix giggled and cast a mischievous grin at her. "I'm very good at nae lettin' Maither and Faither catch me daein' anythin'."

"Beatrix!"

"What? I have tae be," she replied. "If I didnae sneak around, I'd never get tae have any fun. Nae so long as ye remain unmarried."

"Oh, so yer bad behavior is me fault."

"Well... aye. It is," she said with a laugh.

They laughed together in a way they hadn't since they were children. Diana knew it wouldn't last though. It never did. It wouldn't be long before they were at each other's throats for one thing or another again. But she would enjoy the peace and goodwill while it lasted.

"Ye're incorrigible, dear sister," Diana said. "Simply incorrigible."

A cheeky idea occurred to her, so she grabbed her sister's hand and pulled her out of the small antechamber.

"Where are we goin' then?" Beatrix said with a giggle.

"Come with me."

Feeling inexplicably emboldened, Diana marched her sister over to where the man she'd been eyeing was standing. When they were close enough, she gave Beatrix a small nudge with her elbow. Startled, her sister squeaked and dropped the lace and silk handkerchief she'd been holding. Diana watched the small square of cloth flutter and fall to the floor near the man's boots. He offered Beatrix a smile filled with warmth and bent down to pick it up for her.

"I believe ye dropped this," he said.

"Thank ye," Beatrix said in a soft, breathy voice. "I'm Beatrix."

"I'm Gavin, me lady. Gavin Davidson."

Their gazes were locked and the conversation between the two started to flow. They spoke so fervently, it was as if the entire room around them had fallen away, leaving just the two of them in it. Smiling to herself, Diana turned to leave, wanting to give them some time and privacy to get to know each other and ran straight into a large, burly man. She bumped the cup of wine in his hand, spilling it all over the front of her dress, drawing a gas from her.

Och, damn it!

"Apologies, me lady," the man said.

"Dae ye nae watch where ye're goin'?"

Diana raised angry eyes to the man and felt her breath catch in her throat. He was a head taller than her and was broad through the shoulders and chest. His dark hair was wavy and fell just to his shoulders. Although dressed in finery, the man was rugged and handsome with strong features, a smooth, tawny complexion, and pale blue eyes that burned with an intensity that sent a flutter through her heart. But then she noticed that he looked... amused. And anger took the best of her.

"Beg pardon, me lady. 'Twas an accident. I didnae mean tae—"

"Me gown is ruined!"

The fabric of her gown was soaked through, sticking uncomfortably to her skin, clinging to her curves in a way that was almost lurid. When she looked up again, she found the man eyeing her curiously, although she thought she could see desire as well. She felt her cheeks flush and the flutter of hummingbird wings in her heart. They stood there in silence for a moment, neither of them seeming able to find the words.

The air about them was filled with tension and the rest of the ball melted away. She no longer heard the laughter or the music. All she heard was her own breath and beating heart. The man was staring at her in a way she deemed inappropriate and Diana was appalled at herself because she sort of... liked it. She gave herself a shake, pulling herself out of the moment, as the sound of music and crowd around them rang in her ears once more.

The man licked his lips and straightened up. "Is there anythin' I can dae tae help?"

"I think ye've done enough."

Her cheeks still flushed and her heart still racing, Diana turned and fled rather than stand there in front of the man in a dripping wet gown. Instead, she dashed from the hall and sought refuge in her father's salon.

She moved quickly to the table and a dry cloth, which she dipped into the basin of water and dabbed at the wine that had been spilled on her gown. The door to the salon opened behind her. Assuming it was Beatrix, she turned around. The acidic remark about the oaf who'd run into her withered and died on her tongue when she found not her sister, but the oaf himself standing in the doorway. She swallowed the lump in her throat and quickly composed herself.

"I came tae see if ye were all right, me lady," he said.

"I'm fine fer havin' had a cup of wine dumped all over me."

She sniffed and glared at him coldly. A small grin flickered across his lips, stoking the flames of her indignation. How dare he laugh at her discomfort.

"Again, I apologize fer what happened," he said, his voice deep and resonant. "But if ye'd nae spun around so fast, ye might have seen—"

"Oh, so this is me fault?"

The man shrugged his broad shoulders. "Aye. At least partly."

"How dare ye!"

He laughed. "'Tis nae me fault ye werenae lookin' where ye were goin'."

Her face was hot, and she could not quell the tremor in her heart. There was something about being near the man that set her insides ablaze and made her stomach churn. She'd never had that sort of reaction to a man before and it was as confusing as it was infuriating. Although the corners of his mouth continued to curl upward, the man held up a hand, a gesture of peace.

"Forgive me, me lady. I dinnae mean tae laugh."

"Are ye sure about that?"

"Nae really. But it seems the right thing tae say."

She huffed and stared hard at the man. "Ye're an oaf."

"I've been called worse."

"I'm certain ye have."

The sparkle in his eye and the smile that crept across his face only made those strange, disconcerting feelings rampaging through her grow in intensity. Her heart pounded like she was running, and her legs trembled. Fearing they would give out beneath her and spill to the floor of the salon, Diana cleared her throat and patted her hair as she stood with her back rigidly straight, attempting to reclaim some bit of her dignity.

As they stood there staring at each other, Diana became even more aware of the way her body was reacting to him. In addition to the flutter in her belly and the heat in her face, she realized she was growing warmer and feeling a strange flutter in a different, lower part of her body. It was disconcerting. As his icy blue eyes burned into hers, she realized they were alone in the salon. And if her parents happened upon them… it would not be good.

"'Tis inappropriate fer us tae be here alone," she said.

"Aye. Probably."

"Definitely," she countered. "Ye need tae leave."

"I came tae help ye, seein's how it's half me fault ye're in here."

"I dinnae need yer help."

"Are ye sure about that?"

"Aye. I'm sure. Now, please leave."

He didn't move though, and continued staring at her, making that flutter in her belly all the more pronounced. Diana swallowed again but didn't seem able to control her insides. The man was having a strange effect on her and if she was going to regain control over herself, she knew she had to get away from him.

"Are ye goin' tae stand there or leave?" she demanded.

"Dae ye always obey the rules of what's right and proper?"

"Aye. I dae."

He smirked. "'Tis a shame. Slavishly followin' the rules all the time isnae always fun."

"'Tis nae about fun. 'Tis about what's right."

"I disagree—"

"Please... leave."

His gaze lingered on her for a moment longer before he flashed her another smile and nodded. Then, without another word, he turned and walked out of the salon, gently closing the door behind him. When he was gone, Diana leaned against the table and let out a long, deep breath she hadn't even realized she'd been holding.

She poured herself a glass of her father's whiskey and drank it down to steel her nerves, slow her racing heart. It took a couple of minutes, but she finally managed to regain her composure and let out a heavy sigh as she tried to banish images of the handsome, rugged man from her mind. As arrogant and annoying as he was, he'd had a profound impact on her that was unlike anything she'd ever experienced. And it was only then that she realized she'd never learned his name.

CHAPTER TWO

May, 1715
Macgillivray Castle, Dunmaglass

Diana stretched out in her bed, a small smile playing across her lips as she enjoyed the book in her hands. This was her element. Other than healing the wounds of others, this was where she felt most comfortable. She was a simple woman who enjoyed simple things. She despised elegant balls and fancy social gatherings. It was the one thing most of the men who tried to court her did not understand about her. And if they did not understand her, Diana had no desire to marry them.

Her parents were giving her some freedom in choosing her suitors. She was grateful to them for that. However, she knew if she continued to reject suitor after suitor, their patience with her would eventually run out and they would make the decision for her. It was a thought that sent a chill rushing down her spine. It wasn't that they would intentionally pick a bad man. It was just that she felt that nobody really knew her at all and that they might pick a man who was bad for her. It was a conundrum she had been grappling for some time.

Diana yawned and set her book aside. She wanted to sleep and push all thoughts of suitors and marriage out of her head. At least for a while. She knew once she woke, she would have to deal with them all again, as her mother would undoubtedly begin pestering her with a list of names of "suitable men" to court her. Of course, her idea of a suitable man differed greatly from Diana's. She knew the time was coming when she was going to have to find the least objectionable man from the list her mother offered.

With a heavy sigh, she reached for the oil lamp but quickly pulled her hand back at the thunderous crash in the corridor beyond her door. Her heart pounding in her chest, Diana jumped out of bed and grabbed her robe, quickly pulling it on as she dashed to the door. Her hand trembling, fearing what was happening, she pulled the door open and peeked outside. Rather than the soldiers from an invading army as she'd half-expected, she found her sister, Beatrix, crouching down, picking up the remnants of a shattered vase.

"What," she looked around and whispered, "the hell are ye daein', Beatrix?"

Her sister gave a start as Diana rushed over to her. "I—I bumped intae the table and knocked the vase over. Help me clean this up, Diana. Please."

"Where were ye?"

"I was… I was out."

"At this hour? Out doin' what?"

Beatrix's cheeks flushed and a small smile curled her heart-shaped lips, telling Diana exactly what her sister had been out doing. She'd been out with a lad. Of course, she had. Diana sighed. Given that her parents' bedchamber was just around the corner, she knew there was little to no chance they hadn't heard the crash in the corridor.

"I will fix this. We need tae get out of the hallway," Diana urged. "Maither and Faither will have heard ye break the vase fer certain—"

The sound of footsteps echoed around the corridor and sent a bolt of lightning through Diana's veins. The hair on the back of her neck stood on end as she stood up and turned around, unsurprised to see their parents, Dunn and Elayne, standing behind them, cross looks on their faces.

"What is all this?" their father, growled.

Diana knew their parents were with Beatrix than they were with her. It was yet another issue that contributed to their often-sour relationship. It wasn't Diana's fault, but her sister would hear none of it. Her sister blamed her, often accused Diana of trying to ruin her life. It couldn't have been further from the truth, but Beatrix believed it.

As angry as she was with her sister for her ridiculous accusations, some small part of Diana felt bad for Beatrix. She knew her sister was frustrated and only wanted to live her life... something she couldn't do while being forced to live in Diana's shadow. And it was a shadow that would only dissipate once she had married and had begun her life away from her family's home.

"'Tis me fault," Diana said. "I snuck out of me chambers tae fetch some sweetcakes from the kitchens. I bumped the table and Beatrix came out tae see what was happenin'. I'm sorry."

Her father was no fool though. His eyes shifted from her to Beatrix, his face tightening. Diana knew he saw right through her.

"Beatrix, is this true?" Dunn asked.

Her sister's eyes shifted to her then back to their father as she licked her lips. She nodded.

"Aye. 'Tis true," she squeaked.

"Then why are ye wearin' a dress and a cloak?" he demanded. "Daesnae seem like somethin' ye'd wear tae bed."

Diana and Beatrix exchanged a glance, their mouths open, neither of them seemingly able to form a coherent word. Their parents looked at them disapprovingly.

"In me salon," he growled. "Both of ye."

Beatrix stepped forward. "Faither—"

"Now."

Their parents turned as one, stalking down the corridor toward his salon expecting them to follow. Diana and Beatrix sighed and did. Their mother closed the door behind them when they stepped in. The chamber was cold, the fire having been banked long ago. Their father had already lit a couple of oil lanterns, casting the chamber in a dim, gloomy light. He shook out the match in his fingers then turned and crossed his thick arms over his broad chest and glared at them, his icy blue eyes glittering in the dim light.

"Now, what is this all about, girls?" he demanded. "What are ye daein' creepin' around the castle in the small hours?"

Diana racked her brain, trying to figure some way to cover for and protect her sister. Before she could say anything though,

Beatrix stepped forward and raised her chin, her eyes glittering with defiance.

"I took a walk through the grounds," she said. "With a lad."

Their mother's eyes widened, but their father's face darkened. Diana swallowed hard, not sure what to say to mitigate what was coming. She had long known her fascination with men would get Beatrix into trouble at some point, though she never expected her sister to open the floodgates like that. But her sister stood strong, her chin lifted, her face betraying no fear.

Diana held her breath, waiting for the coming explosion from her father. Instead, her mother put a gentle hand on his arm and some bit of silent communication passed between them. His jaw flexed as he gritted his teeth, but he gave their mother a small nod and stepped back, letting out a long breath and tried to compose himself. Their mother stepped over to Beatrix, standing in front of her, a look of compassion on her face.

"And who is this lad, Beatrix?"

"His name is Gavin. Gavin Davidson."

Their parents exchanged a knowing look, and Diana got the idea the name was familiar to them. It was only belatedly that she realized Gavin was the man Beatrix has been mooning over at the masked ball a couple of months ago.

"And what dae ye ken about this lad?" Elayne asked.

"I ken he's the second born son of Clan Davidson. And we exchange letters often," Beatrix said. "I ken that he's sweet. Smart. He writes well."

The way she spoke and the expression on her face told Diana her little sister was over the moon about this man. She could practically see hearts in her eyes as she described meeting him in secret.

She didn't see this situation between Beatrix and this Gavin man ending well for her baby sister. She was going to have her heart shattered like glass. But then, Diana thought it might be for the best. It was time Beatrix learned to be an adult, learned some lessons about life and about love. Maybe it would finally temper her childish enthusiasm for boys.

"And why have ye been sneakin' around behind our backs?" Dunn growled from where he stood across the room. "Why nae talk tae us about it?"

"Because ye never would have let me see him! Because of yer stupid bleedin' rule about Diana always havin' tae be with me," she howled. "Diana only ever wants tae sit in her chamber and read or go muckin' about in the mud fer her precious herbs. 'Tis like I cannae have a life if me sister daesnae have a life."

"Beatrix, love, 'tis nae that we dinnae want ye tae have a life," Elayne said gently. "But there's an order tae things. There's a way these things are supposed tae be done. And until yer sister is wed, ye cannae be courted. Tae dae it otherwise would be invitin' scandal."

"'Tis what I mean, Maither," Beatrix whined. "She is nae interested in bein' married."

Diana bristled at her sister's remarks. But she held her tongue because she could not really refute them. She had no interest in being wed. At least, not to any of the men her parents had been parading in front of her.

"What about Laird Munro?" Dunn asked. "Diana, ye've nae said nay tae him courtin' ye. As I understand it, he's very interested in ye. And he seems like a fine—"

Diana could hold her tongue no longer. "I'm nae interested in Laird Munro. Why would ye want me tae be interested in a man who allies with the English? A man who's arrogant and hungers fer power and naethin' more?"

Her mother turned to her. "Diana, he is a gentleman—"

"Tae yer face. But I had a chance tae talk tae him when ye werenae around and he was hardly a gentleman. He was arrogant and dismissive. He was condescendin' and cruel," Diana said as she shook her head. "Nay. I havenae said nay tae him because I didnae think I had tae. I didnae think ye'd see him as a suitable suitor."

Beatrix stamped her foot. "Dae ye see?" she cried. "She'll never marry. She'll reject every suitor ye deem fit. And she'll keep draggin' this out until I'm old and gray. Ye might as well lock me away and call me a spinster now. I'll never get tae be with Gavin because she'll never find anybody good enough for her."

"Stop whinin' like a bairn," Diana almost shouted. "Nae everythin' is about ye! I willnae marry because ye want me tae, Beatrix."

"Diana!" her mother snapped. "Hold yer tongue. There's nay reason tae be hollerin' at yer sister like that."

Diana fell silent but glowered at her sister who shot her a smug look. Elayne and Dunn exchanged another look, once again giving her the sense they were communicating without words. It was a gift that couples who'd been married as long as they had seemed to possess and one, despite her sister's words, Diana longed to have with somebody. She thought her parents had the ideal relationship. Her father valued her mother, sought her advice and counsel and truly took her words into account before making any decisions. That was the sort of relationship she wanted to have. It was also the sort of relationship she knew she'd never have with any of the men they had paraded before her.

"All right, Beatrix. We'll allow ye tae see this Gavin lad," she said. "But only if he brings his braither, the first-born son of Laird Davidson with him. From what I ken he's nae married yet. Ye can get tae ken them both taegether. And ye'll only ever be in Gavin's presence if his braither and Diana are there as well."

"Maither, Faither. 'Tis nae fair," Beatrix whined.

"Those are our terms," Elayne said.

"Aye. Clan Davidson is an ally of ours and a match between Diana and their first-born son would be beneficial fer all," Dunn said.

Beatrix turned to Diana, her eyes burning with something akin to desperation and anger. Diane looked back at her sister with a cool, frosty gaze. Beatrix was behaving like Diana owed her something. She did not. But thanks to the social norms being enforced by their parents, Beatrix's future truly was beholden to Diana's whims. She couldn't be courted until Diana had agreed to marry. As much freedom as their parents had given them to choose their suitors—a rarity, to be sure—that was the one norm they strictly adhered to.

"Please, Diana," Beatrix begged. "I love him. I dinnae want tae lose him."

Perhaps making this sacrifice would improve her relationship with her sister. She really did want to be on good terms with Beatrix. But she wasn't sure how it was going to help since she already knew this firstborn son of Laird Davidson was, more than likely, not going to be somebody she would be interested in marrying. The fact that he hadn't offered himself up as a suitor already made her question whether he even had interest in courting her, which immediately made Diana uninterested in being courted by him.

But perhaps she could make Beatrix happy, for at least a little while. And perhaps, allowing her to see Gavin would somehow bring them closer together.

"Fine," she said. "All right. "I'll meet this man fer her sake."

Beatrix threw her arms around her waist and thanked her profusely. Diana had to keep from rolling her eyes. But at least she'd make her sister happy.

At least for a little while.

CHAPTER THREE

"Ye cannae be serious," Lorne said. "Ye seriously cannae be serious!"

His cousin and the captain of his guard Gavin winced but said nothing as he turned his eyes away. Lorne guided his horse down the path into the village that lay along the Spey River, one of the final stops on his monthly tour. Knowing his father liked to be informed about the demeanor and needs of the villages around the castle, Lorne had taken it upon himself to check in with the people of the clan every month and report back to his father what he had learned. It was just one of the ways he had tried to gain his father's favor and approval. Something he seemed to have been chasing since he was a child and often wondered if he would ever actually attain, or if it would forever remain just beyond his reach.

"Gavin? Please tell me yer jestin' with me," he pressed.

Gavin turned to him, a sickly look on his face and grimaced. "I wish I was jestin' with ye—"

"What in the bleedin' hell were ye thinkin'?"

"I didnae thinkin' things would turn out this way," he said. "I thought it was just a bit of fun. I never expected tae feel this way."

"Bleedin' hell," Lorne muttered. "What did ye tell this lass?"

Gavin frowned and couldn't meet Lorne's eyes, telling him that whatever tale he had spun for the girl was even worse than anything he'd been imagining.

"Gavin?" he pressed. "Out with it."

"I told her I was yer younger braither," he said quietly. "Yer younger braither and Laird Tiernan's second born son."

Lorne ran a hand across his face, trying to swallow down the lump of anger and disgust that had bubbled up into his throat. Gavin turned to him, his expression inscrutable.

"Come on now, ain't ye ever made somethin' up tae impress a lass?" he asked.

"Nay," Lorne replied coldly. "I havenae."

Gavin bowed his head and lowered his gaze again. "Of course, ye've nae. I sometimes forget that ye're always perfect."

"Oh nye. Ye're nae goin' tae turn this around on me. Ye're the one who lied, nae me. This has nothin' tae dae with me and everythin' tae dae with ye tellin' tales."

He sighed heavily. "I didnae—"

"I ken. Ye didnae mean tae. It just happened. I've heard it before, Gavin."

"Nay. I was goin' tae say that I didnae expect tae fall fer this girl. But I did. I love her. And she loves me back—somethin' else I wasnae expectin'."

"Bleedin' hell," he muttered.

Lorne's mood was as dark and stormy as the sky overhead as they rode toward the village. He had enough to deal with on his own without having to add Gavin's stupidity on top of it all. He had done some ridiculous things before. But never something so outlandish as to tell a woman he was a Laird's son rather than the captain of the household guard that he was.

"Why'd ye dae it, Gavin? What's wrong with tellin' her ye're the captain of the guard? 'Tis an honorable position," Lorne asked.

He pulled a face. "What's more likely tae impress a lass? Tellin' her ye're a household guard? Or that ye're the son of a laird?"

Lorne rolled his eyes again and exhaled noisily as they entered the village. One of the young stable boys rushed out to them as they dismounted, eager to please. Lorne handed him their reins, then tousled the boy's hair and handed him a couple of coins.

"Make sure they're well-watered and fed, lad," he said.

"Aye, Maister Lorne. I'll take good care of 'em."

"I ken ye will, lad. Thank ye."

As the boy led their horses away, Lorne tried to calm himself down. He knew Gavin was a bit of a scoundrel, but he wasn't normally so foolish, and he was certain he hadn't intended to fall in love with this girl. It didn't make what he'd done any less reckless, but Lorne was certain it hadn't been something he'd planned out.

"What is this lass's name?" Lorne asked.

"Beatrix," he replied. "Beatrix Macgillivray."

He sighed. "Ye fell in love with the laird's daughter? The one ye met at the ball?"

"'Twas nae me plan. But… aye."

"Bleedin' wonderful."

The situation got deeper and worse with every passing moment and Lorne had no idea what he was going to do about it. As he studied Gavin though, he could tell there was more to the story than the man was saying. He could tell by the way he kept shifting on his feet and refused to meet his eyes. It wasn't just embarrassment over what happened, there was something more.

Before he could question Gavin further though, Lorne noticed an older woman with white hair and a bowed back up ahead of them struggling with a cart full of goods. He started over to the woman, his glance back at Gavin telling him he expected the man to come along. He did. Lorne stepped to the woman and offered her a warm smile.

"Allow me, ma'am," he said.

"'Tis very kind of ye, Maister Lorne. Thank ye."

"'Tis me pleasure."

Lorne pushed the cart for the woman, escorting her to her home. Once they were there, he and Gavin unloaded the cart for her. When they were done, she took them both by the hand.

"Thank ye, lads," she said. "'Tis very kind of ye."

"Of course. We're happy tae help."

"Would ye stay fer supper?"

"I'd love tae," Lorne said. "But we've still got much work tae dae."

"Next time then," she said.

"Aye. Next time."

They left the old woman's home and made their way around the village, speaking with the people about their concerns. Lorne listened carefully and committed some to memory to present to his father later. All the while, Gavin stalked along beside him quietly, the tension building in the air between them. Truthfully, Lorne was glad to have the distraction speaking with the villagers to help take his mind off his cousin's misadventure.

But eventually, Lorne ran out of people to talk to. He'd addressed everything he could and promised to bring what he couldn't do to his father for a resolution. The sun was slipping toward the horizon when they reclaimed their horses and got back on the road to the castle. Lorne could feel Gavin watching him, the awkward tension between them seeming to grow. As he stared at the road ahead of them, a question occurred to him.

He turned to Gavin. "'Tis been two months since ye told this lie," he said. "Why are ye tellin' me about this bleedin' nonsense now?"

Gavin stared at the back of his horse's neck and muttered something so low, Lorne couldn't make it out. He gave his cousin a moment to repeat himself. He didn't.

"I didnae hear."

He sighed. "I want tae court Beatrix."

"All right. Ye're a free man. Ye dinnae need me permission tae dae that."

He cringed, sending Lorne's heart plummeting into his belly. Whatever it was Gavin was holding back was about to be brought into the light—and whatever it was, Lorne was not going to like one thing about it.

"Gavin? What is it? What arenae ye tellin' me?"

"If I want tae court Beatrix proper, her parents are demandin' that somebody court their elder daughter," he said. "Only when she has a proper suitor will they let Beatrix have one."

Lorne frowned. He failed to see what any of that had to do with him. It wasn't long though, before the reality of what Gavin was saying sunk in. He turned to his cousin, eyes wide, shaking his head vigorously.

"Oh nay. Ye cannae think that I'd go and court somebody I dinnae ken just so ye can court somebody ye deceived intae lovin' ye in the first place."

"Cousin, it'd mean the world—"

"Find somebody else."

"Oh," Gavin sniffed. "Dae ye ken any other proper, firstborn sons who might be able tae court the lass?"

"'Tis nae me problem, 'tis yers. Ye lied tae the girl, 'tis on ye tae figure out how tae wriggle out of yer fairy tales if ye want tae court her."

Just up ahead of them stood the Silver Scale, the oldest tavern in the clan's lands. He and Gavin had a tradition every time they made the loop of stopping for a cup of ale and a bite to eat. But he was so frustrated with his cousin that he didn't feel like doing anything other than going home, so he hesitated for a second.

Yet with a sigh, Lorne steered his horse to the tavern, and they dismounted as usual, tying their horses off, then walked toward the front door.

They walked into the tavern and took their usual table in the corner on the far side of the room. It gave them a clear, unobstructed view of all the tables and the front door. If somebody was coming for them, they would know long before they got to them. As they settled into their seats, the barmaid brought them large cups of ale and a platter of roasted meats and warm, crusty bread. Once she was gone, they dug into the platter, eating and drinking in silence.

Gavin couldn't truly believe he would agree to court a woman, just so he could. His cousin had always been bold, but that bordered on the outlandish, even for him. As he watched Gavin though, saw the way he was still avoiding his gaze, and not saying much, Lorne knew there was yet still more to the story than he was concealing.

He took a drink and set his cup down and leaned forward. "Look at me, cousin."

Gavin reluctantly raised his gaze and Lorne held it firmly for a moment, silently impressing upon him that the time for games was not over.

"Ye're goin' tae tell me the whole and complete story without leavin' a single thing out," he said. "And ye're goin' tae tell me now."

Gavin winced as if Lorne had just struck him. The sinking feeling in the pit of his belly opened into a yawning chasm as he got the feeling the situation was even worse than what he'd been picturing in his mind.

"Yer faither may already ken about it all," Gavin squeaked. "And far from thinkin' ye a disappointment, he thinks it's the smartest thing ye've ever done."

"What are ye talkin' about? What's the smartest thing I've ever done?"

"Tryin' tae arrange a marriage alliance with a clan like that Macgillivrays."

Lorne's eyes nearly popped out of his head and Gavin recoiled in his chair as if preparing to be punched in the mouth. And based on the way this conversation was going, Lorne couldn't promise it wouldn't happen. He was certainly beginning to feel like it.

"Why is me faither thinkin' about a marriage alliance with the Macgillivrays?"

"It could be because when Beatrix was caught out, she may have mentioned tae her faither that she was bein' courted by the son of a laird. And maybe Laird Macgillivray penned a letter tae yer faither invitin' us tae his castle tae meet with his daughters. And maybe, yer faither, confused by the letter, might have heard a suggestion that Laird Macgillivray simply mixed up the names and what they're really askin' is fer ye tae meet with their eldest daughter so ye may begin' courtin' her?" Gavin said, wincing with every word.

Lorne sat back in his chair feeling like he'd just been punched in the stomach. "Bleedin' hell. Please tell me this is all a jest. This cannae possibly be real. Me Faither thinks I'm a disappointment already without ye adding tae it, Gavin."

"Please, Lorne. Come with me tae Castle Macgillivray—"

"I've nay interest in marryin'. I certainly have nay interest in marryin' somebody I dinnae ken just tae pull yer backside out of hot water," he angrily cut him off. "Ye made this mess. Ye find a way tae fix it but keep me out of it."

He frowned. "But yer faither is already expecting that ye'll be courtin' the Macgillivray lass."

"Then I suppose ye're goin' tae have tae tell him the truth of it all, eh?"

"Please, cousin. I love Beatrix. I love her."

"I'm nae goin' tae—"

"Cousin, I'll never get tae be with her if ye dinnae dae this fer me," Gavin countered. "Nobody's sayin' ye have tae marry this woman. Ye dinnae even have tae court her fer real. Just… put on a good show."

Lorne sighed and sat back in his chair, taking a long swallow of his ale, trying to wash the foul, bitter taste out of his throat.

"Me faither thinks it's a good idea, eh?"

Gavin nodded. "Aye. He thinks it's a good idea. He's proud of ye fer comin' up with it."

His father had never been generous with the praise or compliments. Hearing that he thought it was a good idea and that he was proud of him for coming up with it made him want to hold onto that faint bit of praise—even if none of this was his idea. He'd always had trouble saying no to his cousin. And he had to admit, as terribly messy as this whole situation was, it was kind of romantic. Gavin had never been one who seemed to want to commit to a woman and now, there he was, wreaking havoc in everybody's life for one.

Lorne sighed and ran a hand over his face, taking another moment to think things over. "Maybe there's a way I can solidify the alliance with the Macgillivrays without havin' tae marry their daughter," he muttered.

"Now ye're thinkin'," Gavin said, beaming.

"Ye're goin' tae owe me, cousin."

"Of course, I will—"

"I mean, really owe me fer forcin' me tae spend a week or two with a woman I'm sure will be borin', homely, and more concerned with the silk ribbons in her hair than anythin' I'm interested in."

"I will owe ye me life."

"Bleedin' right ye will."

Gavin grinned. "It could always be worse, cousin. Ye could be spendin' time with that shriekin' harpy who spilled wine on ye at the ball where I met Beatrix."

Lorne scoffed. "I'd nae thought about that harpy since that night. She was insufferable."

"Oh? Could have fooled me," he said. "Ye've certainly talked about her a lot fer a man who's nae given her a second thought."

"Shut it, donkey," he said. "And drink. We have plans tae make."

CHAPTER FOUR

The sky was black as night and the rain poured down in sheets, which fit Lorne's mood all too well. He still couldn't believe he'd agreed to that farce. But when he turned to Gavin, who rode beside him, and saw the smile on his face, he couldn't hold on to his anger. His cousin's demeanor had been decidedly upbeat in recent days. Indeed, he'd been happier than Lorne could ever recall seeing him. It was the only thing that made him feel good about this whole fiction.

Although, he did wonder—and worry—about how this all might play out, given that this relationship he sought with this girl, Beatrix, was built upon a lie. She would eventually come to realize that he wasn't the son of a laird, but the nephew of one instead. Being the captain of a household guard was a noble position, but he knew it was not fitting for the daughter of a laird, like Beatrix. He feared what might happen when the truth finally came to light. And it would.

As they crested a small rise, Lorne spotted Castle Macgillivray just ahead in the distance and felt his stomach lurch. This fantasy Gavin had woven was becoming all too real. He turned to his cousin and frowned. Lorne was soaked through to the bone. His cloak, clothing, and even his boots were wet and heavy. But his cousin was smiling and didn't seem to be noticing the rain at all. He seemed to be living in his own ray of sunshine. Gavin turned to him, his smile seeming to widen even more.

"'Tis a beautiful day isnae it, eh?" Gavin asked.

Lorne frowned. "Have ye thought about how all this ends, cousin? When she finds out who ye really are, how dae ye see this playin' out?"

His smile wavered for a moment, but he shook his head, seeming to be pushing all the dark thoughts out of his mind now that the castle, and the woman he loved who he was within, were in sight. It wasn't long before that smile and lovesick look crept across his face again.

"I havenae thought that far ahead, tae be honest," he said. "I guess I'll have tae figure that out as we go, eh?"

"Wonderful," Lorne groaned.

"'Tis too late fer us tae turn back now though, given yer faither has already accepted the invitation fer ye tae court their daughter."

Lorne's stomach churned and he was struggling to fight off the waves of nausea that battered his insides. He could not believe he was there, caught up in Gavin's idiocy. That he'd let his desire to please his father and gain the man's approval lead him to the doorstep of a woman he did not know so her could pretend to court her. And Gavin's giddy optimism that somehow, everything was going to work out just fine only made him more nervous, knowing there was no chance in the world this would end well for any of them.

The rest of the ride was made in a sullen silence, at least on Lorne's part. His cousin sang an upbeat song about love the entire way. It was perhaps even more annoying than the constant deluge of rain. They rode beneath the portcullis in the curtain wall, then through the yard and were just beginning to dismount when the doors to the castle flew open. A small army stepped out—the household staff along with a tall, striking man and woman whom he assumed were Laird and Lady Macgillivray.

"Welcome tae our home," Laird Macgillivray called. "We are honored tae have ye here."

"Thank ye fer yer hospitality. 'Tis our honor tae be here," Lorne called back.

"Please, come inside where it is warm and get out of this miserable weather, eh?" Lady Macgillivray beckoned warmly.

As the Laird and Lady's retinue turned and walked back into the castle, a small, but striking young woman with thick auburn curls, eyes as green as emeralds, and a smile as wide as Gavin's came flying out, heedless of the falling rain or the mud she was running through. She threw herself at his cousin and he scooped her up, embracing her tightly as they spun around, laughing with one another.

Lorne's eyes drifted to the sallyport, where another woman stood, cloaked in shadows. It was too dim for him to see her clearly, but she seemed slender and lithe. Four men in livery and cloaks bustled out of the castle and dashed over to them, a pair of them taking their horses to the stables and the other pair taking their bags and disappearing inside.

"Ye both are soaked through tae the bone," Beatrix, Lorne supposed, said with a giggle. "Come inside where it is warm and dry."

She took Gavin by the hand and pulled him in, both of them giggling like fools. Shaking his head to himself, Lorne walked up the stairs that led to the sallyport and got his first glimpse of the woman he was there to pretend to court. She was stunning and when his eyes fell upon her, Lorne's breath caught in his throat. She was also somehow... familiar. He would have said he'd met her somewhere before, but he knew that wasn't true. Even still, there was something about her that rang the bells of familiarity in his head.

The woman was elegant with soft, delicate features, hair the color of gold that was tied back in a braid that fell over her shoulder, and eyes a dark, rich shade of brown that were bottomless. Her bow-shaped lips were full and red, contrasting with her soft, velvety skin, which was the color of cream. She wore a simple dress that was unadorned, made of wool, rather than silk. The dress, rather than making her seem plain and unadorned herself, actually made her even more beautiful to him. She was a woman who didn't need finery to make herself look like royalty.

"I'm Lorne Davidson, me lady. It's a pleasure tae make yer acquaintance, " he said with a polite bow.

She didn't speak or move for a long moment, save for her eyes, which moved up and down, taking him all in, assessing him. The rain had made a mess of him, and he could see in her eyes that she was unimpressed. It was a reaction he was familiar with. She was not the first woman he'd encountered who seemed to believe she could assess him, and his worth, with naught but a single glance. She may not dress like royalty, but she had the cold gaze of one.

"Apologies fer me appearance," he said. "'Tis a bit of rain out. Perhaps ye'd noticed."

The corners of her mouth flickered with what appeared to be a grin, but she quickly got herself back under control. She tilted her head and seemed to be staring at him from a different angle. In her eyes though, he could see that she too, saw something familiar in him.

"Ye're Diana?" he said.

"Aye, I am. And ye're the man who ruined me dress with a glass of wine and laughed."

Lorne opened his mouth to respond but found no words. Not that she gave him a chance. With a flip of her braid and a roll of the eyes, Diana turned and walked back into the castle, leaving him standing alone in the sallyport. Lorne grumbled to himself as he stalked inside after her.

After he and Gavin had been shown to their rooms to get cleaned up and change into some dry clothing, they made their way down to the great hall. A fire roared in the oversized fireplace on the far side of the room, casting off waves of heat. Lorne made his way over to it and let the warmth leech into his bones. He had been so wet, cold, and miserable, feeling the heat washing over him was curative.

Beatrix and Gavin stood close by, whispering and giggling to each other like a couple of besotted children. Lorne tried to hold on to his anger but seeing the smile on his cousin's face made him feel as warm inside as the warmth being cast off by the flames. Diana stood nearby as well, holding a cup of wine, and stared into the fire, the expression on her face telling

Lorne she didn't want to be there any more than he did. Like him, she also seemed bound by duty to be there.

Lorne cleared his throat. "Ye... ye look lovely."

A pained sigh passed her lips. "Thank ye."

She continued staring into the flames, seeming to be lost in her own thoughts. Or perhaps she was plotting her escape from the hall.

"So," Lorne said. "Did ye get the wine out of yer gown?"

He grimaced as the words came out of his mouth, knowing just how lame the question sounded. But the air between them was thick with tension and he knew he had to say something. If he was to pretend to court her, he had to be able to converse with her. But when she turned her dark-eyed gaze to him and he saw the sheer contempt it held, Lorne found himself wishing he hadn't said a word. Or had at least asked a better question.

"Nay," she said coldly. "I had tae throw it out."

"Dinnae listen tae her," Beatrix said. "The wash women worked a miracle and that gown is hangin' in her wardrobe right now."

Diana turned a furious glare at her sister, but Beatrix was already lost in Gavin's eyes once more. She snorted and stared down into her cup of wine.

"Again," Lorne said. "I apologize fer bumpin' intae ye at the ball."

"Oh. So ye admit 'twas yer fault then, eh? All these months later?"

Lorne felt his cheeks flush as the anger began to burn in his belly. "Nay. I was bein' polite," he said. "Ye're the one who wasnae watchin' where ye were goin'. If we're speakin' plainly, ye're the one who bumped intae me. Ye spilled the wine all over yerself."

"Wait," Gavin said. "This is who ye spilled wine all over at the ball?"

"She bumped intae me," Lorne huffed. "She did it tae herself. Were ye nae listenin'?"

Diana raised her cup and took a drink of her wine, but not before Lorne had seen a small smile flickering across her lips. The more flustered he got, the more amused she seemed to be. Not wanting to give her the satisfaction, Lorne tried to swallow down his frustration and put on the most pleasant, charming smile he could muster. Before he could say another word though, the doors to the hall opened and the girls' parents strode in.

Tall and broad with hair so fair it was almost white and an imperious blue-eyed gaze, Dunn Macgillivray, father to Diana and Beatrix, wore dark breeches and a blue velvet doublet with silver scrollwork up the sleeves and around the collar, knee-high boots and a dark blue cape. A ghastly-looking white scar, thick and jagged, cut across his face, running from the scalp to his jaw. Even at his age, he still moved with the easy grace of a swordsman. Between that and the scar, Lorne knew the man had seen his share of battle. He was still formidable.

Elayne, mother to the girls, shared Beatrix's auburn locks, but had Diana's dark eyes, full, bow-shaped lips, and smooth, supple skin like both of her daughters. She was petite, with delicate features and a look of fragility about her. But Lorne could tell by the way she caught and held his gaze she was anything but. He got the sense that beneath that delicate exterior was the heart and ferocity of a lion. Which, of course, reminded him of Diana.

The doors at the other end of the hall banged open and an army of servants came flooding in carrying trays heaped with food. The hall was instantly filled with an array of mouth-watering aromas that made his stomach rumble. The staff laid the elegantly set table. The fact that they were there under false pretenses made Lorne feel all the worse about it.

"Faither. Maither," Beatrix exclaimed as she dragged Gavin over to them. "Let me better present ye. This is Gavin Davidson. Gavin, these are me parents, Laird Dunn and the Lady Elayne."

"Me laird, mc lady," Gavin said. "'Tis wonderful tae meet ye both."

Dunn and Elayne looked at him coolly, and Gavin cast a nearly panicked glance at him, silently asking Lorne to pull their attention away from him. With a small sigh, he stepped over bowed to them courteously.

"Me laird, me lady, I am Lorne Davidson," he said. "Son of Laird Tiernan. 'Tis truly a pleasure tae meet the both of ye."

They both favored him with a warmer smile than they'd given his cousin. Laird Dunn gripped his forearm in the warrior's embrace and gave him a nod. He turned and inclined his head as he took Elayne's hand and placed a respectful kiss on the back of it. If there was one thing he'd learned from his father, it was proper manners.

"'Tis a pleasure tae meet ye as well, Lorne," Elayne said.

"Aye. And I see ye've already met our daughter, Diana," Dunn said, his voice deep and gruff.

Lorne cut a glance at her and felt his stomach lurch. Despite her less-than-pleasant demeanor, she was the most beautiful woman he'd ever seen. She stared at him, her gaze cool and detached.

"Aye," he said. "We actually met once before. At yer masked ball."

"Oh, aye," Dunn said, his chuckle booming around the hall. "'Twas a fine evenin', that."

"Aye. 'Twas very fine," Lorne agreed.

"All right," Beatrix said. "I'm sure the lads are famished. Let's eat then, eh?"

CHAPTER FIVE

"Would ye care fer some of the wonderful meats?" he asked brightly. "Yer kitchen staff is absolutely fantastic."

Diana didn't even bother turning to him when she sniffed and said, "Nay. Thank ye."

From the corner of her eye, she saw a small frown flicker across the man's lips as he set the tray he'd offered her down. It was petty, but it made her grin to herself. Diana did not want the man getting comfortable in her home. And she wanted to throttle her sister for sitting him next to her. Beatrix sat across from her, too wrapped up in Gavin to even notice. Diana knew her father expected her to be open to being courted by the oaf seated next to her. He thought it was a good match, especially since it meant gaining an ally like Clan Davidson.

But she had no desire to talk to Lorne Davidson, let alone be courted by him. The man was ruggedly handsome, she had to give him that. His dark chestnut-colored hair framed the strong jaw and sharp features of a face that was golden brown, as if he spent much of his time outdoors. The man's eyes were his most distinctive feature. As much as it pained her to admit, the icy shade of blue was captivating. It was easy to get lost in them, which was one reason she was doing her best to keep from looking at him.

Lorne cleared his throat. "Ye have a lovely home, me laird and lady."

"Oh, thank ye," Elayne said.

"I understand yer lands are prosperous as well," Dunn said.

Lorne nodded. "Aye. the soil is fertile and the land is good fer farmin' and raisin' animals."

"Our lands are nae quite as fertile as yers," Dunn said. "But we do have plenty of woods and a thrivin' timber trade."

"Aye. Me faither says ye also have some terrific smithies."

"Ah yes," Dunn said, seemingly pleased. "Our smithies dae very good work."

Diana listened to Lorne laugh, talk, and carry on with her parents like they were old friends. Beatrix and Gavin were sitting close, lost in their own conversation as if the rest of the world around them had ceased to exist long ago. They simply whispered and giggled to each other as if they were the only two people in the entire world.

She knew the longer she took to settle on a match for herself, the longer Beatrix would have to wait for Gavin. And part of her wondered how long the man would wait for her sister. Men had notoriously short attention spans and she didn't know if Gavin's seeming devotion to Beatrix would last if he had to wait a year for her hand. Or two. Or longer. As devoted to her as he seemed to be right now, would that affection continue to flourish if they were forced to wait to be together? Diana didn't know. But she wasn't overly optimistic about Beatrix's chances.

The meal dragged on interminably. Lorne tried to engage her in conversation a number of times and it was all Diana could do to mask her utter indifference. She replied to him in the fewest number of words she could without being considered rude. It wasn't that she did not think he was handsome. He was quite striking, and if she was being honest, he was quite cleveras well. He intrigued her. But she did not want to marry anybody. Not even a man as dashing as he seemed, so she feigned her indifference. She was no doubt going to hear about her behavior later.

"The meal was wonderful," Beatrix announced as she jumped to her feet. "I think we should retire tae the drawing room tae play some games, eh?"

Their parents got to their feet. "Ye head tae the drawing room, we have other matters tae attend tae," Dunn said. "Feel free tae enjoy some time taegether. It sounds like a wonderful idea."

Diana saw her opportunity to escape and got to her feet, starting to excuse herself, but her mother shot her a glance that immediately made her stop.

Diana knew her mother's glares well enough to know not to try anything else. With one last withering look at her, their parents turned and left the hall.

"Come, sister," Beatrix said. "And boys. Let's go play games."

It was a silly, childish thing to suggest, but Gavin looked like he thought it was the best idea in the world and Lorne wore a small, bemused grin on his face.

When they walked into the drawing room, the household staff was already busy getting the fire going and laying refreshment out on the table for them. When they were done, they quickly bowed and left the room. Predictably, Beatrix and Gavin dropped onto the sofa in the far corner of the room and lost themselves in each other rather than start up a game. It annoyed Diana since it had been her idea to begin with. Beatrix had probably suggested it knowing their parents would decline so she could have some time alone with Gavin out from beneath their eyes.

Diana sighed as she stood in the center of the room, contemplating leaving. She knew though, her mother would hear of it —likely from Beatrix herself—and stripe her hide for being impolite to the man who had come to court her. She knew her parents were keen on forging an alliance with Laird Davidson and although she didn't know all the ins and outs of it, she had heard enough over lunch to know that both clans would benefit from such an arrangement. It was a realization that turned her stomach.

Was there a way they could work an alliance without her having to get married to Lorne? What if they found a different way for everybody to get what they wanted? But she knew that for Beatrix it would not be good, since her sister's courting and marriage depended upon her getting married.

Her relationship with Beatrix had pained Diana for a very long time and all she wanted was to make her sister happy. She longed for the sort of relationship where the sisters could be confidants, but they were such different people with such opposite interests and personalities that Diana had never known how to bridge that gap between them.

It was why she had agreed to this ruse in the first place. She thought maybe, if she showed Beatrix she was trying to be mindful of her happiness, the first planks of that bridge might be built between them. What she hadn't expected was to find the man who'd accompanied Gavin to be so handsome and intriguing, and she didn't exactly know what to do with herself.

She knew she couldn't afford to let herself give in to those strange, foreign feelings. She didn't understand them, which scared her. She had never felt the gossamer wings of a butterfly brushing the inside of her heart around a man, or the sudden churn in her belly. It was… alarming.

As she looked around the room, she turned to see Lorne pour himself a cup of wine then sit down at the table in front of her father's chess board. If she was going to find a way to make an alliance without marriage, thus perhaps preserving her sister's courtship with Gavin and making her happy, she was going to have to talk to Lorne. She was going to have to find a way to not just get along with him but convince him that making the pact with her father while not requiring her hand in marriage would be better for both of them. It was a tall task, but she had to find a way.

Lorne looked up as she sat down across from him. He took a drink of his wine, eyeing her over the rim of the cup as a long, awkward moment stretched out between them.

"Dae ye play?" he finally asked.

"Aye. A little," she replied. "Dae ye?"

"A little."

Diana offered him a small smile, the first genuine smile that had crossed her lips in what felt like days. She poured herself a cup of wine and sat back. She had spent countless hours playing with her father, who was a skilled player and had taught her everything he knew. She wasn't the player her father was, but she was better than average. Perhaps losing a game to her might stick a pin in that giant ego of Lorne's and let some of that hot air out.

"I'll let ye go first," she said and gestured to the board.

"Ladies first," he replied. "I insist."

"Quite the gentleman."

"I have me moments."

A small laugh drifting from her mouth, Diana sat forward and made the first move. Lorne countered. As they moved in turns, she quickly realized he was a skilled player. He was at least as good as she was, and Diana found that she was enjoying the challenge. As they played, they made pleasant conversation, which surprised her. Diana hadn't thought she'd be able to have a civilized conversation with the man to save her life.

"Ye're quite good at this game," she said unexpectedly.

"Aye. I've got a keen strategic mind. Nobody back home has ever been able tae beat me," he replied with a chuckle. "And ye're just as good yereslf, I have tae say."

"'Tis the logic of the game I enjoy. And ye say nobody's ever beaten ye?"

"Never."

"Then it will be me honor tae be the first."

He scoffed. "I admire yer confidence, lass. But I think ye're outmatched here." The man had an ego and thought very highly of himself, that much was obvious. But Diana got the feeling that was simply the face he presented to the world. As they chatted, he said a few things that hinted at a depth to him that wasn't as apparent. He was intelligent, well-read, and clever. He'd said a few things that had her laughing harder than she could remember laughing in quite a while. But he also had a very logical, calculating mind and seemed to anticipate her moves on the board in ways few others could. Which was frustrating.

The pleasant conversation and lighthearted banter were a mask for the war they were engaged in on the board. Move and countermove. Thrust and parry, neither of them willing to give an inch. Neither of them willing to give in. As she pondered her next move, which could be her last if she was not careful, Diana raised her gaze. She found herself staring into his icy blue eyes and felt a flash of lightning crackle through her veins. Her heart thumped inside of her and her stomach churned. Her mouth went dry but her palms grew damp and she bit the inside of her cheek, trying to stop the flurry of physical reactions she was having to him.

She played her move then turned away, finding Beatrix and Gavin watching them both intently. Her sister gave her a knowing smile and a wink, which made Diana's cheeks flush. She quickly turned back to the board and tried to focus on the game. She was alarmed to see just how close to winning Lorne was. She frowned. She couldn't let him win. Not only would she be ashamed of herself, she feared she'd never hear the end of it from the insufferably egotistic man.

A devious smile curled the corners of Diana' mouth as a plan formed in her mind. If there was one thing she knew about men, one thing they all shared in common, it was a fascination with the female form. They could not help themselves but to look at a woman's body. She had to keep from laughing at how petty her desire to win was and how low it was making her stoop, but she was not above it. She was not going to let herself lose to this man.

As he studied the board, looking for the move that would be a killing blow, Diana casually took a sip of her wine. And as she set her cup back down, she casually tugged the bodice of her dress down, putting her cleavage on prominent display. She leaned forward and with one arm tucked subtly beneath her breasts, further accentuated her cleavage, then cleared her throat while she pretended to be intently studying the board.

Lorne looked up and she had to keep from laughing out loud as she watched the color drain from his face. His eyes remained locked on her cleavage for a long moment and when she raised her eyes, locking gazes with him, a choked cough burst from his mouth. His cheeks turned an unhealthy shade of scarlet and he sat there, completely frozen. She arched an eyebrow at him, a mischievous glint in her eye, and an almost flirtatious smile on her lips.

It looked to her like he had to make a Herculean effort to tear his eyes from her bosom and when he did, he grabbed his cup of wine and drained it as if his mouth had grown drier than a desert. Diana hid her mouth behind her hand and had to savagely fight the urge to laugh. Lorne cleared his throat then proceeded to make the one move on the board he couldn't make. Diana pounced and took advantage of his mistake.

"Checkmate," she said.

His face blanched and his mouth fell open as he stared at the board, searching for some way to prove her wrong.

"Bleedin' hell," he muttered.

Grinning like a fool, Diana got to her feet. "Thank ye fer the game. 'Twas more fun than I had expected," she said. "But I'll take me leave now."

Diana turned on her heel and headed out of the drawing room, her laughter echoing around the stone corridors as she made her way back to her chamber. She closed the door behind her and flopped onto her bed, her eyes on the ceiling above as she thought about what she'd just done and then laughed some more. She couldn't believe her need to win had made her stoop to such petty, childish measures. But she didn't like to lose.

The door to her chamber opening made her sit up straight. Beatrix slipped inside and closed the door behind her then leaned her back against it.

"That was low. Usin' yer bosoms tae win a game?" she said, though with a smile.

Diana shrugged. "We dae what we have tae dae tae win."

"Ye looked like ye were havin' a nice time with Lorne," she said. "I've nae heard ye laugh like that in a long, long time."

"He's clever. Witty."

"And handsome."

"I suppose."

"Ye say that, but the way ye were lookin' at him across the chess board says somethin' else," Beatrix said. "I ken that look. 'Tis almost the way I look at Gavin."

"Bollocks," he said. "'Tis naethin' like the way ye look at Gavin."

"If ye say so."

"I dae say so."

She laughed softly but gave her a grin that said she didn't believe her. Diana sighed and threw her hands up. Beatrix was going to see what she wanted to see regardless of what she said.

"Why are ye here? Why arenae ye with Gavin?" she asked.

"I wanted tae thank ye fer what ye did taeday," she said. "Fer goin' along with... all this. I truly dae appreciate it."

It was the first time Beatrix had ever thanked her for anything. Diana was touched. But then she saw the gleam in her sister's eye and knew she wasn't done.

"What is it?" she asked.

Beatrix shuffled her feet and grinned at her. "I was hopin' ye might come on a ride with us before supper? The rain has stopped and 'tis a nice evenin' outside."

"I'm tired and want tae lie down."

"But I cannae go with Gavin unless ye're there," she said. "And I want tae get away from Maither and Faither and show him around a bit."

"Beatrix—"

"Please, Diana. I'm beggin' ye?"

Diana sighed. There was such earnestness in her sister's voice. She truly seemed to care about Gavin. However, Diana really was tired and felt the first throbbings of a headache coming on... yet Beatrix couldn't go anywhere with Gavin without her. That had been a condition their parents had set. But that also meant that Lorne would very likely be accompanying them on their ride.

As the thought crossed through her mind, so too did the image of those pale blue eyes of his and the intensity that burned within them. It made her heart skip drunkenly in her breast.

"Please, sister. I'm beggin' ye."

"Fine," she sighed. "Let's go."

Beatrix squealed and threw her arms around Diana, making her laugh as she embraced her little sister. It was the most laughter and affection they'd shared… maybe ever. And though Diana was irritated she had to leave her chamber when she didn't want to, she couldn't help but feel her heart swell at the smile on Beatrix's face.

"Thank ye, Diana."

She shook her head but kept grinning. "The things I dae fer ye."

Beatrix kissed her on the cheek. "And dinnae think I dinnae appreciate it. Now, let's go."

CHAPTER SIX

The rain had stopped but the air was crisp, cool, and the sky overhead was still clogged with thick, dark clouds and thunder rumbled somewhere in the distance. Lorne didn't think it would be long before a fresh storm rolled in. But Gavin had badgered him into coming on a ride with them before supper. He said it might be a good time for him to try and get to know Diana and keep up with the façade of trying to woo her. It was a game he was quickly growing tired of.

It didn't help that Diana didn't seem to want to get to know him. He'd thought there had been a thawing between them while they'd been playing chess. They had talked and laughed together. And then of course, there had been... her bosom. It had been intentional, he knew. A tactic, a gambit. A way to throw him off his game. And he had silently cursed himself for letting such a cheap ploy work on him.

That being said, he couldn't stop thinking about it. He wasn't a man who normally lost his head over a woman's beauty or her physical assets. But there was something about Diana that captured his imagination in ways no other woman ever had. And having her act so brazenly, all but shoving her cleavage in his face, had driven him crazy. Just thinking about it now stirred something deep within him. Her flirtation aroused him, and he couldn't stop seeing it in his mind's eye.

Not that it mattered all that much. After the game she had turned frosty once again. With Gavin and Beatrix riding well ahead of them, lost in their own world, Diana rode ahead of him, not speaking, nor looking back at him. She ignored him like he wasn't even there. The abrupt switch and then switch back in her demeanor toward him made Lorne's neck hurt.

The ground was muddy and made wet, sucking sounds beneath the horse's hooves as they rode. Lorne stared at Diana's back, not understanding how she could go from being so flirty to being so cold. Did winning a game matter that much to her? It was a thought that made Lorne grin to himself knowing he would probably have done something similar if he had been in the same situation. He hated losing too. It seemed to him they had more in common than expected and he didn't see any reason they couldn't get along.

A mischievous smirk crossing his lips, he gave his horse a nudge and caught up with Diana, falling into step beside her. Her gaze was cool, and the corners of her full, red lips curled down. Lorne offered her a wide grin. She chuffed and gave her horse a nudge, riding ahead of him again. Chuckling to himself, Lorne caught up and rode beside her. She sighed heavily and turned to him, a baleful expression on her face.

"What dae ye want?" she asked.

"I want ye tae admit ye cheated tae win our chess match."

"I did nay such thing."

Lorne raised his eyebrow and smirked at her. "Ye ken ye did. Admit it."

"How dare ye impugn me honor."

"So, ye ken what I am talking about then," he chuckled. "Ye practically shovin' yer bosoms in me face?" he asked playfully.

Diana blushed furiously.

"I dinnae ken what ye're talkin' about. I didnae dae what ye are suggesting," she huffed. "Ye must think the world of yerself tae think I'd actually shove me bosoms in yer face."

She would not look at him as she spoke and her cheeks flared bright red, drawing another chuckle from him that seemed to make her face burn brighter.

"Just admit it. Admit ye cheated. Ye distracted me," he teased.

"Even if that was true, which it's nae, it wouldnae be me fault that ye're so feeble minded as tae be distracted by… by somethin' like that," she hissed.

She seemed to sulk as they rode in silence for a few minutes, which only amused Lorne even more. He moved his horse closer to hers and grinned at her.

"It takes a lot tae distract me, lass," he said. "Take that as a compliment on yer bosoms."

She spun in her saddle, her face surprised. That expression quickly changed though to one of horror and her face drained of color. Lorne realized she'd spun in her saddle too quickly and had thrown herself off balance and was slipping off the back of her horse. Moving on instinct, Lorne leapt from the back of his horse, landing on the muddy road with a splash and lunged for her.

Diana landed in his arms but was squirming so hard, she slipped through his grasp and landed in the mud on her backside with a wet splatter. A squeal of outrage burst from her mouth, and as she tried to keep herself steady, she slammed her hands down on the ground, managing to splash herself with yet more mud. Lorne couldn't stop the laugh that burst from his mouth. She stared at him with wide eyes, her lips curled back in a sneer.

"It isnae funny" She screamed.

Lorne reached for her, but she slapped his hand away with a snarl and started to get to her feet on her own. Her foot slipped in the muck, though, and she started to fall. Diana pinwheeled her arms, her face white and etched with surprise as she once again fell into the mud, twisting and splashing in the muck that covered her from head to toe.

Lorne tried but couldn't keep himself from laughing. Diana screeched in frustration and slapped her hands in the mud puddle she was sitting in, splashing herself with yet more mud. Not that it made any difference that Lorne saw. She was already covered head to toe in thick, black mud. He doubled over, slapping his knees, laughing hysterically.

"Oh, I'm glad ye're havin' a good time over there," she howled.

"I tried tae help," he gasped through his laughter.

She howled again in impotent rage and splashed in the puddle again like a child. He took a deep breath and let it out slowly, trying to get himself under control. He wanted to defuse her anger and the only way to do that was to stop laughing at her. But it was hard.

"I'm sorry," he said. "I didnae mean tae laugh at ye."

"For somebody who didnae mean tae laugh at me, ye certainly seemed tae be enjoyin' yerself at me expense," she grumbled.

"Well… 'tis an amusin' situation."

"'Tis nae."

"I shouldnae have laughed."

Even as he said the words, he felt the laughter bubbling up in his throat again. The sight of her covered head to toe in black mud, her eyes startlingly wide and white in the dark mask, was too much. He tried to choke it back but lost the fight. Laughter erupted from his mouth and once he started, he couldn't stop.

"I'm sorry," he gasped. "I'm really sorry."

Diana looked down for a moment. She seemed to be fighting with herself, but perhaps recognizing how ridiculous the moment was, began to laugh along with him. As Lorne listened to her laughter, high and musical, he felt something between them shift and the wall of ice seemed to thaw again. At least, for the moment. Her mood was like the weather—it was subject to change at the drop of a hat. But he was determined to enjoy the easy laughter as long as it lasted.

"Here," he said as he extended his hand. "Let me help ye up."

She hesitated but reached out and took his hand, allowing Lorne to haul her up and out of the mud. When she was finally upright again, he gave her a crooked grin.

"I'd offer tae brush ye off, but there doesnae seem tae be much point tae it," he said.

She laughed and shook her head. "Bleedin' donkey."

"Are ye two all right?"

Lorne turned to see Gavin and Beatrix riding back over to them. He scoffed.

"Ahh, ye pulled yerselves out of each other's backsides long enough tae notice what was goin' on around ye. Thanks fer that," Lorne said.

"Couldnae have said it better meself," Diana said.

"Well, ye two looked pretty busy playin' in the mud, so we wanted tae give ye a minute," Gavin said with a grin.

Lorne fought the urge to pull Gavin off his mount and into the mud. Diana cast a small grin at him as if she knew what he was thinking.

"Come," Diana said. "We need tae go home so I can get cleaned up before supper."

Gavin and Beatrix looked at each other and let out a pained sigh as if the thought of going back to the castle was almost too much for them to bear.

"Let me help ye back ontae yer horse," Lorne said.

She looked at herself and then at her saddle and shook her head. "Nay. I cannae bear the thought of muckin' up me saddle," she groaned. "This mud is goin' tae be hard enough tae get out of me dress as it is."

She took her reins and started the walk back to the castle. Gavin and Beatrix shared another longing look and a sigh then rode on ahead. Lorne frowned as he weighed his options. He could—and probably should—mount up and ride on. He didn't think Diana would appreciate him falling into step beside her. But then, he changed his mind and, taking his own reins in his hand, he caught up to Diana and together, they walked down the road. Neither of them spoke, but she had offered him a small smile and hadn't launched into a verbal assault on him, so he took that as a positive sign. Perhaps, it was the first step toward something that might pass for cordiality between them.

CHAPTER SEVEN

*A*fter a long, hot bath, Diana put on some fresh clothes and sat at her table before the looking glass as she tied her hair back. It had taken her forever to get all the mud off and despite nearly scrubbing her skin raw, she still didn't feel clean. If supper weren't already on the table, she would have had an even longer soak.

The door to her bedchamber opened and one of her maids stuck her head in. "Me lady, supper is bein' served. They're waiting on ye."

"Thank ye, Alyth," she said. "I'll be along shortly."

"Very good, me lady. I'll let them ken."

The door closed and she turned back to her reflection. If she had any say in this at all, she would skip the dinner altogether. But her parents were insistent she let herself be courted by Lorne. and while she understood the logic, she didn't want to play the game.

If she was being honest with herself, there was some small part of her that hated what she was doing to Lorne. Not that she cared about him, but he was trying to court her. He had no idea she was simply going through the motions and playing the game to earn her sister a little time with a man she cared for. And to lead Lorne along like this, when she had no genuine interest in him made her feel like a heel.

But only a little bit. The man was an oaf. He was arrogant and condescending and incredibly full of himself. He was insufferable. Infuriating. But for some reason, she could not stop thinking about him. It boggled her mind, but she couldn't stop seeing his ruggedly handsome face in her mind—his tousled chestnut-colored locks and those icy blue eyes. And the harder she tried to push those images of him out of her mind, the more she couldn't.

She had to admit that he could be clever and charming. He was witty and when those eyes held hers, Diana felt a flutter in her heart she'd never felt before. Diana didn't understand the effect this man had on her and yet, she couldn't deny that he did. She warred within herself because she found him so annoying on so many levels, it was as confounding as it was maddening. And it was for those reasons, and a host of others, that she wanted to avoid the man altogether.

The door opened again and Alyth stuck her head in. "Beggin' pardon, me lady, but yer maither and faither are askin' after ye. They instructed me tae clap ye in irons and drag ye down tae the dinin' hall if I had tae."

Diana sighed at her reflection. "I suppose tellin' 'em I've taken ill wouldnae work?"

"I fear nae, me lady. They're quite insistent."

"Bleedin' wonderful."

Unable to put it off any longer, Diana got to her feet and walked out of her bedchamber, feeling for all the world like she was being dragged to the gallows. Alyth walked silently behind her, as if to ensure she did not dash for the front gates rather than walk to the dining hall, which only added to the sense that she was heading for the headsman's block.

Alyth slipped around her and opened the door for Diana and ushered her inside. Conversation stopped when she entered, the only sound the crackle and roar of the flames in the fireplace. Everybody was already there, the table had been laid out, but nobody was eating yet. They had obviously been waiting for her. As she made her way to her seat, which of course, was beside Lorne, her parents cast disapproving scowls at her.

"I apologize fer me tardiness," she said lightly as she sat down. "'Twas quite the feat washin' all the mud off me."

She offered her parents a smile, trying to make light of the situation, but they didn't look amused. Her father turned to Lorne, his expression turning apologetic.

"Me apologies fer me daughter's tardiness. Sometimes I wonder where her manners go."

"'Tis nae a problem," Lorne said and offered her a grin. "I cannae imagine it was easy gettin' all that mud off, as she said."

She was grateful for the cover he was giving her and gave him a small nod. Across the table from her, Gavin and Beatrix looked amused. Her father gestured for the servants who stepped forward to refill wine cups.

"Well, now that we're all finally here," Dunn intoned. "Let us eat and talk. I think it would be good fer us all tae get tae ken each other, eh?"

"'Tis a wonderful idea," Elayne echoed.

Most of the talking was done by Lorne and her parents who seemed to be growing entirely too fond of the man. She cast a look at her sister, searching for some rescue from this farce, but as usual, Beatrix was too caught up in Gavin to notice. There was a small part of Diana that wanted to stand up and confess to what was really happening, to declare she had no intention of choosing Lorne as her suitor, and to tell them this had all been a ploy her sister had set up from the start to allow Gavin to court Beatrix.

The hope had been that their parents would see what a suitable match they were, both as the second children of lairds, while still allowing Diana to go unwed. The weight of it all was pressing down on her so hard, she was having trouble even breathing. Her heart thundered in her ears and her stomach churned wildly. And even worse, Beatrix didn't seem to either notice or care.

"Are ye all right?" Lorne whispered to her. "Ye look like ye are goin' tae be sick."

"I think I might," she whispered back.

"Diana, dear, what is the matter with ye?" her mother asked.

"She's bein' difficult," her father grumbled. "As usual."

"I'm nae bein' difficult," she squeaked.

"Apologies again, fer me daughter," Dunn said, his voice cold and tight. "She is sometimes too free with her tongue."

Diana looked up, her face burning with anger and humiliation. "Apologies. 'Tis nae me intent tae be rude, Faither."

"Ye look unwell, sister," Beatrix said, throwing her an unexpected lifeline. "Maither, Faither, perhaps it would be better if we let her retire fer the evenin'."

"Perhaps she ate too much of the mud out there on the road today," Lorne said lightly.

The table erupted in laughter, making Diana's face burn even brighter. She was sure he had meant it in a lighthearted way. He was trying to defuse the tension that crackled in the air around them and to that end, it seemed to have worked. But his comment had the opposite effect. While everybody else thought it a fine jest, Diana had never felt more embarrassed or humiliated in her life. She felt the sting of tears in her eyes and had to fight to keep them from falling.

Her head was down but she felt Lorne's eyes burning into her. She turned and cast a withering glare at him, which he recoiled from as if she'd just slapped her. His face fell as he seemed to realize what he'd just done.

"I'm sorry. 'Twas a jest," he said. "I didnae mean tae make ye feel bad."

His voice was earnest and sincere. He said he didn't mean to humiliate her, and she believed him. But, as her father had said just moments before, there they were anyway. He reached for her hand but seemed to think better of it and withdrew, but the look on his face told her he felt terrible about making her feel as she did. It didn't change the way she felt, but it was appreciated.

The effect on the whole though, was what he'd intended. Gavin and Beatrix managed to pull themselves out of their little bubble and engaged in conversation with their parents. Laughter echoed around the hall and the mood turned lighter and somewhat festive. The servants came around to clear the plates and laid out dessert in front of them.

Their parents seemed happy to be chatting with Gavin and her sister—finally—and seemed to have forgotten about her altogether. A respite Diana was grateful for. She cut another glance at Lorne, who was still looking at her, his expression crestfallen.

A frown upon his lips, he cut his sweetcake in half and as if he knew she enjoyed sugary treats, slid half of it onto her plate. She stared at the sweetcake for a long moment. It was obviously his way of trying to make peace. It was a bit pathetic as far as olive branches went, but it was something. She gave him a small smile, feeling her tears ebbing, and ate the cake.

CHAPTER EIGHT

*L*orne entered the bedchamber he shared with his cousin to find him pacing the room like a caged lion. Wringing his hands together, a dark, tight expression on his face, the man was clearly agitated. Lorne closed the door and walked over to the table, poured himself a cup of wine, and sat down, watching Gavin walking back and forth, waiting for him to speak. He had made it through half his cup before his cousin stopped and turned to him.

"I almost told her taenight," he said. "As we walked through the gardens taegether after supper... I almost told her."

"Almost told her what?" Lorne asked.

"The bleedin' truth."

Lorne cocked his head. "The truth about... what?"

"About me. About me nae bein' a laird's son and bein' the captain of the household guard instead," he screeched.

He walked over and sat down in the chair opposite Lorne, but immediately jumped up again, unable to contain his agitation.

Lorne sat back in his chair and crossed one leg over the other and sipped his wine as his cousin practically climbed the walls.

"And what stopped ye from tellin' her the truth?" Lorne finally asked.

Gavin stopped and turned to him, a dumbfounded expression on his face. He stared at Lorne like the answer was the most obvious thing in the world. Lorne shrugged.

"If I tell her, I'll lose her fer sure," he said.

"Seems tae me like ye're delayin' the inevitable. She's goin' tae find out, lad. And I firmly believe ye should be honest with the lass. Nay one should be deceived like this."

He sighed and ran a hand through his sandy blond locks. "I ken. I just... I didnae expect tae feel the way I feel about her. Me feelin's fer Beatrix have only grown since we've been here. Whenever I look at her, I feel like me bleedin' heart's goin' tae burst. I love her, Lorne."

Lorne knew what a big statement it was coming from Gavin, a man who'd sworn off love and relationships a long time ago. Truthfully, Lorne never figured his cousin would ever do anything but enjoy every last chambermaid he could get his hands on. For so long, he had been happy with that. To see such a radical shift in him and hear him declare his love for a woman was shocking.

"What am I goin' tae dae, cousin?" he asked.

"I dinnae ken."

"When she finds out I'm nay laird's son, she'll lose her mind."

"I hate tae say it, but what did ye think was goin' tae happen when ye told that lie tae begin with?" Lorne asked.

"I wasnae thinkin'. I was havin' a good time with Beatrix and I just... I wanted tae be somebody in her eyes."

"Ye are somebody—"

"I'm a bleedin' guard, Lorne. A soldier. Tae somebody like Beatrix, the daughter of a laird, a soldier is nobody. Nothin'."

"If she loves ye like ye think she does, she'll love ye regardless of what ye dae."

He looked at Lorne like he'd lost his mind. "Maybe she will and maybe she willnae," he said. "But her faither will care fer certain. He'll never let his daughter be with somebody like... me."

"Ye dinnae ken that. Ye are a laird's nephew."

"Of course, I dae!" he shouted. "I've naethin' tae offer. Nay lands. Nay money. I've got naethin' tae offer up as a bride's price. Laird Macgillivray will never give me her hand."

Lorne refilled his cup and took a long drink. Gavin probably wasn't wrong. Laird Macgillivray seemed more liberal with his daughters than other lairds he had known, but it was probably fair to say he would still demand a bride's price for Beatrix's hand. One that Gavin would not be able to give him. It made falling in love with Beatrix every bit as stupid as lying to her about who he was in the first place. He felt terrible for Gavin, but at the same time, the outcome of his deception was entirely predictable.

"I cannae believe ye didnae see how this was the inevitable end of this," Lorne said.

"I dinnae need ye tae lecture me, cousin."

"Then what dae ye need?"

"I need ye tae help me figure a way out of this," he said, his voice tinged with desperation. "A way that allows me tae keep Beatrix's hand."

Lorne frowned and stared into his cup as he swirled the wine around inside of it. His mind raced and his stomach lurched. He knew the answer to Gavin's question, but he also knew his cousin was not going to like it and was hesitant to give it.

"Please, cousin. I need yer help," Gavin pleaded.

He shook his head. "Honestly, I dinnae see any way this ends with ye bein' able tae keep Beatrix's hand—"

"There has tae be a way."

"If there is, I dinnae see it."

Gavin scrubbed his face with his hands and sighed heavily as he began to pace the room again. Lorne had never seen his cousin so upset before. But this was a mess of his own creation. He should have known better than to lie about who he was. He hated seeing Gavin so torn up about the situation, but he did this to himself. And if there was one thing his father had ingrained into him, it was having to accept responsibility for his mistakes. It was time for his cousin to learn that lesson.

Gavin stepped to the window and looked at the darkened world beyond it. "I never meant tae fall in love with her. I thought we were just havin' a good time taegether and didnae expect fer it all tae happen this way."

"I understand that. But maybe the best thing ye can dae fer yerself is tae tell her the truth," Lorne said. "Maybe ye and her faither can find some way forward fer ye and Beatrix."

He felt the falseness of his words even as they slipped from his lips. There was only one way this was going to end and judging by the stricken look on Gavin's face, he seemed to know it. The truth was, Lorne was going to be glad when this farce was finally brought to an end. The Macgillivrays were good, kind people and didn't deserve to be deceived the way Gavin—and he—were deceiving them.

He didn't want to keep pretending to be courting Diana just so his cousin could keep seeing Beatrix, knowing their entanglement would come to an unhappy end. The guilt of what they were doing sat like a stone in his chest. And not just for them. The ramifications of this farce were as wide ranging as they were dangerous. They were things he should have thought about before he agreed to help Gavin.

Gavin sighed. "I dinnae ken what tae dae."

"The only thing ye can dae is tae be honest with her, cousin."

"I cannae—"

"Ye must. And ye need tae dae it before she figures out yer deception," Lorne said. "Have ye even stopped tae consider what the repercussions will be if Faither hears about all of this? What will happen if the Macgillivrays tell him about yer —about our—deception? Wars have been fought over lesser things than what we did here."

"I think ye're bein' a bit dramatic."

"If anythin', I'm nae bein' dramatic enough," Lorne said.

"We cannae let him find out. Ye need tae help me."

"I've helped ye enough."

"Which means ye're intae this as deep as I am," he replied.

Lorne snarled. "Are ye threatenin' me?"

"Nay. I'm askin' fer yer help. I'm askin' ye tae help me find a way tae get out of this mess and still keep Beatrix."

"And I'm tellin' ye, there is nay way. I should've put a stop tae this before it started. That's me fault," Lorne said firmly. "But 'tis time fer this tae be done."

"Lorne—"

"Ye tell her, or I will."

And with that, Lorne stormed out of the chamber and down the corridor, searching for the door to the gardens. He needed some fresh night air to cool his blood and clear his mind. He never thought things would go this far or that his cousin would be stupid enough to fall in love with a woman he could never have. But he had. And now, Lorne needed to find a way to extricate them from the hole Gavin had put them in.

CHAPTER NINE

Diana trudged down the hall that led to her father's study. She had managed to escape to her bedchamber after the morning meal and had spent a little time reading and enjoying the solitude. But Alyth had come and ruined all that, telling Diana that her parents requested her presence. It had sounded entirely foreboding and Alyth had had no idea what it was about. And as she walked down the corridor, her footsteps echoing in her ears, a thousand different scenarios raced through her mind, each one worse than the last.

She stood just outside the door gripping the handle. Diana closed her eyes and drew in a deep breath, counted to ten, then let it out slowly. Her nerves hadn't steadied much but there wasn't anything she could do about that. She couldn't keep her parents waiting. As it was, they were probably already going to read her the riot act about being late for supper. The last thing she wanted was to give them even more fuel for that fire.

Gritting her teeth, she opened the door and stepped inside. Her father sat behind his large and ornately carved desk while her mother sat on the sofa near the fireplace. She had a cup of mead in her hand and looked at Diana as she closed the door, an amused smile playing across her lips. Her father though, stared at her with a darkly serious expression on her face.

"Sit, daughter," he said.

She did as he bade and sat down in the chair before his desk, wringing her hands together in her lap and biting the inside of her cheek, doing everything in her power to keep from looking as anxious as she felt. Her father sat back and took a long drink from his cup, his eyes never leaving her. He set the cup down then picked up a sheet of parchment, holding it up for her to see.

"Dae ye ken what this is?" he asked.

"I fear I dae nae."

"'Tis a letter from Laird Finley Munro."

He fell silent, still holding the letter up, watching her closely. Her mother said nothing either. She just sat on the sofa, sipping her mead, the flames in the fireplace glittering in her eyes.

"Am I meant tae guess what Laird Munro's letter says?"" she finally asked.

Her father set the letter down and slid it across the desk to her. With a sigh, Diana picked it up and quickly scanned the page, her heart sinking deeper into her belly with every word she read. She grimaced, noticing how much the page shook in her trembling hand. Swallowing hard, she set the letter down on her father's desk and sat back, trying to absorb what she'd just read.

"It seems that ye made quite the impression on Laird Munro," her father said.

She shuddered and lowered her gaze. Munro had made quite an impression on her as well and it wasn't a good one. He was arrogant and self-absorbed. He didn't seem to care about her thoughts or opinions and liked to hear himself speak more than he wanted to listen to her. Diana could tell that he didn't value women the way she wanted the man who would be her husband to value her. His attitude told her he saw women as possessions or things to collect rather than somebody to be cherished.

"He's made quite a generous proposal fer yer hand," her father said.

Diana frowned and said nothing but shifted in her seat, growing more uncomfortable with this conversation by the moment. It was far worse than what she'd been imagining. She would have preferred being berated for being tardy to supper and being so cold to Lorne.

"Laird Finley seems like a good man," her mother finally said. "He's handsome, wealthy, possesses quite a bit of land and—"

"And an alliance with him would be good for us strategically as well," her father added. "And for him. As much as want tae respect yer feelings in this situation, ye've got a duty tae the clan tae consider."

"More than anythin' though, Diana, we love ye and want ye tae be happy," her mother said. "We want tae see ye filled with joy—"

"And a home filled with kids," her father said with a smile. "I want a passel of grandkids tae spoil and laugh with. What I dinnae want is tae see ye wanderin' the halls of this castle alone. Any thought of alliance aside, it breaks me heart tae think of ye livin' yer life alone."

"Ye've got so much tae offer, Diana. We hate tae see ye hidin' yerself away."

"I'm nae hidin' meself away."

In truth though, she knew she was. She feared the emotions and the passion that coursed through her veins. She didn't understand them. And truthfully, she had always feared she would never find a man who treated his wife with the love and care her father showed her mother. Their relationship was the sort the poets wrote about and deep down, there was a longing inside of Diana for just that sort of love.

She wanted to be respected by her husband the way her mother was. And she certainly hadn't felt that sort of respect from any of the men her parents had sent her to choose from, especially Laird Munro. The man was arrogant and dismissive.

Lorne though. He seemed different. He could be brash and arrogant, of course. She had yet to meet a man who could confidently wield a blade who wasn't. But she had to admit that he had been trying to get to know her.

As those thoughts passed through her mind though, she pushed them away. She had engaged in this entire farce because she wanted to be closer to her sister. This wasn't about her finding love. And yet… she still could not deny that as she thought about Lorne she didn't feel some whispered hint of intrigue.

"What is yer hesitation tae allow Laird Munro tae court ye?" her mother asked.

"Why dinnae ye at least let him try tae court ye?" her father asked. "Ye never ken. Ye've been so intent on pushin' him away, ye may find that he surprises ye. That ye two might… find some common ground and that ye enjoy his company."

Diana knew already that would never happen. Not with a man like Munro. But Lorne… she still wasn't sure what to make of him.

"I just… I am sorry fer bein' so indecisive," Diana said. "I just… this is the rest of me life, so I want tae make sure I find the right man fer me."

"And ye dinnae think Laird Munro is that man?" Her father asked.

"I ken he is nae."

Her mother sat forward. "Is this because of Lorne? Dae ye have interest in him?"

Diana got the feeling that if she said no, they might accept Munro's proposal. As she considered that possibility, her stomach churned, her heart raced, and she seized on the question her mother had just asked her.

"Aye. Aye, Maither," Diana said quickly. "'Tis exactly that."

Her father eyed her curiously. "Ye've got interest in Lorne?"

"Aye."

"Then why have ye been givin' him the cold shoulder?" he asked. "From where we're sittin' it hasnae appeared that ye've got that least bit of interest in the lad."

She offered them a quavering smile. Diana knew what she was saying was a lie, but if it kept her parents from accepting Munro's proposal, it was a good lie. So, she took hold of it tightly, determined to run with it. She would sort the rest out later.

"I cannae make meself too easy tae obtain, now can I, Faither?" she said sweetly. "How would that look then, eh?"

Her parents exchanged looks, both of them wearing the same small frowns and expressions of skepticism. But some silent bit of communication passed between them, and they nodded to one another, as if they'd come to some sort of accord. It made her stomach clench as her throat grew dry. She feared what that accord her parents had come to might be.

"All right," her mother said. "If ye truly want tae allow Lorne tae court ye, I think ye're Faither will be agreeable tae that."

"Aye. 'Tis what I want," she said.

Her father leaned back in his chair; his lips pursed as he stared at her for a long, silent moment. Diana's stomach twisted and turned over on itself as waited for her father to render his judgment on the situation. Finally, he nodded.

"All right. If this is what ye want, then I'll write tae Laird Munro and decline his proposal," he father finally said. "Are ye certain this is what ye want?"

"Aye, Faither. I'm certain."

"All right," he said.

Relief immediately flooded Diana's body. She'd managed to deflect Munro's advances and had bought herself some time to figure out what to do about Lorne. How much time, she wasn't sure, so she'd have to figure it out quickly.

"Diana, I'd like ye tae accompany yer sister and Gavin intae the village. There are some things I'd like ye tae pick up fer me," her mother suggested. "And why dinnae ye take Lorne with ye? Make a day of this."

Diana was about to retort when her mother arched an eyebrow. "Is there a reason ye dinnae want to spend some time with Lorne? I'd think ye'd welcome the chance tae get tae ken him better, bein' that ye're choosin' him tae court ye rather than Laird Munro?"

Diana knew instantly that her mother was testing her, trying to see how truthful she was being when she said she preferred to be courted by Lorne. And if she didn't pass her mother's test, they would seal a pact with Munro for her hand. She offered her mother a smile she hoped looked more genuine than it felt upon her face.

"Of course, Maither. I'd be happy tae. Sounds like a fun day," Diana said.

Her mother smiled. "Good. I'm glad tae hear it. Yer sister already has the list of things I need ye tae pick up fer me."

That confirmed for her that this has been a set up from the start. It was their way to force her to either choose or have them choose for her. And like it or not, Lorne was the lesser of two evils. She got to her feet and gave them both a smile and a polite curtsy.

"I should ready meself then," she said.

"We shall see ye fer supper," her father said. "We look forward tae hearin' about yer day."

A forced smile on her face, Diana turned and headed back to her bedchamber. She'd been wrong. The walk to her father's study hadn't been her walk to the gallows. Walking to her bedchamber to ready herself for a day with Lorne was.

CHAPTER TEN

The day was bright, the air crisp and cool as they made their way from the castle to the small town in the foothills below. Gavin and Beatrix, of course, rode ahead of them, lost within each other. Lorne watched the way they looked at one another, noting their smiles and the affection that shimmered in each other's eyes. He sighed, the frown tugging at the corners of his mouth.

Truthfully, there was a part of Lorne that longed to have a woman look at him the way Beatrix gazed at his cousin. That longed to be held with the same sort of esteem and affection she more than obviously held for Gavin. He was glad to see that his cousin's love was being returned, but as he watched them, he couldn't deny that some bit of pain and perhaps even jealousy echoed through the empty chambers of his own heart.

But this was all a fiction. And one he knew was going to come crashing down around them at some point, sooner rather than later. Gavin's lie would eventually be exposed. And when it was revealed that he was not the son of a laird, but the nephew of one instead, the fallout was going to be catastrophic. Gavin would lose Beatrix and for all Lorne knew, the resulting chaos would spark a war between their clans.

He hoped he was being dramatic, but he wasn't so sure. What he did know was that when this farce was exposed and his father found out, the chaos at home would probably make Lorne wish for a war instead. It might be less painful to fall in battle than endure what his father was going to do to them. He shook his head, trying to figure out for the thousandth time why he'd agreed to take part in this mummery in the first place.

Trying to push all those thoughts from his mind, Lorne turned to Diana, who rode silently beside him. Her face was pinched, her eyes narrowed, and her lips softly turned downward. She looked like a woman in deep contemplation.

"Are ye all right?" he asked.

She gave herself a shake, as if the sound of his voice cutting into her thoughts had startled her. Diana turned and offered him a smile that didn't reach her eyes.

"Aye. I'm fine," she replied.

"Ye just look like ye're thinkin' about somethin' serious."

She gave him a small shrug. "Naethin' too serious."

He flashed her a roguish smile. "Then what are ye thinkin' about?"

A small smile flickered across her lips and was gone in an instant as she lowered her gaze. Diana had a strange expression on her face that Lorne couldn't identify. He thought it looked uncertain. Perhaps tinged with fear. But what would she be afraid of?

"Naethin'," she said. "Just enjoyin' the day."

"Ye dinnae look like ye're enjoyin' yerself."

She chuffed. "As if ye'd ken what I look like when I'm enjoyin' meself or nae."

"'Tis true," he replied. "But when somebody's enjoyin' themselves, they tend tae smile rather than look like they're walkin' tae the gallows."

That got a genuine laugh out of her. It sounded like music in Lorne's ears and the sparkle in her eye that accompanied it made his breath catch in his throat. She was already beautiful, but the authentic smile on her face made her absolutely radiant.

"I suppose so," she replied softly. "I dinnae mean tae look that way."

Diana intrigued him. He had come into this expecting to have to put on a show and endure the farce of courting her. But the more time he spent in the presence, the more he felt surprisingly drawn to her. Feeling a pull towards her was not what he'd expected when Lorne had first seen her standing beneath the sallyport with a scowl on her face.

But now, having spent a few days in Castle Macgillivray, Lorne found himself seeking her out. Craving her presence when she was not in the room. When he'd learned they would be going into town today, his first feeling had been one of excitement.

"So, what has ye lookin' so gloomy then?" he asked.

He watched the thoughts scrolling across her face and could see she was trying to figure out what to say to him. She was being very guarded, her words calculated. She was careful to not give too much of herself away or let him see too deeply into her thoughts. It was something he could relate to and respect since he was very much the same way.

"They look like they're gettin' on well, eh?" she said, motioning to her sister and Gavin.

Lorne nodded. He was curious about her deflection and change in conversation but decided to not press her too hard on it. She was entitled to her thoughts.

"Aye," he said. "I suppose they are."

"Dae ye think they'll marry?"

Lorne shrugged. "I dinnae. There are a lot of things that need tae happen before that."

"Such as ye marryin' first?"

He had actually been thinking about Gavin confessing his lie and them needing to find a way past it together if they were to marry. If her father would even permit it. The laird's permissiveness with his daughters gave him some small bit of hope that Gavin, being that he was the captain of his father's household guard, might possibly be seen as a suitable suitor. But he didn't know. Worse, he still wasn't sure how they were going to approach Laird Macgillivary with the truth.

With every passing day, the shadow of guilt upon Lorne's heart grew darker. The Macgillivrays were warm, kind people and he liked them enormously. The fact that they were there under false pretenses, that they were lying to their faces with their every breath was an increasingly growing burden on his shoulders.

As he glanced at Diana riding beside him, he decided to not think about any of that for the day.

He cleared his throat. "Aye," he said. "Such as me marryin' first."

The lie slipped from his lips so effortlessly, he frowned, feeling a lance of guilt pierce his heart. Lorne quickly reined it all in and controlled the emotion on his face. Diana's cheeks flushed and she turned away, as if only just realizing what she'd said—and what it implied for her, for them given that he was supposed to be there to court her.

"I think they look good taegether," she said, changing the subject once again.

"Aye. They dae," he agreed, happy to let her.

They rode into the village and turned their horses over to the stableboy who approached them. Lorne handed the kid a few coins.

"Make sure they're well fed and watered," Lorne admonished him.

"Aye, me laird."

"I'm nae a laird."

The kid nodded and smiled vacuously before turning and leading their horses away to the stables. By the time he turned back, Gavin and Beatrix were already gone. He glanced at Diana who gave him a wry grin and a shrug.

"Where did they go?" he asked.

"Off tae be with each other, I suppose," she groaned. "Beatrix said they would meet us at the Lion and Lamb fer somethin' tae eat later."

He sighed and shook his head. "Well, I suppose we're on our own tae get the things yer maither asked fer, eh?"

"Would ye mind if we stopped somewhere first?"

"Lead on," he said.

She gave him a small, grateful nod and led him through the crowds that packed the streets of the small town. He followed her to a small shop that sat between a butcher and a baker. The aromas wafting from the bakery made Lorne's stomach rumble.

They walked into the shop and Lorne was immediately assaulted by a mélange of different scents. Dried herbs hung in batches from the ceiling and the shelves along either wall were lined with pots of different tonics and ointments. The smell inside the apothecary, though not unpleasant, was overpowering. It was cloying.

"Morag, are ye here?" Diana called out.

"I'm in the back lass," a voice responded from behind a curtain. "I could use a hand, actually. Come on back."

Without waiting for him, she pushed the curtain aside and stepped through, letting it fall back into place, leaving Lorne standing in the middle of the shop.

"Bollocks this," he said to himself with a frown.

He followed Diana into the back room and his frown deepened. A child, no more than eight or nine summers old, sat in a chair with a wicked looking gash that ran from his wrist to his elbow. A pile of bloody rags sat on the floor beneath him. Diana knelt beside the boy whose face was streaked with tears and twisted with agony. She whispered to him and stroked his hair, doing her best to soothe him as an older woman, plump and gray, stitched the wound.

Diana didn't flinch from the sight of so much blood and helped the older woman apply an ointment and stitch the boy up. She was so smooth and gentle with the needle and thread while simultaneously keeping the boy calm. Her skill was impressive, as was her dedication.

"There ye go, lad," said the older woman, presumably this Morag.

Diana finished wrapping a long strip of cloth around his arm then tied it tightly. She patted the kid's knee and offered him a smile.

"That should dae it," she said gently. "Yer arm should heal up just fine."

"So long as ye dinnae go playin' with her faither's bleedin' sword again," Morag grumbled.

"Dinnae listen tae her. She's just grumpy," Diana said with a smile.

"Of course, I'm grumpy. I dinnae like seein' foolish children almost cuttin' their arms off because they're too foolish tae not play with swords bigger than they are," the woman says.

"Come back and see her in a few days," Diana said softly. "She'll need tae change the dressin' on yer arm and put on some more ointment."

"Aye, me lady. Thank ye," the kid said with a polite nod.

He got to his feet and gave Lorne a strange look before dashing out of the shop. Diana and Morag chatted amiably as they cleaned up the room, throwing all the bloody rags into a large pot that would be filled with water and boiled later.

Lorne saw they were close and that the older woman served as Diana's mentor.

"Oh, fergive me," Diana said after several minutes. "This is Lorne. He's… uhh… he and his cousin are stayin' with us fer a little while."

Being described as somebody who was staying with them for a while cut him in a way he didn't expect. It wasn't that he expected her to make some grand declaration of love or anything like that, but hearing her describe him as a stranger sheltering beneath her parents' roof, no different from a squatter, was like a lance of ice had pierced him.

"What are ye apologizin' fer, lass?" the older woman said. "The man's got a mouth and a brain of his own. He could have introduced himself if he'd wanted tae."

Lorne chuckled. "Aye. I suppose ye're right."

He watched the two women interact for a little while and found himself admiring Diana in ways he hadn't considered before. She was talented as a healer and, as he'd seen with the child, dedicated to the craft. He could simply tell that she was passionate about it and he respected that more than he could express.

"We should be goin', Morag. We have tae meet me sister," Diana said.

"Aye. I'm glad ye stopped by," the older woman replied. "Also, I dried some of the herbs ye asked about. They're out front, so just bundle 'em up and take them."

"Thank ye."

The woman waved her off. "Nay, thank ye fer yer help with the bairn. Ye've got a natural touch calmin' 'em down that I dinnae have. Should come in handy when ye have bairns of yer own."

Morag tipped Lorne a wink as she said it, which made him shift on his feet uncomfortably while Diana's face flushed and turned a bright pink. The older woman laughed and the tension in the air quickly dissipated.

"I'll come by in the next day or so," Diana said.

"Aye. See ye then."

Diana led him back into the front room. She walked over to a barrel where some stalks of dried herbs had been laid out and began to bundle them. There were quite a few of them—far more than what she could hold in her small, delicate hands. Without thinking, Lorne stepped forward and picked up the stalks of dried herbs. Their hands brushed together, and they both paused. He felt like lightning had shot through his veins and when he met her sparkling green eyes, he felt that lurch in his belly he only got when she was around.

He cleared his throat. "Sorry."

Her smile was small, but genuine. "'Tis all right. Just... hold those like that, please."

"Aye."

As he held the herbs, she fetched a roll of ribbon then as quickly and deftly as she's stitched up the boy, she tied the stalks together. They repeated it with two more bundles and when they were done, she looked up at him, her gaze lingering on his.

"Thank ye," she said, her voice suddenly thick.

"Ye're welcome."

Diana put the herbs into a bag and they left the apothecary. Neither of them spoke as they made their way through the crowd, but a heavy sense of anticipation settled down over them. They made their way to the Lion and Lamb inn to find Gavin and Beatrix already waiting for them. They had cups of mulled wine in their hands and were staring into each other's eyes.

"We've already ordered plates of food," Beatrix said, tearing her eyes away from Gavin to look at her sister.

"Thank ye," Diana said.

"Well, if it isnae Diana Macgillivray."

They all turned at the sound of the man's voice. He was tall with dark hair and darker eyes, broad through the chest and shoulders, and although he wore a sword on his belt, he moved like he wasn't comfortable with it. It seemed to be more for show than anything. Which stood to reason given the fact that he wore silks and velvet—a nobleman who sent others to fight in his stead, Lorne judged.

Diana cringed and shifted in her seat, her face betraying how uncomfortable she was as the man sauntered over. That look of discomfort only deepened when he braced himself by placing a hand on their table and leaned down, looking at her closely as if none of the others at the table existed.

"'Tis good tae see ye, lass. 'Tis been a while," the man said.

"Aye. 'Tis been a while indeed, Laird Munro," she said.

The man finally cast a glance around the table, his eyes lingering on Lorne's for a long moment, a challenge in the silence, before he smirked dismissively, and turned back to Diana.

"Why dinnae we go somewhere else tae get a drink," he said. "Someplace a little less crowded and more intimate, eh?"

"I'm flattered, of course, but nay thank ye. We need tae be gettin' home after we eat," Diana replied. "Me maither will be expectin' us."

The man chuckled low and leaned forward, saying something into Diana's ear. It looked completely inappropriate. It was too low for Lorne to make out the individual words, but he recognized the honeyed insistence of the man's tone. He was trying to persuade Diana to do something she clearly didn't want to do. She looked ready to crawl out of her skin.

"Leave her alone. She said nay," Lorne said.

The man turned back to him, his eyes dark and angry. "I dinnae believe I was speakin' tae ye."

"Nay. Ye werenae," Lorne said. "But I'm speakin' tae ye."

The man stood and squared up to Lorne, his face hard, his gaze dark. But in his eyes, Lorne could see the uncertainty. The fear. He knew without a doubt, the nobleman who stood before him had never been in a fight in his entire life. Lorne amused himself with thoughts of the man stabbing himself as he tried to draw his blade.

All around them, the common room fell silent and the air crackled with an electrical charge and the whispered promise of violence. Lorne felt the eyes of everybody in the tavern on him, but he held the nobleman's gaze firmly, standing with the ease of a man who was comfortable in a fight—something the nobleman was not.

"The lady said she daesnae want tae go with ye," Lorne said, his voice low. "I suggest ye respect her wishes and bugger off."

"Dae ye ken who I am?" he sneered.

"Nay. And I dinnae really care tae, either," Lorne replied coldly. "The lady asked ye tae leave her be. So, leave her be or ye and I are goin' tae have a problem."

"Is that so?"

"Aye," Lorne said. "'Tis so."

The man reached for Diana as if he was going to grab her. Before anybody could react though, Lorne delivered a punch that rocked the man's head back. He looked at Lorne, dazed. His eyes were wide with surprise that somebody had put their hands on him. Diana watched the scene unfolding with horror... but not without some bit of fascination as well. She was almost flattered to see Lorne taking up for her. She was shocked to feel her heart swell and a warmth fill her belly.

That warmth quickly faded to fear though, when the man reached for his sword, fumbling with the hilt as he tried to draw. Lorne was quicker though and delivered a pair of hard punches to the man's stomach. He doubled over, gasping and sputtering as he tried to reclaim the breath that had been driven from his lungs.

"Thae woman asked ye tae leave her alone," Lorne said, his voice cold. "Now I'm askin' ye tae leave us all alone and get out of here before this gets worse. Dae ye understand?"

Still gasping and wheezing, the man straightened up. He stared at Lorne with pure hatred as he licked his lips, cutting a glance at baleful Diana. He wiped the blood from his lip and glared at Lorne before turning back to Diana. He looked at her for a long moment, scowling.

"Ye're nae worth the trouble," he sneered.

The man turned and stormed out of the tavern, nearly tripping over his sword in his haste. Lorne chuckled darkly to himself then turned and sat down again. Diana said nothing, but she offered him a wide, warm smile and a look of gratitude. And in her eyes, Lorne saw something he had never seen from her before when she looked at him: respect.

CHAPTER ELEVEN

Despite how enjoyable the time at lunch had been, Diana was reluctant to give in to the feelings that coursed through her. The situation had shaken her. While it had been in defense of her, she feared violence, was not accustomed to it, and seeing Lorne punching the man had left her a bit rattled.

"Are ye all right?" Lorne asked.

"Aye. I'm fine."

"Ye seem... tense."

Diana met his eyes. "It's just that... What happened with the man—"

"He was out of line with ye," Lorne replied. "I am sorry if ye felt that it was out of me place, but I acted impulsively. I didnae want him touching ye."

"I could have handled it meself."

"Ye shouldnae have tae," he countered. "Ye asked the man tae leave ye alone—"

"I ken. But I could have handled him on me own and things wouldnae have had tae become violent."

Lorne's face clouded over, and his expression grew tight. He stared at her like he didn't understand why she was so upset with him. The truth was, she didn't know either. She appreciated that he had taken up for her, nobody had ever done something like that for her. He could have put himself in real danger if that man had drawn his blade, but he'd stepped in and defended her like it was nothing. And she was not ungrateful for that, she respected him for his bravery.

But she also didn't like that he thought she was something that needed to be coddled. She would have handled the man who was bothering her if he'd given her the chance, and she would have done it without resorting to violence or other brutish tactics.

The mood outside the inn was suddenly thick with tension, the good humor they had enjoyed inside gone. Lorne stared at her with consternation and bewilderment. She stared back at him with a simmering anger in her eyes.

The bright sunlight of the day was gone, the sky choked with slate-gray clouds. Somewhere in the distance, thunder rumbled, and judging by the sound of thunder, a storm was coming soon. As if to underscore that point, a cold gust of wind blew down the street, making Diana shudder.

"We need tae get home. I've got a headache and need one of yer tinctures, Diana," Beatrix complained.

Her sister sometimes suffered from terrible, nearly debilitating headaches. She had since they were young. They would sometimes lay her out for several days at a time, leaving her incapable of doing anything but lie on her bed and moan in agony. Diana had always found it frightening.

"Aye. I'll take ye home and get ye fixed up," she said then turned to Lorne. "Would ye and Gavin be so kind as tae pick up what me maither needed while I take Beatrix home?"

"I dinnae think 'tis wise fer ye tae be travelin' these roads by yerself," Lorne said. "Especially nae with this storm bearin' down."

Diana turned to him, offended. "We have been travelin' these roads all our lives. We ken them like the back of our hands," she spat. "We dinnae need ye tae tell us what's safe and nae safe in our own lands. Ye've only just gotten here."

She sniffed and folded her arms over her chest, glaring at him coldly. She didn't like being told what to do and although she was sure he thought he was being a gentleman; she did not appreciate his overprotectiveness. It was unnecessary and it wasn't his place to tell her what to do. These were her lands, not his, and she knew them best.

"Why dinnae I escort Beatrix back tae the castle?" Gavin offered. "That way, she's nae alone and has somebody tae watch over her in case there are bandits on the road—"

"There are nay bandits on these roads," Diana huffed.

"Says everybody until they're set upon by bandits with bad intentions," Lorne said.

She glared coldly at him. Bandits weren't entirely unheard of, and she wasn't that naïve that she didn't know bad people did bad things all over the world. But she didn't want to give him the satisfaction of telling him she agreed with him. The truth was, it was starting to get dark, so she would be glad to have a man as skilled with a blade accompany her sister back to the castle. But it was partly, if not mostly, because she didn't trust the men to get what her mother needed. She realized it the moment she'd first suggested it.

"Fine," she said coldly. "But get me sister home safely or I'll have yer head."

"She'll make it home safely. Ye have me word," he agreed.

She grumbled under her breath but nodded. "All right then."

Beatrix grabbed Diana by the hand, and she could see the agony etched into her sister's features. It broke her heart.

"I'll see ye at home," Beatrix said.

"There's a bottle of yer tincture in me chambers," she replied. "I'll make ye some more when we return."

Gavin escorted Beatrix away, his arm wrapped around her shoulder protectively. Her sister leaned into him, and it made Diana smile. Though the day hadn't ended the way she had hoped or expected, Diana couldn't help but feel like she and her sister had taken another step closer, that chasm that existed between them narrowing. It filled her heart with joy.

"All right, so where dae we go?" Lorne's voice cut through her thoughts like a scythe.

"Come," she said.

She led him through the crowd around the marketplace. There were many vendors who sold what her mother required, but the quality varied between them all. As did the pricing. It was one reason she didn't trust anybody but herself to purchase the goods.

"Did ye nae think I could complete yer maither's purchase?" he asked, his tone teasing.

She gave him a deadpan expression. "Nay, I didnae."

His cheeky grin faltered, and a strangled gasp burst from his mouth. He hadn't been expecting her to say that and clearly did not know how to respond. She grinned to herself.

"What is yer maither after, anyway?" he asked, finally recovering.

"She wants her favorite bottle of wine and sweetcakes."

He gave her a strange look and she couldn't help but laugh. She knew it was ridiculous, but the household staff didn't make the sweetcakes the way she liked, and the wine she wanted was only made by a specific vendor in town.

"Me maither is very particular about her sweetcakes and wine," she said.

"It seems so."

"Then come. Let's find what me maither asked me tae fetch."

They made their way from stall to stall, searching for her mother's items. The rumble of thunder drew closer and the air about them grew colder. The storm was coming. Even worse, the day was growing long, and night would be upon them soon. And after what felt like hours of searching, they still had not found what they were looking for.

"Just grab somethin'," Lorne said grumpily and pointed to a table lined with bottles. "That wine there. I've had that before and 'tis quite good."

"'Tis nae what me maither wants though."

"But it's good wine."

"I told ye. Me maither is very specific."

He sighed and ran a hand over his face. "'Tis gettin' dark and bleedin' storm is bearin' down on us. Dae ye want tae go home with soggy sweetcakes?"

"Ye dinnae understand."

"Nay, I dinnae."

"Maybe ye should go back tae the castle without me. I'll stay and find—"

"I'm nae leavin' ye here alone."

"I dinnae need yer protection," she said. "I'm quite capable of takin' care of meself."

"Are ye then?"

His tone was mocking, and it made her face grow warm. He subtly motioned to three men who stood to the side of the crowd. They were rough looking. Hard men. And the way they were looking around, eyeballing everybody—and the purses on their belts—told Diana they were up to no good. She frowned.

"Dae ye think ye could fight all three of them off and keep them from stealin' yer purse and then ravishin' ye?" he asked.

"Ye dinnae need tae be so crude."

"If it gets the point through yer stubborn, thick skull, I think I dae."

She huffed and turned away, unwilling to give him the satisfaction of admitting he was right. She would not be able to fight off those three men. She likely wouldn't be able to fight off one of them. But he was right about one thing… she was stubborn. She had inherited that from her mother.

Her despair at not finding the things quickly gave way to elation though, when she spotted what she was looking for. The vendor was tearing down her booth for the storm was approaching. Panic-stricken, she sprinted over.

"Please, I need tae buy a bottle of yer wine and a box of yer sweetcakes," she said.

"Miss, I'm closin' up. The storm's goin' tae be here—"

"Please. I'll be quick."

The woman sighed and looked irritated by the interruption. A crash of thunder overhead made them both jump and the woman looked as if she wanted to be anywhere but there.

"Please, I'll give ye double yer askin' price if ye just unpack—"

Lorne sauntered over to the table and gave the woman a wide, warm smile. Diana watched as the woman's expression changed from one of surliness to a blush. An actual blush! She looked back at Lorne like a besotted girl.

"Surely, ye can give us enough time just tae buy a couple of things before ye send us on our way, cannae ye, love?" he purred.

"The storm's comin' and I really need tae get me things packed up before it arrives," she said. "'Tis goin' tae be a nasty one, I'm sure of it."

"We only need a couple bottles of that wine and a couple of boxes of those incredible sweetcakes," he cooed. "From what I hear, those treats are legendary in these lands and I have been dyin' tae get me hands on some."

"I dinnae ken about legendary—"

"'Tis what I heard," he replied. "And what I've also heard is the woman who makes them is every bit as sweet as her cakes."

Not only did the woman's entire expression change when she spoke to Lorne, her voice did too. Her tone became softer and she actually giggled! Diana watched the entire exchange completely aghast at what she was seeing. For his part, Lorne leaned into the flirtation with the wide smile and practically mooning eyes as he looked at her.

"So, how about it? Can ye take just a minute tae sell us yer wine and cakes? I promise we'll get out of yer hair long before the storm gets here. And I'll tell ye what, I'll even help load yer boxes intae yer wagon."

The woman giggled again and swayed on her feet as Lorne gazed her, his blue eyes sparkling like he was a man in love.

"Oh, all right. But let's be quick about it then," she said.

The woman rapidly set about putting their order together as Lorne, true to his word, began stacking her crates and boxes into the wagon that sat nearby. By the time Diana had finished her transaction, he had her loaded up and ready to go.

"Thank ye so much fer helpin' me out with me stuff," she said. "Ye're a true gentleman."

Diana scoffed. Lorne gave her a smile then turned to the woman and took her hand, planting a soft kiss on the back of it.

"And thank ye fer bein' so kind tae us," he said and tipped her a wink. "Have a pleasant evenin'."

He took the bottles and boxes from Diana and together, they walked through the crowd, rapidly thinning with the coming storm, toward the stables.

"Ye acted like a bairn back there," she said.

"Sometimes, ye have tae," he said. "Didnae anybody ever teach ye how tae have fun?"

"Is that what that was then? Fun?"

"Aye. Ye should give it a try sometime."

He grinned and waited as the stable boy brought their horses out to them. They quickly packed their things into saddle bags then mounted up and got on the road back to the castle. She cut a glance at Lorne, the image of him dashing around the table with the vendor chasing him flashing through her mind. She shook her head and laughed, and he shot her a roguish grin. Her breath caught in her throat and her face warmed. He was a handsome man ordinarily, but when he smiled at her, it felt like it had the power to stop her heart. He was devastatingly handsome, and she hated the power his smile had over her.

Thunder crashed overhead so loud and sudden, it felt like the earth was splitting open. The horses reared and whinnied loudly, terrified by the sound and it was all they could do to keep them under control. A moment later, a frigid gust of wind was accompanied by the spattering sound of fat raindrops beginning to fall.

"This is bad. Very bad," Lorne said. "The storm is here."

"Aye," she replied. "Come. We have tae get out of the rain and wind."

She nudged her horse on, following a trail that was familiar, but one she hadn't traveled in a very long time. The path wound through the tall, wide trees of the forest, the thick canopy overhead shielding them from most of the rain. For the moment anyway. Wind howled with an eerie, ghostly sound among the trunks as they rode, sending a wave of chills down her back.

"Where are we goin'?" Lorne called.

"I know of a place we can find shelter!"

Peals of thunder crashed one after the other in an endless cascade. It sounded like the sky was being torn apart. Rain poured down through the canopy overhead and gusts of wind that chilled her to the bone swept through the trees.

"There!" Diana called.

She led Lorne to an old cottage she'd seen abandoned long ago. They reined their horses to a stop and tied them off, giving them as much shelter as possible, then dashed inside and closed the door behind them. Outside, the loudest peal of thunder yet crashed, shaking the walls around them.

Diana leaned her back against the door and used her cloak to wipe the raindrops off her face. As Lorne walked around the inside of the cabin as if searching for threats, she took a moment to catch her breath. The flight from the storm had been exhausting.

He paused and turned to her. "I guess we'll be stayin' here the night then."

She nodded as her heart dropped into the pit of her stomach. "Aye. I suppose we will."

CHAPTER TWELVE

The thunder crashed overhead, shaking the floor beneath their feet. It was such a loud and violent noise, it sounded like the mountains around them were being torn asunder. Lorne studied the interior of the small one-room cottage Diana had led them to. It smelled stale and of disuse. Cobwebs clung to the corners and debris from the forest, twigs and leaves, littered the ground around them.

Somewhere in the distance, he heard the sharp crack and thunderous crash of a tree falling victim to the storm. Diana gave a start, worry crossing her face. She looked uneasily at the ceiling above them, no doubt picturing one of the massive trees outside crashing through it and crushing them both beneath its weight. He offered her an encouraging smile.

"This cottage is sturdy enough, lass. I'm sure it's held up through many a storm. We'll be perfectly fine," he said.

"Aye. Probably," she said, though she didn't look so sure.

"Look," he offered brightly. "There's already a stack of wood here. We'll ride out the storm warm and dry."

She nodded then flinched as another peal of thunder split the heavens outside. The flash of lighting that followed lit up the forest around them with a pulsing, strobing light that was as bright as the sun. Diana seemed to be growing uneasier by the moment, so Lorne busied himself with stacking wood in the small fireplace. Once he had that done, he used his dagger and a piece of flint to spark the blaze to life, immediately casting the cottage in light and warmth.

"There we go," he said. "Better?"

Diana offered him a small smile and though she still seemed on edge, he watched as the tension in her shoulders started to ebb. He cleared a large patch in front of the fireplace, using his cloak to sweep away the twigs and leaves that had gathered, them motioned.

"Have a seat," he said. "Get dry and warm."

She sat down without a word but favored him with a grateful smile. Once she was seated, he dropped down next to her and held his hands out, soaking in the warmth of the flames. Aside from the roar of the storm outside and the crackle and pop of the fire inside, the cottage was silent. A tense, awkward air filled the space between them. From the corner of his eye though, he noticed her stealing glances at him, seeming as if she wanted to speak, if only to fill the silence, but wasn't sure what to say. She wasn't very good at small talk. But to be fair, neither was he.

"I hope yer sister is feelin' better," he said.

She nodded stiffly. "Aye. As dae I," she said, then added, almost to herself, "There should be enough tincture tae get her through the night…"

"Does she get these headaches often?"

"Often enough tae worry me," she said. "Me faither's healer says there's naethin' tae be worried about, that it is normal, but…"

"But ye're her sister, so of course ye're goin' tae worry."

A wry smile crossed her face, and she nodded. "Aye. I've always worried about me sister."

"Have ye always been close?"

Her bark of laughter was sharp and brittle. "Oh, we're nae close. We never have been."

"Really? Because ye two seem—"

"I'm tryin'. We're tryin'," she said. "I've always wanted tae be close tae her. We just… we're two very different people and 'tis nae always easy."

Lorne cocked his head. "How dae ye mean?"

"Me sister… she's always been more comfortable around people than I. She needs tae be around them. She likes the grand parties and the attention she gets…"

"And ye dinnae?"

She shook her head. "Nay. I prefer me books. I prefer learnin' tae be a better healer. I prefer tae be of service than bein' a thing tae be fawned over and pursued," she said. "She loves playin' dress-up in fancy silks. Beatrix wants tae be married and loved. She wants tae be adored…"

"And ye dinnae want those things?"

"Me parents want me tae want those things. 'Tis never been important tae me."

Her voice trailed off and her gaze fell to the floor beneath her. Diana's full lips curled down and it wasn't hard to see the pain she felt. Knowing it would be unwelcome, Lorne fought the urge to take her into his arms and comfort her. But the look of sadness on her face and the way her shoulders bowed as if she carried some tremendous burden broke his heart. But there was more in her expression than simple sadness or regret.

"Ye feel guilty because yer relationship with Beatrix isnae what ye want it tae be, eh?"

"I'm the older siblin'," she replied. "'Tis it nae me responsibility?"

"From where I sit, it takes two people tae make a relationship," he replied. "Or break one."

She raised her head, her eyes cold. "Ye and Gavin dinnae seem tae have that problem. Ye both seem thick as thieves."

Guilt racked him and he cringed. His hands balled into fists and he fought the desire to come clean. To tell her this had all been a farce his cousin concocted because he'd allowed himself to fall in love with a girl above his station. The words bubbled up in his throat, but he choked them back down. He couldn't do that to Gavin.

"Nay. We dinnae have that problem," he said through gritted teeth.

"Then ye dinnae ken what ye're on about."

Lorne bristled but held his tongue in check, cleared his throat and adopted a conciliatory face.

"I dinnae need tae have a strained relationship with a siblin' tae ken about relationships," he said softly. "The things we dae fer those we love—and the things we dinnae dae. I ken all about the guilt fer nae thinkin' we've done enough fer them. That we've nae showed them the kind of love we think they deserve. And I ken what it is tae be so different from somebody we love."

She opened her mouth as if she was going to say something but closed it again without speaking. Instead, she stared into the flames and said nothing. Lorne sat silently, admiring the way the light of the fire made her skin glow warmly and sparkled in her emerald-green eyes. Her beauty put a stitch in his heart and filled him with a plethora of feeling as unexpected as they were unfamiliar. He cleared his throat and tried to swallow it all down.

They sat together quietly for several long moments. The fire crackled and the storm raged outside with a ferocity that made even Lorne nervous. Sharp cracking noises echoed in the distance as large branches and trees were felled by nature's fury. As he listened to the rain and wind battering the cottage, a thought occurred to him.

Lorne turned to her. "Can I ask ye a question?"

She grinned wryly. "Can I stop ye?"

"Probably nae."

"Then ask."

"If ye're so dead set on nae marryin', then why are ye allowin' me tae court ye?"

Her eyes glittered as she laughed. "Is that what ye're daein'?"

"Well... I mean... I'm tryin'," he said with a weak shrug. "Ye dinnae make it easy."

Diana turned away, giving him her profile again. She seemed to be weighing her words carefully, torn between telling him or remaining silent. As he gazed at her and absorbed the silence, Lorne was starting to get the feeling that her acceptance of his pledge to court was as false as his offer to court her in the first place. It was a thought that made him want to laugh and he wanted to find out if he was right.

"'Tis all right," he said. "Ye can tell me."

She sighed heavily and nodded to herself; her decision made. "The only way our parents would allow Gavin tae court Beatrix was if I allowed ye tae court me as well," she said. "'Tis why we have tae accompany Beatrix everywhere she goes. She's nae allowed tae be on her own with yer braither. 'Tis improper and unseemly."

"Aye. I understand that. Traditions and propriety must be followed."

"Aye," she said. "Fer as much freedom as our parents give us, which I ken is more than most, they are still very traditional in some ways."

"So, ye're daein' this fer yer sister," he said. "Nae because ye actually want me tae court ye."

Her face colored and her full lips curled down. Regret tinged her features and it wasn't hard to see just how guilty she felt. It was all he could do to keep from laughing. To think they were both doing this for somebody else... Lorne found it hysterical.

"I'm daein' this because I want me sister tae be happy. Bein' with yer braither is the happiest I've ever seen her. And because I'm helpin' her, this is the closest we've ever been," she said.

Lorne grinned fiendishly. "So, after our courtin' is done, if I proposed marriage, ye'd accept just tae make yer sister happy."

A sneer touched her lips, and she turned to him, eyes icy cold. "Ye've nae seemed any more interested in marryin' me than I am in ye. So, let's stop the farce. Ye're dain' this fer yer braither. Same as I'm daein' fer me sister. That's all this is, eh?"

"And if it's nae?"

She held his gaze for a long moment, her full lips parted, a look of consternation on her face. She didn't seem to know how to respond to that. The crack of a log in the fire sent a shower of sparks rising up the chimney like a swarm of fireflies and Lorne gazed longingly into her eyes, admiring the way the light and shadow flickered across her face, making her seem sultry, then mysterious in turns.

The air between them grew charged. It felt like the air right before a lightning strike. The hair on his arms stood on end and goosebumps broke out upon his flesh. The distance between them seemed to be shrinking and all he could see were her full, red lips. Diana's eyes shimmered and her cheeks reddened, but that distance between them continued to diminish.

A crash of thunder outside rattled the walls around them and she gave a start, quickly pulling back. And just like that, the spell that had been cast was broken and as Lorne sat back, he noted a sense of regret bubbling in his chest. He longed to feel her full, pillowy lips against his and silently chastised himself for it.

"We should get some sleep," she said, then cleared her throat.

"Aye. Probably so," he replied.

They laid their cloaks out on the ground then stretched out on top of them. Belatedly, Lorne realized just how close together they were lying. He smelled the floral scent of her perfume and felt the heat radiating from her body. Diana's eyes opened wide, and she looked at him then quickly turned her face up to the ceiling, seeming to realize how close they were lying as belatedly as he had. Her cheeks reddened but she said nothing. Nor did she move away.

Perhaps it was the warmth he offered, perhaps it was the feeling of safety. Whatever it was, Diana remained where she was, as rigid as a piece of iron. Lorne smiled to himself. It probably was a practical matter that kept her where she was —heat and safety. But given how close they had come to kissing and the desire he'd seen in her eyes, momentarily though it was, Lorne preferred to believe it was something else that kept her lying beside him.

For it certainly was something more that kept him beside her.

CHAPTER THIRTEEN

Laird Finley Munro stood at the window in his study, staring out at the land beyond. Thunder crashed in the darkened sky above, sending torrents of rain cascading down like a waterfall. Gusts of frigid wind blew with enough strength to take a man off his feet if he was not paying attention, sending ghostly howls echoing throughout his castle. The weather outside seemed perfectly suited to his mood.

He held a parchment in his hand that was crumpled and battered, mostly by his own angry fist. Munro turned away from the window and threw it down onto his desk, picked up his cup and took a deep draught of the ale inside. His mood was black and it was all he could do to keep his rage in check. He drained last of the ale and with a vicious snarl, hurled the cup against the far wall. It hit it with a sharp bang and clattered to the floor of the study.

The door opened and one of the guards who stood outside poked his head in. "Everythin' all right in here, me laird?"

Munro waved him away. "Everythin's fine. Stand yer bleedin' post."

"Aye, me laird."

The door closed with a resounding bang as Munro dropped into the chair behind his desk. He picked up the crumpled parchment and read the words for what had to be the thousandth time. He had read the missive so many times, he could probably recite it by heart. The message on the page enraged him every bit as much on this read through as it had on the first.

The door to his study opened again and Munro was just about to give his guard yet another tongue lashing when he looked up and let the acidic words wither and die on his lips. His advisor, Graham, entered the room. The older man looked at the cup on the floor and frowned. He picked it up then walked over to the table and poured him another cup of ale before bringing it back to the desk and setting it down in front of him.

"Yer cup must have fallen, me laird," Graham said.

"Aye. Must have."

Graham nodded and groaned as he lowered himself onto the chair in front of his desk. Munro had inherited the older man from his father when he had taken over as laird. His first instinct had been to set the man loose. Munro thought he was too old to be of use. But Graham had proven to be intelligent, shrewd, and cunning. His advice was always sound, and he seemed to be able to see several moves ahead of their adversaries.

It was with Graham's guidance and his own daring that Munro had increased his clan's lands and riches in ways his father would have never imagined. For as great a man as his father was, he played things too carefully at times. Far too carefully. Munro was ambitious, he had a bold vision and was unafraid to do what it took to see it come to fruition.

"What has ye so vexed, lad?" Graham asked.

Munro picked up the discarded parchment. "Ye've seen this?"

The man nodded sagely. "Aye. I've seen it. What of it?"

"She declined me offer of courtship," he growled. "She declined me offer tae marry her."

"It happens."

"Nae tae me, it daesnae. Naebody says nay tae me."

Graham offered him a patient smile. "Daes it really matter, me laird. She's but one woman. There are plenty of other beautiful women fer ye tae choose from—"

Munro slammed his fist down on the table so hard, his cup nearly fell over. He snatched it up before it did and took a long swallow. Graham said nothing to him, giving Munro a moment to settle down. That was also one of the things he appreciated about the old man the most—he had a way of calming him down that others did not. Perhaps it was his experience. Or perhaps he was simply just a patient man. Whatever the reason, Graham had always known when the right time to fire him up was and when it was better to preach calm.

But Munro's veins felt like they were filled with liquid fire. Nobody said no to him. He had wanted Diana from the first moment he had met her at the ball. She was every bit as comely as he'd been told and had a fiery personality he had been looking forward to taming. He had always had a talent with horses and like any good steed, Diana just needed to be broken. It was something he had been very much looking forward to. It never occurred to him that she would refuse his offer of courtship and eventual marriage.

It was something he had never experienced in his life. No woman ever refused him. Ever. And that this tart was comfortable enough to refuse him filled him with the blackest of rages. It wasn't that she was the fairest woman in all his lands, it was the simple fact that she thought she could refuse him that set his blood boiling.

"I think there are bigger things we need tae be focused on," Graham said.

"Ye're the one who said I should take a wife," Munro reminded him. "Ye're the one who's been prattlin' on and on about producin' an heir."

"Aye. And fer good reason. Ye dae need an heir if ye want yer line tae continue as laird," Graham said. "But again, there are plenty of lasses we can find who—"

"And if I dinnae want those other lasses? If I've me mind made up on Lady Diana?"

Graham sighed and sat back, his lips curled down in a frown. He pinched the bridge of his nose like he was trying to stave off a headache. It was something Munro had noticed a long time ago that he did whenever he was being particularly obstinate. But on this, he would not budge. Diana Macgillivray was a nobody. A nothing. A marriage to him would only raise her up in society. Who was she to say no to him?

His logical and rational mind told him that Graham was right. That side of his brain pleaded with him to listen to the wise old man and focus on other, more important things. But the other side of him could not. Diana had wounded his pride.

"Me laird, we have a few matters that need—"

"Did ye find out if the rumors are true?" Munro cut him off.

Graham sighed heavily and pinched the bridge of his nose again. He lowered his gaze and stared at the floor. Munro gave him a moment to speak, his impatience growing with every passing second. He leaned forward, a snarl upon his lips.

"Graham, I gave ye a very simple task. Did ye confirm the rumors?"

"Me laird, 'tis nae important what one girl—"

"'Tis fer me tae decide what is important and what isnae," he snapped. "I am the laird, nae ye. Are ye presumin' tae tell me what I should be concerned with?"

"Of course nae, me laird. I'm simply tryin' tae offer ye counsel as I have done—"

"Ye've always offered sage counsel, I dinnae deny it. But ye're also tasked with followin' me orders. And I told ye I wanted tae ken if thae rumors are true."

The older man's face darkened, and he could not meet Munro's eyes. "The rumors are true, I'm afraid, me laird. It seems that Diana Macgillivray is spendin' quite a bit of time with Lorne Davidson, son of Laird Tiernan Davidson."

"I'm aware of who he is," he said, his voice harder than steel.

Munro sat back in his chair, his stomach churning, white-hot fury flowing through his veins. It wasn't insult enough that she had refused his courtship and potential marriage. She had made it ten times worse by spending her time with a lesser man like Lorne Davidson. A hundred times worse. His lips curled back over his teeth as his anger swelled up like a dark tide within him.

Munro leapt to his feet so quickly, his chair toppled over behind him, hitting the ground with a sharp crash. He howled in rage as he swept up his cup and launched it across the room again. It hit the wall with a dull thud, spraying ale across the stone floor as it landed with a clatter. Munro grabbed the dagger from the top of his desk and shouted a string of curses as he stabbed the parchment from Laird Macgillivray over and over again.

Through it all, Graham sat silently in his chair, watching Munro with patient eyes. It wasn't the first time he had endured one of Munro's outbursts. When he had finished, out of breath and with sweat streaming down his face, he perched on the edge of his desk, twirling the dagger he was still holding in his hand.

"Are ye quite done, me laird," Graham asked.

"Fer the moment."

"'Tis nae worth this amount of upset."

"'Tis the point of the matter," he said.

"And what will ye dae now? If this lass is so important—"

"I will write tae Laird Macgillivray. He needs tae be reminded of what he is losin' by allowin' his daughter tae turn down this alliance," he said. "There will be consequences. Dire consequences. Nobody says nay tae me. Nobody humiliates me the way that tart has by denyin' me and takin' up with that bleedin' Davidson."

"Me laird—"

"I ken what ye're goin' tae say. And I ken we have other important matters tae attend tae," he said. "But this is important tae me so we'll be handlin' this as well."

"And what are ye goin' tae dae, me laird?" Graham asked with a heavy sigh.

Munro looked away for a moment, his mind spinning with dark plans of retribution. They would suffer for this disgrace. As an idea flitted through his mind, he grinned and turned.

"Fetch me one of the chambermaids, Graham," Munro said coldly. "I've an idea."

CHAPTER FOURTEEN

Diana was awakened not by the sound of the storm ravaging the world beyond the cottage, but by the silence. After a whole night of unrelenting howling of the wind and lashing of the rain, the quiet of the forest was surprising. And a bit eerie. Part of her feared the world beyond the door of the cottage might have ended. She got to her feet and walked to the door, quietly opening it, and when she wasn't greeted by fire and chaos or the sky crashing down around them, stepped outside and looked around in wonder.

The relentless fusillade of thunder had stilled and the only sound she could hear was the steady drip-drip-drip of water from the boughs above, still heavy with moisture. The air still felt thick but the clouds overhead, while still slate gray, seemed less threatening. Diana closed her eyes and took a long, deep breath, savoring the scent of the forest around her as she tried to quell the tempest in her mind and heart.

Last night, she had been so close to kissing Lorne. If not for that peal of thunder, she might have. It was like God himself had sent that as a warning for her. She had almost given away her virtue. And what troubled her the most was that she realized she had wanted to. Even now, in the still light of the morning, she wanted to. It was most troubling indeed.

"Looks like the storm let up, eh?"

His sudden voice behind her, shattering the perfect stillness of the morning, startled her. Diana jumped and felt her heart leap into her throat. She turned around and scowled.

"Dae ye need tae sneak up on me like that?" she hissed.

Lorne looked confused and frowned. "I wasnae sneakin'. I just walked out."

She blew out a loud breath and patted down her hair. Diana felt it coming out of its braid and was sure it looked a mess, which embarrassed her. The last thing she wanted was to look a fright in front of him. Lorne's eyes lingered on her and she felt the heat creeping up her neck and into her cheeks. He looked at her like she was the most beautiful thing he'd ever seen. Which, after a night sleeping on the floor of the cottage, she was most assuredly not.

"With the break in the weather, we should get back," she said crisply.

"Aye. 'Tis what I was thinkin' too."

She couldn't help but hear what sounded like a tinge of regret in his voice as he spoke the words. Or perhaps she was just imagining it.

The horses had, amazingly, weathered the storm. They'd sheltered behind the cottage, soaked through and spooked, but were otherwise unharmed. They quickly gathered their things, mounted up, and got on the road home. The sound of thunder in the distance sounded like it was chasing them, so they picked up their pace.

"I guess the weather may nae be done with us yet," he said.

"Daesnae sound like it."

The horse's hooves made a wet, sucking sound as they marched through the mud, silent for the most part, until they reached the castle. As they approached, the gates in the curtain wall opened and they rode into the yard. They quickly dismounted and handed their horses off to the stable boy, just as the front doors to the keep flew open and Beatrix came flying out, auburn locks streaming behind her, with Gavin hot on her heels.

"Where have ye been? We've been worried tae death about ye!" Beatrix cried.

"Are ye all right?" Gavin asked.

"Aye," Lorne said. "Got caught out in the storm."

"We found shelter in the old healer's cottage," Diana said.

Diana's parents stepped out and stood on the steps that led to the front doors of the castle, their faces tight, eyes cold. She shuddered, knowing she was in trouble.

"Ye're alive then," Dunn called.

"Aye, Faither," Diana replied lightly. "A little too worse fer wear, but alive."

"Good," he replied. "Then join yer Maither and I in me study. Both of ye."

And with that, they both turned on their heels and disappeared back into the castle, expecting Diana and Lorne to follow. He cast an uneasy look at her.

"'Tis nae good, eh?" he asked.

"'Tis nae."

"Maither and Faither have been up all night, worried sick about ye," Beatrix said.

"And growin' grumpier by the hour," Gavin added.

Diana sighed. That her parents stayed up all night worrying about her meant she was in trouble. She turned to Lorne.

"We may as well get this over with," she said.

"Good luck," Beatrix said and squeezed her hand.

Gavin patted Lorne on the shoulder as they passed by and climbed the steps then walked into the castle. As they made their way through the labyrinth of corridors, Diana once again felt as if she was headed for the gallows. Except this time, she wasn't sure that feeling was unwarranted. The fact that she had stayed out all night with a man was improper and for her still somewhat traditional parents, it was not something they were going to be happy about.

"How much trouble are we in?" Lorne whispered.

"A lot."

"But we did naethin' wrong."

"Didnae we?"

As they made their way to her father's study, the fear that her parents had somehow found out about her near indiscretion took root in her mind. It was impossible for them to know, of course. They hadn't even known where she and Lorne were. But even knowing that didn't stop the icy grip of paranoid fear from seizing control of her mind.

The guard standing beside the door of her father's study opened it and allowed them inside. The hard bang of it closing behind her reminded Diana of the closing of a prison cell door. Her father sat at his desk and her mother stood behind him, her hand on his right shoulder, both of them staring at her with icy expressions on their faces. Diana was suddenly reminded of being eight years old and getting caught sneaking into the kitchens in the middle of the night and eating her mother's special sweetcakes. Her parents had looked at her then much the same way they were now.

The air in the study was heavy and thick with anticipation. Her parents remained quiet, letting the awkward tension in the air grow even thicker, until Diana felt as if she was choking on it. Lorne though, stood at attention, his hands clasped behind his back, his face blank and neutral. If he had any sliver of fear coursing through his heart, he was not showing it, unlike her.

"And where were ye two last night," her father finally said.

His booming voice sliced into her thoughts like a scythe, impossibly loud. It startled her the way the thunder had been exploding overhead last night, making her jump just as much. She turned to her parents, eyes wide and a hard lump in her throat. She licked her dry, cracked lips, and tried to swallow it down. For a long moment, all she seemed able to do was stand there and gape at them as her words refused to come out.

"Well?" her mother pressed. "Answer yer Faither, Diana."

Her mouth opened and closed but nothing came out. It was as if the fear that choked her had robbed Diana of her power of speech. Seeing her distress, Lorne took a step forward.

"Laird and Lady Macgillivray, 'tis me fault and I must apologize," he said. "I dithered too long in the market last night—"

"We didnae ask ye, Maister Davidson," Dunn said coldly.

"Nay. Ye didnae. But even still, I feel compelled tae speak up fer what is me fault," he said. "We had a long meal in town—Diana, Beatrix, Gavin and meself, I mean. Beatrix came down with a headache, so since we hadnae acquired the items we went tae town, but first we sent Beatrix on tae get one of Diana's tinctures while we searched for the wine and sweetcakes Lady Macgillivray had requested."

As if suddenly rediscovering her voice, Diana stepped up beside Lorne. "We were on our way back when the storm broke. 'Twas wicked, Maither and Faither," she said. "We sought shelter in the old healer's cabin just outside of town. If we hadnae, we might nae have made it back at all."

Lorne stepped forward and set the bag he was carrying down on the desk in front of her father. She watched as her mother's neck flushed scarlet, the color slowly creeping into her face. She reached for the bag, but her father was quicker and snatched it away. He opened it up and pulled out the boxes of sweetcakes and bottles of wine, setting them down on the desk then turned to her.

"Ye sent them intae town fer this?" he asked incredulously.

She shrugged as a sly smirk crossed her lips. "'Tis nae like I kent the storm was comin'," she said with a smile. "Besides, I thought a day in town might be good fer all of 'em. And as I remember it, ye thought it a good idea too."

"I didnae think ye were sendin' 'em out fer wine and sweetcakes."

"Well, 'tis yer fault fer nae askin' then," her mother said.

A grin flickered at the corners of Diana's mouth… then quickly vanished when her father turned his cold, hard eyes on her again. His lips curled downward, his face marked with disapproval.

"And ye two stayed in the old healer's cottage last night?" he asked. "Alone?"

Lorne cleared his throat. "I offered tae sleep outside in the storm with the horses for propriety's sake, but lady Diana was kind enough tae insist I sleep by the fire instead."

Diana felt her face blanch at Lorne's cheeky response. Her mother hid a smile behind her hand and turned away. Even her father's eyes glittered with amusement, but he composed himself quickly, his gaze turning steely, staring at Lorne with something darker than disapproval.

"Me daughter's virtue—"

"Remains intact, me laird. I promise ye," Lorne said, his tone a bit more conciliatory. "We sheltered in the cottage from the storm. Naethin' more. 'Twas a matter of keepin' safe."

Her father stared at him for a long, tense moment as if trying to determine whether or not he was telling the truth. Diana cleared her throat.

"I swear it, Faither. Me virtue has nae been sullied. Lorne was a perfect gentleman the whole night," she said. "Ye ken me, faither."

He nodded, his expression sober. "There is somethin' else."

"What is it then?"

He picked up a parchment from his desk. "We received a letter from Laird Munro. It seems he's nae taken ye declinin' his courtship well."

"How so?" Diana asked, as her flesh prickled with goosebumps.

"He's promisin' retribution of some kind," her father said. "Says he daes nae appreciate bein' denied and will make us pay. Make ye pay specifically. Also promises that he'll make ye his bride if it's the last thing he daes."

Diana shuddered and shook her head. "Seems me instincts about the man were correct."

"Seems so," her father said. "In any event, I dinnae want ye or yer sister tae stray far from the keep. And on those occasions when ye dae need tae go outside the walls, I want ye tae have an escort. Maister Lorne, fer example."

"Aye, Faither," she said.

He stared at them both for another long, tense moment, as if trying to decide once and for all whether they had told him the truth about their adventure in the cottage. He finally nodded to himself, seemingly satisfied they had.

"All right. Go clean up and get somethin' tae eat," he said.

"Me laird, if I may, I just wanted to mention that there was an altercation yesterday at the inn we stopped at tae eat. Laird Munro approached yer daughter and spoke disrespectfully tae her. He insisted she go somewhere quiet with him fer a drink, after she said nae more than once and told him she had tae get back tae the castle tae bring things fer her maither," said Lorne.

"Is that so? And then what happened?" asked Dunn, his forehead corrugated.

"I asked him several times to leave, that the Lady Diana didnae want tae go. When he didnae listen, we came tae hands, I'm afraid. He finally left in a sulk," Lorne told him. "I fear his anger is partly me fault fer affronting him, and I am sorry fer that," he added.

"Ye only defended me. Laird Munro was being horrible, ye have naething tae be sorry about," Diana cut in in his defense.

Dunn tookin what he had heard and nodded.

"Thank ye, Lorne, fer defending me daughter and making sure she made it back safely. Ye may have angered him more, but I am sure he would have been angered by our response nonetheless," replied Dunn, patting Lorne on the back.

"Thank ye, Faither. I'm sorry we worried ye," Diana said.

"Aye. Me apologies as well," Lorne added.

As they walked out of the study, she reflected on what her father had said about Munro's letter. It made her all the more glad she had rebuffed his interest in her.

"May I accompany ye fer somethin' tae eat?"

She nodded. "Aye. After I clean up. And ye could use with a bath yerself. Ye smell terribly."

He laughed. "Very well. I'll see ye soon."

CHAPTER FIFTEEN

*A*fter a hot bath and some fresh clothes, Lorne was feeling human again. But as he stalked down the hall, a dark cloud hung over his head. There was a tightness in his chest, and it felt as if he carried a stone in his belly that he just could not shake, no matter how hard he tried. And he knew why.

"There ye are."

Lorne stopped and turned around to find Gavin rushing up to him from behind. The man smiled and he pulled him into a tight embrace, pounding him on the back.

"I was worried half out of me bleedin' mind about ye," he said. "What happened out there?"

"Storm broke and we had tae take shelter."

"Did ye now?" he asked slyly. "And how were the... accommodations then, eh?"

As he looked into the grinning face of his cousin, he felt that darkness inside of him swell and he had the sudden urge to slap the smile off his face. The tightness in his chest and the stone in the pit of his belly were because of him. As if sensing his mood darkening, Gavin's expression sobered and the smile slipped from his lips.

"What's wrong?" Gavin asked.

"I cannae keep daein' this," Lorne replied.

"Daein' what?"

"Lyin' tae Diana!"

Gavin's face blanched and he motioned for Lorne to quiet down. He grabbed him by the arm and dragged him into an alcove just off the main corridor, looking around as if afraid they might be seen or overheard. When he saw nobody else around, Gavin turned back to him.

"What happened out there?" he asked. "What's got ye in such a state, eh?"

"Naethin' happened. But ye turned us both intae liars and the bleedin' burden is gettin' too heavy tae carry, Gavin. I cannae keep daein' this."

"Cousin, I need ye tae calm down."

"How am I supposed tae calm down when I feel like I'm bein' torn apart inside?"

Gavin recoiled like Lorne had just slapped him, his face a mask of fear and confusion. He opened his mouth and stammered for a moment then ran a hand across his face.

"What dae ye mean? Torn apart?" Gavin asked. "I dinnae understand."

Lorne sighed and raked his fingers through his hair as he tried to find a way to explain it. The problem was, he didn't understand it himself. All he knew was that he felt something for Diana. He couldn't define the feelings he had for her because they were so foreign to him. But he knew it was tearing him to pieces knowing he was lying to her.

"We have tae stop this farce, Gavin," he hissed. "The longer this goes on, the harder it's goin' tae be tae get out from under the lie."

"Dae ye think we'll be able tae get out from under it now?" he replied. "We're in too deep, cousin. We're trapped in our own lie."

"Yer lie."

Gavin grimaced. "Which, is now yer lie since ye went along with it."

"Ye son of a—"

"'Tis nae what I meant. This is all me fault. I ken that," he said, holding his hands up in surrender. "All I mean is that ye're trapped in it sure as I am. And aye, 'tis me fault. 'Tis me who told the lie that got us intae this."

Lorne sighed and turned his face up to the ceiling, his mind racing with a thousand different thoughts. As much as he blamed him for their predicament, his cousin had spoken true —this now was as much his lie as it was Gavin's. He hadn't put a stop to it when it had started because he wanted to see his cousin happy. But things had gone too far.

"The question is how are we goin' tae get ourselves out of this?" Lorne asked.

"I dinnae ken," Gavin said somberly. "Is there a way we can get out of this without me losin' Beatrix? I dinnae ken if I can bear tae lose her."

Lorne pinched the bridge of his nose and squeezed his eyes shut, doing his best to contain the sudden flash of anger that was boiling over inside of him. Screaming at his cousin wasn't going to do anybody any good. He let out a long breath and stared at him for a long moment.

"What is it ye're nae understandin', Gavin?" he asked, his voice trembling with frustration. "I ken 'tis nae yer fault, but ye arenae goin' tae be allowed tae be with her."

Sadness streaked his face. "Lorne—"

"And when ye tell her who ye are and that ye've been lyin' tae her this whole time, she's nae goin' tae want tae be with ye anyway," he presses. "The sooner ye can learn tae accept that, the better it will be fer ye."

He shook his head miserably. "If I cannae have Beatrix, it will never be better fer me."

"Ye should have thought about that before ye lied," Lorne said with exasperation. "Where did ye think this was goin' tae lead?"

Part of his anger was directed at Gavin. But part of it was directed at himself for going along with this farce. More than that, it was the growing realization that Gavin losing Beatrix meant Lorne was going to lose Diana. And that thought sent a dagger of pain straight through his heart. It was unthinkable when they first got to Castle Macgillivray, but Lorne couldn't deny that he had grown increasingly fond of Diana.

Gavin looked at him, a strange expression crossing his face. "Ye fell fer her, didnae ye?" he asked. "'Tis why ye're so surly, isnae it?"

He moved his eyes away for a moment, unable to look at his cousin. Lorne hated to think he was so transparent, that his feelings for Diana were so clear. This situation was growing more complicated by the second and Lorne didn't know what to do with all the emotions that were swirling around inside of him.

He glowered at his cousin. "What's botherin' me the most is that we're lyin' tae this family. They're good people and dinnae deserve tae be deceived, Gavin."

Gavin frowned and turned away, his face clouded over with emotion. Lorne felt bad for his cousin but he was also very worried about the ramifications this was going to have for their clan. In addition, Lorne's father already held him in low esteem. This scandal was only going to make him think even less of him as a son, and as a man.

"Gavin, we need tae think of what's goin' tae happen at home when the truth comes tae light," Lorne said. "We'll be lucky if we can avoid war with the Macgillivrays."

"Then what are we goin' tae dae?"

Lorne rubbed his chin. "I'm nae sure yet. But we need tae figure out how tae get out of this as painlessly as we can. And that starts with ye tellin' Beatrix the truth."

"But—"

"Nay. I've got a responsibility tae protect the clan. Tae think about what's best fer it," Lorne said. "I've got tae dae me duty tae the clan, Gavin."

Gavin lowered his gaze, his expression both fearful and grief-stricken. Lorne leaned forward and lowered his voice.

"I mean it, Gavin. Ye need tae tell her," he said. "Or I will."

Lorne left him standing in the alcove and stepped into the corridor again. Movement in his peripheral vision drew his attention. He thought he saw somebody disappearing around a corner at the far end but couldn't be sure. He shook his head and mumbled to himself about seeing things and jumping at shadows. This situation with Gavin had him on edge.

Doing his best to shake it off, he stalked off, determined to enjoy a meal and a little time with Diana while he was still able to before everything came crashing down around him.

CHAPTER SIXTEEN

Diana had managed to avoid Lorne most of the day, doing everything she could to not be alone with him, but when the bell for dinner rang, she had no choice but to attend. It had been a stiff, cold affair. He'd tried to engage her in conversation multiple times, but she had rebuffed him, drawing curious glances from her mother. Her father had been so engaged in conversation with Gavin and Beatrix, he hadn't noticed and for that she was glad.

As soon as the evening meal had ended, Diana had excused herself, telling everybody she had a headache and just needed to lie down. They seemed to believe she was still suffering the effects of her night out in the storm combined with the stress of Laird Munro's not so subtle threats on their life and safety. And she was happy to let them think that.

She lay in bed staring up at the ceiling as she'd been doing for what felt like hours. The castle around her had gone silent as everybody else had retired for the night but Diana hadn't been able to sleep. Her mind was filled with Lorne's voice, talking to Gavin about duty and responsibility. Just hearing those words echoing through her head sent a fresh wave of anger washing through her.

After freshening up, she had gone in search for him, looking forward to sharing a meal with him after their ordeal the night before. Something between them had shifted. She'd felt it. And the way he'd looked at her made Diana think he had as well. But when she heard him speaking to his brother in the alcove, although she hadn't been able to make out everything they were saying, she'd heard enough to know she'd been very wrong.

The idea that Lorne viewed her as a duty, or a responsibility sent a dagger of pain through her heart. It made her see that all this they had been doing had been a farce. That she was simply something he had to put up with so his brother could be with Beatrix. Lorne didn't want to be with her. Didn't want to court her, let alone marry her. He was doing this for his brother. The same way she was doing this for her sister, she supposed.

With a growl of frustration, Diana threw the covers back and climbed out of bed. Lying there staring at the ceiling was only causing more frustration to grow and fester within her. Throwing on a thin robe and her slippers, she padded out of her room and down the corridor, swift and silent as a shadow. Usually, when she was this frustrated, there was only one thing that helped get her out of that mood.

Sweets.

Diana made her way down to the kitchens and poked around, then moving into the cold room. A smile stretched across her lips when she found what she was looking for. Grabbing the tray, she brought it out and set it down on the table. She picked up a sweetcake, admiring the moist, spongy texture for a moment before taking a bite.

Diana's eyes rolled back in her head, and she groaned with pure pleasure as the sweet, lemony taste hit her tongue. Yes, she thought, this was exactly what she needed. She felt her disposition lightening almost immediately. She finished off the first cake then greedily grabbed another.

She was halfway through her second cake and was already thinking about a third when she felt a presence behind her.

"Diana—"

The voice shattered the quiet in the kitchens, making her jump out of her skin. Without thinking, she spun around and collided with a large man. As her instincts took control of her body, her knee came up hard, crashing into the man's soft groin. The man grunted and stumbled backward. He pinwheeled his arms, trying to keep on his feet, but he tripped over a box on the floor that sent him staggering. Diana watched in horror as, just before he found the purchase and pulled him out of the spin, he crashed face-first into a cabinet with a sharp grunt.

"Lorne!" she called.

He managed to avoid going down completely, but he still fell to a knee, his hand clapped over his nose. Blood, thick and scarlet, squeezed between his fingers. Lorne took a beat to gather himself then got to his feet and turned to her. He pulled his hand away, revealing the blood flowing from his nose. His normally handsome visage was streaked red and looked like something straight out of Diana's nightmares and she shuddered.

"What in the bleedin' hell are ye daein'?" he roared.

Planting her hands on her hips, she glowered at him as she bristled. "What in the hell am I daein'? What in the hell are ye daein' sneakin' up on me like that?"

"I wasnae sneakin'! I've been lookin' fer ye!"

Lorne grabbed a cloth on the counter nearest to him and put it to his nose. They're gazes were locked and the kitchen was filled with a strange and awkward tension. She felt the smile flickering across her lips and before she knew it, she was laughing out loud. Laughing like it was the funniest thing in the world. And a moment later, Lorne joined her.

They laughed long and loud for several minutes, both of them doubling over, tears of mirth squeezing out of their eyes. They laughed without knowing exactly what they were laughing at, but it broke the tension in the room. And when their hysterics finally tapered off, the mood in the room was far lighter than it had been just a couple of moments prior.

"I'm sorry," he said. "I didnae mean tae sneak up on ye."

She stared at him and sighed, then pointed to a stool that sat beside a counter. "Sit."

He did as she told him while Diana gathered a basin, water, and some fresh cloth. She carried it all over to where he sat.

"Ye're a mess," she said.

"Well, if ye'd nae busted me nose, maybe I wouldnae be."

She giggled. "Maybe this'll teach ye ta nae sneak up on a lass."

"Aye. I'll be sure tae wear a bell next time."

She laughed as she tended to his wound, losing herself in the work. Things between them felt easy once more and the anger she'd been holding on to all day somehow melted away like butter in the summer sun.

"Why were ye lookin' fer me, anyway?" she asked.

"I wanted tae talk, so I went tae yer chamber, but ye werenae there," he said. "With Munro's threat, I got worried, so I've been lookin' all over the castle fer ye."

His concern for her was touching and Diana felt her heart swell. But then she heard his voice echoing through her mind again, talking to his brother about duty, and the shadow over her heart returned, dark and thick. Once she had the blood washed away from his face, she stepped back and stared at him. She wasn't going to say anything to him about what she'd heard, but as she looked into his piercing blue eyes, she decided she wanted to. If only because she wanted answers about all of this and why he was pretending with her.

"I heard ye talkin' tae yer braither earlier," she said. "When ye were in the alcove. I heard ye sayin' that ye were courtin' me because ye felt it was yer duty."

He frowned and didn't say anything for a moment as if he was trying to recall what she was talking about, but then comprehension dawned on his face.

"Nay. I was nae talkin' about ye," he said. "We werenae talkin' about ye."

"Then what were ye talkin' about?"

"About me co—about Gavin," he replied. "I was remindin' him that he has a duty tae the clan and that he needs tae always be truthful."

A shadow crossed his face, and Diana got the idea there was more to the story. But she knew she couldn't demand he tell her everything he and his brother spoke about, especially when they had been speaking in private. But when he said he was not referring to her, she had heard the sincerity in his voice and saw the earnestness in his eyes. She believed him.

"Ye truly werenae speakin' of me? Ye dinnae see me as a duty tae yer clan?" she asked.

He shook his head. "Nay. Ye're nay a duty. Ye're naethin' but a joy and a pleasure."

"Ye're a man strictly bound tae duty though, eh?"

He frowned and seemed to think about it for a moment before nodding. "Aye. I suppose that's a true statement."

"Why is that?" she asked, curious to learn more about him.

He sighed and seemed to be debating with himself whether to open that door inside of him, perhaps fearing what lay behind it. But when he raised his gaze to her, she saw a steely determination in his eyes. She could see that he wanted to be open and honest with her but she also saw a tinge of fear, perhaps because he was a man who didn't open himself up to anybody.

"What is it?" she asked gently.

"Me faither… he's never approved of me. He's never been proud of me. And it's foolish, I ken, but I've been chasin' that approval from him all me life. I take me duty very seriously hopin' that one day, me faither will see me. That he'll be proud of me," he admitted.

Lorne's shoulders slumped, as if speaking those words had taken a toll on him. Diana's heart went out to him, and she reached out, taking his hand, and gave it a gentle squeeze. He met her eyes and Diana felt something inside of her lurch.

"Ye're a good man, Lorne Davidson," she said. "Ye're kind. Loyal. Honest. I've only kent ye a small time now, but even I can see that."

A shadow crossed over his face at her words, and he shook his head. "Yer words are kind and I'm grateful fer them, but I dinnae deserve such a compliment. I dinnae feel like a good man. I dinnae think I'm loyal or honest."

She frowned and gripped his hand tighter. "I've seen the way ye are with yer braither. Ye're loyal tae him. Kind tae him. If nae fer ye tryin' tae make him happy, ye'd nae be here right now, eh?"

A wry grin curled his lips. "That's more true than ye'll never ken."

"Then, see? Me words are true."

His grin was tight and she got the feeling there was more behind his eyes. And that was all right. She wouldn't pry. He looked down at her hand, still clasping his and smiled. He raised it and placed a soft, gentlemanly kiss on the back of it.

"Thank ye," he said.

Diana felt the heat creeping up her neck and spread through her face. Her cheeks burned hot and that familiar feeling of gossamer wings brushing the inside of her heart returned. She walked over and grabbed the plate of sweetcakes and brought one to him.

"Friends?" she said.

He took one of the small treats. "Aye. Friends."

As they devoured their treats, she noticed Lorne's eyes widen as he took her in. His cheeks flushed and she could see he was trying to avert his gaze but couldn't seem to manage to.

Diana looked down and felt an instant rush of sheer mortification. In all the commotion, she hadn't realized her thin robe had fallen open and that her night shirt was cut so low, it left little to the imagination. The outline of her full, round breasts was more than clear.

She quickly pulled her robe closed and tied it, her cheeks burning furiously. Lorne finally managed to look away but not before she'd seen the smile playing across his lips. Her heart thundered wildly and although she was mortified, she had seen his admiring gaze on her body and didn't entirely hate it, although she would never admit it, least of all to him. He looked at her like she was a living work of art and it never failed to stir the embers of desire deep inside of her.

Clearing her throat, she stared to clean up the mess on the table. She then made the mistake of meeting Lorne's eyes. He held her there, unable to move, barely breathing. But then he did. Lorne took her hand in his and brought it to his lips, placing a soft kiss on her knuckles again. This time, it was less gentlemanly and more passionate. Diana's body was instantly aflame as tingles like little bursts of electricity raced across her body.

Lorne turned her hand over and kissed the palm then the inside of her wrist. His lips were velvety soft as he planted a line of kisses up to the inside of her elbow, never taking his eyes off her. Diana's body vibrated and her breath caught in her throat. The desire to kiss him pulled at her heart, her soul. And Diana felt herself leaning forward. Slowly, inch by inch, the distance between them closed and she was keenly aware of the heat radiating from his body.

Diana licked her lips and tried in vain to slow her racing heart. Her legs trembled and she feared they would give out beneath her. It was a struggle to remain on her feet, but she managed it. Lorne's breath was warm upon her skin and smelled faintly of lemon and sugar. Her body felt as if it was hot to the touch and her heart felt like it was pounding so hard, it would leave bruises on the inside of her chest. The insides of her thighs grew warm and uncomfortably slick. Diana had never felt anything like it before and was terrified… but also exhilarated.

A loud cough and shuffling footsteps rang out, startling them both. They leaped back and turned to see one of the older chambermaids stepping into the kitchen. The older woman looked up, seeming to be as startled to see them as they were to see her.

"Beggin' pardon," the woman said, her voice raspy. "Just gettin' an early start on me chores. Should I come back later then?"

"Nae," Diana said quickly. "We were just leavin'."

With one last look at Lorne and a smile on her lips, she turned and rushed from the kitchen, sure the heat in her face was going to make her head burst into flame any second. She had almost kissed Lorne—again. If not for the maid, she would have. The desire to kiss him was only growing greater by the minute and Diana wasn't sure what to do with that, other than to give in to her desire.

CHAPTER SEVENTEEN

*L*orne spent the balance of the night, tossing and turning, unable to get a wink of sleep. As he stared at the ceiling, all he seemed able to see were Diana's luscious lips biting into the sweetcakes. He couldn't stop seeing the bits of cream and jam stuck to her lips. And of course, couldn't stop seeing her body. When her robe fell open, he'd gotten a good look at her and had immediately felt the fires of desire spring to life inside of him. He couldn't unsee those round, full breasts and the puffy, pink nipples that poked against the fabric of her nightshirt.

She was absolute perfection, her body having been chiseled with loving care by God himself. Lorne could confidently say he had never seen a more exquisite creation in all the world than Diana Macgillivray. He pressed the heels of his hands to his eyes and groaned, trying to shut the images of Diana's perfect body out of his mind. The harder he tried though, the firmer they stuck. They were like a splinter stuck just beneath his skin and try as he might, he couldn't dig it out.

As he lay in bed, feeling his arousal mounting, the sky beyond the windows grew lighter. The sun rose behind a screen of iron gray clouds, casting the world outside in a dim, murky light. With a grumble, Lorne threw the covers back and slipped out of bed. He walked straight over to the wash basin and splashed cold water on his face. He scrubbed his eyes, then splashed yet more water onto his face. He stared at himself in the looking glass, noticing the dark shadows beneath his red, puffy, bloodshot eyes.

"I look like bleedin' hell," he muttered to himself.

After washing his face, Lorne stripped out of his night close, tossing them onto a nearby chair, then pulled on black breeches, black boots, and a mustard-colored shirt. He slipped a dark coat over that, then turned back to the looking glass and inspected himself. He looked tired—the consequence of a long, sleepless night. But at least he was presentable.

Despite feeling wrung out and exhausted, Lorne was in a chipper, upbeat mood. He was in a far better mood than he had any right to, given that he was so tired. But last night's antics in the kitchen with Diana had put a charge into his heart he couldn't deny. He had almost kissed Diana—again—and he knew if not for that servant walking in at the wrong time, he would have.

As he had lain in bed during the night, thinking about everything that had happened, he realized for the first time that this farce Gavin had dragged him into had become very real for him. And that's what made this whole situation so painful.

Dressed and ready for the day, Lorne headed out of his room. He had hoped to catch up with Diana and spend a little time with her. He knew what he was doing was foolish, that the entire house of cards he and Gavin had built was going to come crashing down soon enough. Allowing himself to get even more caught up in Diana and the feelings she inspired within him was stupid. It was not going to end well, and he knew it.

And yet, despite that knowledge, he couldn't stop himself from wanting to spend time with her while he could. What she'd said the night before about him being a good man with a good heart—he hoped she would still be able to feel that way when she found out he had been abetting his cousin's lie all this time.

He knew it was going to be an uphill battle. But it was a fight he was more than willing to take on. Lorne knew, beyond the shadow of a doubt, that he wanted to be with Diana. He wanted to court her properly, and if she was willing, ask for her hand. Yes, an alliance with the Macgillivrays would benefit his clan. Perhaps enough that it might please his father. But for the first time in his life, Lorne wasn't thinking about his father's pride or esteem.

As he rounded the corner, he saw Gavin slipping into the alcove where they'd spoken yesterday. His cousin hadn't seen him, his gaze had been fixed on something—or rather, somebody—already in the recess whom he assumed was Beatrix. But the quick glance he'd gotten of his cousin had left him troubled. Gavin had looked pensive. Fearful.

Lorne slipped down the hallway on soft, quiet feet and pressed his back against the wall just outside the alcove and listened. As he'd expected, he recognized Beatrix's voice with Gavin. They were speaking in hushed whispers, but he strained his ears and could hear them just fine.

"I need tae tell ye somethin'."

That was Gavin. Lorne's stomach lurched as he realized his cousin was about to confess their deception. That house of cards was about to come down.

"Are ye goin' tae tell me ye love me?" Beatrix said with a breathless giggle. "Because, if that's what ye're goin' tae say, I already ken. And just in case ye were wonderin', I love ye too."

Even standing out in the corridor as he was, Lorne could feel the tension radiating from his cousin as he struggled with telling her the truth. It was thick and oppressive and despite the fact that Gavin was doing the right thing and was finally setting things right, he couldn't help but feel for his cousin.

But then, he felt his own stomach churning. Once Beatrix knew, Diana would know and so would end any chance of him being with her. So, perhaps he did know and could relate to turmoil tearing the guts out of his cousin.

"Aye," Gavin said, a tremor in his voice. "Ye're right. I love ye, Beatrix."

"And I love ye, Gavin Davidson."

"Then I'm the luckiest lad in the world."

He heard the rustle of clothing as they likely embraced and kissed. Lorne frowned. Gavin hadn't been able to go through with it. The lie remained intact and the house of cards they'd built remained standing.

He knew he shouldn't be happy about that and that he should be the one to tell Diana the truth and end this charade. He had a duty to protect his clan. A responsibility to always be upright and forthcoming. Those were values his father had ingrained him all his life.

And yet, as he practically skipped down the hall, all he could think about was having more time to spend with Diana. More time to see her smile. To hear her laugh. And maybe, just maybe, to steal a kiss or two before his whole world imploded.

CHAPTER EIGHTEEN

Diana watched her sister in the looking glass. A small smile playing across her full, heart-shaped lips, Beatrix stood behind her, brushing out her long blond locks. She felt her heart swell as a smile of her own touched the corners of her mouth.

"Ye've never brushed me hair out for me before," Diana said softly.

"I suppose I havenae," Beatrix replied with a gentle laugh.

"So, what is the occasion?"

She shrugged her thin shoulders. "I suppose I felt 'twas time I remedied that."

Beatrix giggled, that shy, secretive smile flashing across her lips. Diana grabbed her sister by the hand and pulled her down onto the bench beside her. Taking her other hand in hers, Diana squeezed Beatrix's hand, only making the girl giggle and blush furiously. She refused to meet Diana's eyes, but her smile widened and the blush in her cheek flowed down her neck, turning it a shade of red that couldn't be found in nature.

"What is it then?" Diana pressed.

Beatrix raised her gaze. "Can ye keep a secret fer me?"

Diana's breath caught in her throat. In all their years as sisters, Beatrix had never once asked Diana to keep her confidence about anything. She felt a hitch in her heart and had to genuinely fight to keep the tears from welling in her eyes.

"Of course, I can keep a secret fer ye," Diana said.

"I'm in love."

Diana laughed. "I already ken that."

Beatrix cocked her head and frowned. "Ye did?"

"Aye. I can see it all over yer face whenever ye're lookin' at Gavin."

Her blush deepened and she turned impossibly red, but she looked happy. And it filled her own heart with a joy that mirrored Beatrix's.

"Well, I cannae help it," Beatrix said. "He makes me feel things I've never felt before."

"And? Daes he love ye back."

Her smile was so wide, Diana feared Beatrix's face might split in half. Her joy was infectious though and Diana couldn't stop her own smile from matching that of her sister's. Never before, in all their lives together, had she felt so close to Beatrix as she did in that moment.

"Aye. He told me he loves me back," Beatrix said.

They both squealed like giddy girls and still clutching each other's hands, bounced together on the bench. She truly was over the moon that her sister had found a love that filled her so completely, that brought her the sense of wonder and jubilation she saw on Beatrix's face. But then Diana's smile faltered and she looked at her sister with serious eyes.

"Beatrix, have ye… ye and Gavin…"

Diana let her words trail off, the implication in them more than clear. Beatrix giggled and clapped her hands over her mouth, squeezing her eyes shut as an expression of mortification crossed her face. She shook her head.

"Nay, Diana. Naethin' like that," she exclaimed. "He's been a perfect gentleman. More than a perfect gentleman if ye ask me. If he'd wanted tae, I might have given meself tae him."

"Beatrix!" Diana said with a shocked laugh.

"But true. 'Tis how much I love him."

"Ye cannae give yer maidenhead tae a man ye're nae married tae!"

"Who would ken, sister?"

"Beatrix!"

She squealed with laughter. "I havenae given meself tae him. Breathe, Diana. I was teasin' ye. I'm nae that much of a harlot."

A wry grin twisted her lips. Leave it to Beatrix to nearly stop her heart dead in her chest like that. But she had to wonder if there was some bit of truth in her sister's words. Diana knew Beatrix had long wanted to feel like a grownup, to feel love and all that came with it. So far as she knew, her sister remained pure and untouched but given the feelings she saw in Beatrix's eyes when it came to Gavin, she wondered how long that would last.

"We have kissed though," Beatrix admitted. "I like kissin' him."

"Beatrix!"

"What? 'Tis nae the same as givin' him me maidenhead!"

"Still. 'Tis more than ye should be daein' with a lad."

Beatrix looked at her with a mischievous glint in her eye. "Believe me, sister. I may have kissed a lad or two, but here is nay lad in all of Scotland who thinks me legs are easy tae open."

"Scandalous!"

Her sister giggled and covered her mouth with her hand—it was a gesture that reminded Diana of their mother. Beatrix had always looked their mother in many ways, physically, using the same sort of gestures, and the fiery attitude of defiance that oozed from her every pore.

Diana on the other hand, was more like their father. Coldly calculating at times. Practical. More thoughtful. She had a strong sense of morality and propriety. She'd never had the same interest in men as Beatrix did, preferring her books and learning about the art of healing to fancy social gatherings. It made people like Beatrix think she was prudish or shrew-like. She had never been one to chase love or affection and if she was being honest with herself, she would admit it was mostly because she feared it. She feared being hurt. So, she simply avoided it altogether. It was safer that way.

"'Tis nae as scandalous as ye think, sister," Beatrix said. "And ye cannae tell me ye've nae thought of kissin' Lorne. I've seen thae way ye look at him too, ye ken."

Her sister smiled at her conspiratorially and winked! Diana felt the heat creeping up her neck and spread out into her cheeks. She knew her face was a shade that matched the unnatural shade of red in her sister's face just a few minutes ago, when she'd been talking about Gavin. She cleared her throat and sat up primly.

"I dinnae ken what ye're talkin' about," she said.

"Oh, I think ye dae."

Images of her encounter with Lorne in the kitchen flashed through Diana's mind as she recalled the way his gaze had lingered on her breasts when her robe had fallen open. She bit her bottom lip to suppress the low groan bubbling up in her throat. She sniffed and looked away for a moment, trying to compose herself.

"See? There, that look," Beatrix chortled. "I ken it. Ye were just thinkin' about him. Ye always get that look of rapture on yer face when ye're near him."

"Stop it," Diana said. "Ye're incorrigible."

"But I'm nae wrong."

Diana glanced at herself in the looking glass and cringed when she saw just how red her cheeks actually were. No. Beatrix wasn't wrong. Diana couldn't control her thoughts, or the color of her face apparently, whenever Lorne was around. Or simply when she thought of him. He was not like what she'd thought when they'd first met. Yes, he could be an oaf. He could be arrogant and snide. And he could be entirely too cocky to be taken seriously.

At the same time though, there was a depth to him she had not expected. He was kind, thoughtful. He could even be soft spoken and self-deprecating. The man was like an onion, with many layers to his being, and yes, Diana had very nearly given him her first kiss. It was only fate—or perhaps divine interference—that had kept her from crossing that line. And though she was thankful for it, she was also frustrated. Deep down, she wanted to kiss Lorne.

"Dae ye like him?" she asked.

Diana gave herself a small shake, as if trying to snap herself back to the present. She had never stopped to consider what her feelings for him really were or what they meant. All she knew was that she did indeed feel something for him.

"Diana? Dae ye like him?"

"I dinnae ken, Beatrix," she replied. "But... 'tis fair tae say I feel a certain interest fer him."

She laughed. "Ye sound so rigid and formal about it. 'Tis like ye dinnae really feel it at all."

"But... I dae. Feel it, that is."

"Are ye certain?"

Diana gnawed on her bottom lip and lowered her gaze. Talking about her feelings had always been uncomfortable for her. She was much better at engaging her brain and her logic than her heart and emotions. But she had to admit that talking to Beatrix and really sharing her feelings with her sister, for the first time in her life, felt... good. She felt closer, bonded to her. It was what she had always wanted but had never known how to obtain.

She nodded. "Aye. I'm certain," she said, finally raising her eyes to meet her sister's. "When I'm with Lorne, I feel things I've never felt before."

"So, ye like him."

Diana laughed. "I wouldnae go that far. Nae yet. But what I feel fer him, I feel deeply," she said then leaned closer and lowered her voice, speaking quietly as if there was somebody else listening. "And if ye can keep me secret, I almost gave him me first kiss. Twice."

Beatrix's eyes widened. "Twice?"

Diana's face was burning so hot, she thought it might burst into flames, but she nodded and laughed. "Aye. Once in the cottage we hid in from the storm, and again last night in the kitchens. If nae fer old Hilda coming in, I might have."

Beatrix threw her arms around the back of Diana's neck and pulled her tightly. Diana laughed and hugged her sister back, feeling a rush of warmth and closeness she'd never dared imagine she and Beatrix would share. It made her want to cry.

"Then maybe ye and Lorne will marry after all?"

Diana laughed. "I wouldnae go that far. This is all new tae the both of us. And I dinnae ken how he really feels. I mean, it might just be lust that I think is somethin' more—"

Beatrix shook her head. "Just as I've seen the way ye look at him, I've seen the way he looks at ye, sister. He's more than just smitten. He's in love with ye."

Diana's heart leaped into her throat, and she gasped. Those wings that lightly brushed her insides when she was near him turned insistent and harder than normal and an intense but not unpleasant heat formed in the pit of her belly and spread outward. She could hardly contain her smile or the giggle that threatened to burst from her mouth.

"Dae ye really think so?" she asked shyly.

Beatrix rolled her eyes. "Sister, if there is one thing I ken, it's men."

"I suppose ye ken them far better than me," she replied with a laugh.

"'Tis because ye've always got yer nose in a bleedin' book," Beatrix said. "Anyway, I ken men very well. So, when I tell ye he's in love with ye, believe me. He's in love with ye."

"But he's nae said as much."

"Have ye?"

"'Tis nae fer me tae say."

"Says who?" Beatrix asked.

"Says… propriety."

Beatrix scoffed and waved her off. "If ye stand around waitin' fer propriety, ye may never get what ye want. Sometimes, ye've got tae reach out and take it fer yerself."

"I could never," Diana gasped.

"If ye can never, then ye may never," she responded. "Sometimes ye have tae be bold and go after what it is ye want in life."

Diana leaned back and frowned as Beatrix's words echoed in her head. She looked at her with a small smile playing across her lips.

"When did me baby sister get so wise?"

"I've always been wise," she replied with a grin. "Ye've just never noticed 'til now."

The door to Diana's bedchamber opened and they both turned to see one of the chambermaids poke her head in.

"Beggin' pardon, me ladies, but yer parents are requestin' yer presence out in the rear grounds," she said.

"Rear grounds?" Diana asked. "Whatever fer?"

"They've set up some games fer everybody tae play."

"Everybody?"

"A few families have arrived."

"Families?"

"Friends of yer parents, I imagine," the chambermaid replied.

Diana sighed. "All right. Thank ye," she said. "Tell them we'll be along promptly."

"Aye."

The chambermaid closed the door, leaving her alone with Beatrix again, but that bubble of closeness they'd shared had been popped. If their parents had guests, it meant they were expected to put on a smile and act as proper daughters would.

"Games could be fun," Beatrix offered lightly.

"Aye. I suppose so."

"Come," Beatrix said as she pulled Diana to her feet. "Let's go and have some fun. Let's try tae be bold and take what we want taeday, eh?"

"Maither and Faither will have our hides if we act the fool."

She grinned and tipped Diana a wink. "Sometimes, 'tis worth it fer a little fun."

Laughing together, they strode out of her chamber and down the corridor, hand in hand. Diana felt good. Better than she had in a long time.

"Dae ye think Maither and Faither will allow us tae marry?" Beatrix asked hopefully.

"I dinnae ken," Diana admitted. "I hope so. I've never seen ye this happy, Beatrix. And it suits ye well."

"Ye think so?"

Diana nodded. "Aye. I ken so," she said. "Now, let's go be bold and have a little fun."

Beatrix laughed, her smile infectious. "Now ye're talkin' like me sister."

CHAPTER NINETEEN

"Games?" Lorne said. "What fresh hell is this then?"

Gavin chuckled and nudged him in the ribs. "Have an open mind then, lad. There's naethin' wrong with havin' a little fun on a beautiful day."

The sun shone down from a cloudless field of blue above and Lorne turned his face up to soak in a bit of the warmth. Several families, friends of the Magillivrays, gathered on the rear lawn of the castle, having been invited to take part in feasting and games. The reason for the festivities escaped Lorne. It seemed like they were hosting this party for no other reason than because they could. It was a frivolity he was not accustomed to.

He turned in time to see Beatrix and Diana walking out onto the rear grounds and felt his breath catch in his throat. The sun glinted off Diana's golden hair and warmed her fair skin. Dressed in a simple blue dress, she was radiant and he couldn't take his eyes off her as she seemed to glide, rather than walk.

"Pick up yer jaw off the ground, cousin," Gavin said. "'Tis unseemly."

His cousin gave him a laugh and a wink, nudging him in the ribs. Lorne gave himself a small shake and chuckled wryly. They stood off to the side, watching the festivities from a distance. They weren't part of the family, nor their group of friends, and Lorne was feeling out of place. Laird Dunn stepped onto a small dais that had been erected and held his hands up, calling for quiet. The conversations stopped and all eyes turned his way.

"Thank ye all fer comin' taeday," he said. "'Tis a beautiful day and I thought we'd mark the occasion with a bit of feasting and fun, eh?"

His words were met with applause and cheers from the small crowd. His wife, Elayne, stepped onto the dais beside her husband and smiled.

"We have a series of challenges. Contests of skill and teamwork that will test ye all," she said. "And in the end, the team that works best taegether and scores the most points will win. Sounds easy, eh?"

"What are the odds they'll have contests with a blade?" Lorne muttered.

"Nae bleedin' likely," Gavin replied softly.

"Now, we've divided ye all intae teams," Laird Dunn picked up. "I, of course, will be teamin' with me beautiful wife, Elayne. Beatrix, ye're with Gavin, Diana, ye'll be with Lorne..."

Lorne was, of course, thrilled to be teamed up with Diana—though her face didn't reflect the same enthusiasm. But he was also concerned about it. Depending on what the challenges they'd designed were, he ran the risk of falling flat on his face and making a fool of himself. The last thing he wanted to do was look like a fool in front of her.

"Well, I suppose I should go with me teammate, eh?" Gavin said and sauntered away.

Lorne swallowed hard as Diana strode across the grass to where he stood. Her expression was tight and pensive, but a small smile played across her lips.

"It seems we've been paired up," she said.

"Aye. Seems that way," he replied. "Dae yer parents dae this often? Hold games?"

She shrugged. "Sometimes. They dae enjoy a bit of fun now and then," she replied. "Dae ye nae have games at home?"

He shook his head. "Nay. Me faither isnae one for frivolity and fun."

"'Tis a pity."

Lorne watched as the household staff set up what appeared to be archery targets. He smiled. He was good with a bow and the chances of him looking like a fool were low. It seemed he was going to have a chance to impress her after all.

"Archery," he said. "We may have a chance to win this."

She looked uncertain. "I dinnae. I'm nae good with a bow. In fact, I'm terrible."

"Dinnae worry. I'll teach ye."

"Aye?"

He nodded. "Aye."

"All right," Dunn intoned. "Let the games begin then!"

Lorne led Diana over to the archery range and they quietly waited their turn. Her body was taught, her expression pinched. She seemed nervous. They watched the other couples firing arrows at the targets, most of them missing terribly. But they all laughed and applauded anyway. Everybody seemed to be having a grand time and despite Lorne's misgivings, the playful energy was infectious. Admittedly, Lorne was not a man used to having fun or playing games, but as he soaked in the lighthearted atmosphere around him, he thought he might be able to get used to it.

"'Tis but a game," he said quietly. "What has ye so nervous?"

"I'm nae comfortable with a bow... with any weapon, really. 'Tis nae me thing," she said. "And I dinnae enjoy lookin' like a fool in front of so many people."

A gentle smile touched his lips. It seemed they had more in common than he thought. Though, his fear of looking foolish was limited to Diana and Diana alone. But wanting to ease her discomfort, Lorne gestured to the crowd of people lining the archery lane just as one of her parents' friends, a tall, strapping man, shot his arrow well over the target. Together, they watched the feathered projectile sail far into the distance until it was out of sight. The small crowd cheered and applauded, laughing with each other, rather than at the man who'd missed.

"Ye see? Nobody's takin' it too seriously," he said gently. "And nobody's goin' tae laugh at ye if ye miss thae target. 'Tis just a bit of fun they're havin'."

"Still," she said. "I dinnae like daein' things I'm nae good at."

He fixed her with a serious gaze. "If we only did the things we're good at, we'd never dae very much in our lives, would we?"

She frowned but Lorne could tell his words had hit their intended mark. Her frown faltered and something approaching a smile touched her lips. They were the only couple that had not taken their shots yet and her father was calling for them. She tensed up again, but Lorne put a hand on her shoulder, offering her a nod of encouragement.

"Now, come on," he said with a sly smile. "Let us show them how this is done."

"I'm goin' tae make ye lose this contest."

"Rubbish," he said. "Ye'll probably outshoot me."

That got a laugh out of her as he walked her into the shooting lane. Lorne picked up the bow and tested its weight in his hand with an appreciative nod. It was a well-crafted bow. He pulled an arrow from the bucket and turned to Diana.

"All right, watch what I dae," he said.

She nodded. "Aye."

Lorne planted his feet and lowered his center of gravity, giving him steadier balance. He raised the bow and nocked the arrow, drawing it all the way back in one fluid movement. He took a moment to let out a breath as he sighted the target, then released. The arrow flew true and straight, sinking into the bale of hay close to the center. The small crowd erupted in cheers and applause. He turned to Gavin and smiled.

"Looks like I bettered yer mark, lad," Lorne teased.

His cousin glowered at him then laughed. The only person standing in Lorne's way of winning the game was Diana's father, who was stroking his chin as he looked on. The corner of Lorne's mouth quirked upward as he nocked another arrow, took a moment, then released. The arrow flew true and sunk deep into the very center of the target. The cheering and clapping rang in his ears and when he turned to Laird Dunn, the man laughed and gave him a bow.

"Well played. Looks like ye've won yer side of this contest," he said. "But there's still another side tae go and me beautiful wife made a pretty good shot."

"'Tis true. The Lady Elayne made a very fine shot indeed," Lorne said. "But I've got a feelin' Diana's goin' tae better it."

He turned back to Diana who looked horrified. Her face blanched and her lips trembled as she shook her head.

"I cannae dae this," she said.

"Of course, ye can," he replied and thrust the bow into her hands. "Now, come. Let me show ye how tae dae this."

Lorne stood behind her, putting one hand on the small of her back and the other on her hip as he maneuvered her into position. He was all too aware of the soft curves of her body as they touched. Her skin felt hot to the touch and when his fingers trailed from her back to her other hip, he heard her gasp. He cleared his throat.

"Bend ye legs ever so slightly," he said quietly. "Get a firmer base and steady yer footin'."

She did as he instructed and brushed her firm backside against his swelling staff. Lorne's cheeks flushed and his desire for her grew. If she noticed him growing firm, she was good enough not to mention it. But the space between them filled with an awkward tension and a sense of anticipation. Lorne had to bite the inside of his cheek hard enough to make him wince to stave off his arousal.

Putting his hands on her arms gently, he raised them to the proper height and showed her how to nock the arrow, then helped her draw it back.

"The trick is a smooth release," he said. "Take a moment, let out a breath, and close yer eyes. When ye're ready, open 'em again and let go of the arrow, smooth as silk."

He paused, reveling in the feeling of her body pressed to him for just another moment before stepping back. Biting the inside of his cheek again, Lorne tried to push back the desire that raged through him like a river. Diana opened her eyes and let go of the arrow. It sailed wide of the target, and she turned to him, a look of panic in her eyes. The crowd cheered her on though, encouraging her to try again. And it was when she looked around and saw the smiling faces of everybody looking on that Diana seemed to realize they weren't laughing at her. That they were simply enjoying the day.

Lorne stepped forward and helped her with her positioning again, his hands lingering on her hip and back. He felt the heat coming through her dress and caught her stealing glances at him from the corner of her eye. Lorne smiled as he stepped back.

"Whenever ye're ready, lass," he said.

Diana let out a breath and took a moment to steady herself. He watched as she opened her eyes and let go of the arrow, just as he'd showed her. The arrow flew true and hit the target just beside his in the center. Her mouth fell open and a look of shock crossed her features. The crowd exploded with laughter and applause. Diana turned and threw herself into Lorne's arms, hugging him tight. He laughed with her as he spun her around.

"Ye did it," he said as he set her back down.

"I cannae believe it!"

"I told ye that ye could."

"Well played," Dunn called. "But let's nae get tae excited, eh? We've still got two contests."

"And we dinnae plan on losin'," Elayne added.

They both laughed and nodded to him approvingly as the people shouted their congratulations to Diana on her shot. She smiled and seemed to glow as she basked in the applause although she looked a bit uncomfortable with the praise as well. Lorne could tell she was not a woman who enjoyed being the center of attention.

"Come," Dunn intoned. "Ontae the next challenge!"

"Well done," Lorne leaned close to her and said as they made their way to the next event area. "'Twas a fine shot indeed."

"Wouldnae have been possible without yer expert guidance."

"Aye. I guess I am an expert, arenae I?" he preened.

Diana rolled her eyes but laughed.

CHAPTER TWENTY

"Bleedin' hell," Lorne muttered and sucked the small drop of blood off his finger.

Diana laughed. "Ye're nae supposed tae stab yerself."

He scowled at her. "Ye think I'm doin' this on purpose then, dae ye?"

"Are ye?"

"Nay," he grumbled. "I'm nae."

"So, ye're just naturally bad at this."

"Embroidery is nae me strong suit," he responded. "Whoever thought this was a good challenge tae have needs tae be beaten with a wooden stick."

Diana arched an eyebrow. "'Twas me faither's idea. And as ye can see, he's quite good at it."

She pointed to where her father sat with her mother, laughing and chatting away as he worked the needle and thread with ease. She smiled.

"Me Maither introduced him tae it. Said it would help calm him down when he was under a lot of pressure," she said. "He's been daein' it fer years. Personally, I think all men should learn how tae sew, if fer naethin' else than fer practical matters."

"I ken how tae sew," he grumbled. "I just wouldnae have made a contest out of it."

She shrugged. "Why nae then? If archery can be a contest, why cannae embroidery be tae?"

"Because I'm terrible at it," he said.

She arched an eyebrow at him, drawing a deep, rumbling laugh from the man as he realized she'd said the same thing a moment before he'd thrust a bow into her hands.

"All right, all right," he said.

"Ye said ye ken how tae sew?"

"I dae. But 'tis nae the same," he replied. "The sewin' I ken isnae so fine as the needlework needed tae embroider."

"Kennin' how tae sew at all is a place tae start," she said. "Show me."

She handed him a fresh piece of cloth and though he looked at it like it might bite him, Lorne took it from her and started to work the needle again. His movements were a bit clumsy and awkward, but he was managing to get a decent stitch into the cloth.

"Huh," she said.

"What?"

"Maybe ye're nae as lost a cause as I thought."

He flashed her a grin. "Ye say the sweetest things."

"How'd ye learn tae stitch like that anyway?"

"Honestly?"

"Nay, lie tae me," she teased.

Lorne chuckled but kept his eyes on his stitching, still a bit clumsy, but his work a bit straighter as he calmed down and settled into it.

"I learned tae stitch wounds on the field of battle," he said. "Which, as ye can imagine, is a far cry from embroidery."

As she studied his work, she understood what he meant. His stitching was thick and did look like the sort of thing one would need to close a wound. He raised his gaze to her and grinned.

"I'm a sorry excuse fer a healer but kennin' how tae seal up a wound might be the difference between life and death," he said. "If naethin' else, it can give time tae get a lad tae a proper healer like ye."

She watched him work in silence for a moment, pondering over what he'd just said. She'd never heard any man, not even her father, talk about caring for his men on the field of battle that way. Certainly never enough to learn how to stitch their wounds to keep them from bleeding out.

"Ye look surprised," he said.

"I've just never heard a man who commanded others in battle worry about stitchin' them up tae save them before," she replied.

"If they're goin' tae follow me intae battle, it seems like the very least I can dae is try tae take care of them. Save their lives if possible," he said.

Diana sat back and looked at him for a moment. He was a far more complicated man than she had ever guessed and there were depths to him she hadn't even uncovered yet. Every day—every conversation—seemed to reveal some new layer to him she hadn't expected to find. Hearing the care for others in his voice was definitely one of them. It wasn't the sort of way she'd ever heard a laird—or the son of a laird—speak before. Most were entitled, they moved men around like pieces on a chessboard without care or concern what happened to them. But Lorne was... different.

His lips curled downward as he looked up and saw the expression on her face. But then he softened and put his needle down.

"I'm goin' tae be laird of me clan one day," he said. "As laird, 'tis me duty and responsibility tae care fer all those under me charge. I intend tae dae just that. I want tae be kenned as a good man and as a good laird."

"Twenty minutes remainin'," called Helsa, who would be judging the embroidery.

Lorne frowned. "I'm afraid I'm goin' tae lose this contest fer us."

She laughed. "We've got twenty minutes left. Get tae work."

They both picked up their projects and got busy. Diana showed him what to do as he worked the needle and thread. And when time was called, Lorne held up his work and grimaced. Diana couldn't help but laugh. He grinned along with her and shook his head.

"I tried," he said.

"Aye. Ye did," she replied. "And 'tis nae the worst thing I've ever seen. I think ye beat most of the other men in this room—includin' yer braither."

At the mention of Gavin, Lorne's face clouded over for a brief moment, but it quickly cleared and his smile, wide and warm returned.

"Nae as good as yer faither though," Lorne said, pointing to her father's work.

"Well, like I said, he's been at this quite a long time."

Helsa announced that Dunn and Elayne had won the embroidery competition to rounds of cheering and applause. She and Lorne had finished second after the judging.

"I think we are tied with yer parents," Lorne said.

"With one contest left."

He laughed. "I hope 'tis nae somethin' I'm nae good at."

Helsa, the longtime kitchen staff manager, stood in the center of the room and raised her arms, signaling for quiet. When the laughing and conversation stopped, she grinned at everybody.

"And fer our third contest, we will be headin' tae the kitchens," she announced. "Ye'll be judged by yer bakin' skills."

"Bleedin' hell," Lorne muttered.

Diana laughed. "Come. We can still win this."

"I'm nae so sure," he replied. "Why couldnae this have been a contest with blades or some sort of combat? We'd be sure tae win."

"Because bakin' is somethin' fair tae us all."

"All? I bet most of the men in this room have never baked a thing in their entire lives—and that includes me."

"Then ye'll need tae watch and learn," she said.

He sighed and rolled his eyes dramatically, drawing a laugh out of her. They walked to the kitchens and were given their instructions. They were to bake a set of lemon sweetcakes— the exact sort of cake her mother favored.

"Now I see why we're havin' these games," Lorne said.

"Why is that?"

"Ye're maither is testin' everybody tae see who can make those little sweetcakes she loves so much so she daesnae have tae depend on the vendors in the market anymore."

Diana laughed. "'Tis quite clever if ye ask me."

"Aye. I suppose it is clever indeed," he said with a chuckle. "I didnae expect yer maither tae be so... devious."

"Nor did I," she replied.

Together, they set about trying to make the lemon sweetcakes her mother loved so well. Though she was a better healer than baker, Diana did all right in the kitchen. In the past, she'd had the household staff give her some lessons on how to make various things. They'd showed her how to make some pastries and something similar to her mother's sweetcakes, so she thought back to those lessons and tried to recreate them.

She and Lorne worked surprisingly well together. They had a certain rhythm that she hadn't counted on them having. But when she tasted the batter, she frowned.

"Somethin's missin'," she said.

"What is it?"

She gave him a face then chuckled. "If I kent that, I'd have added it intae the mix by now, wouldnae I have?"

He gave her a sheepish grin. "I suppose so."

Lorne stuck his finger into the batter then tasted it, a thoughtful look on his face. The day they had gotten the sweetcakes for her mother, they had split one of them and she racked her brain, trying to think of what he'd tasted in that cake that he wasn't tasting in her batter now. She seemed to be doing the same thing.

"A bit of honey, I think," he said.

"That might be it," she said. "But I feel like we're missin' somethin' else."

"I'm nae sure what it could be."

"Me neither. That's the problem."

Lorne went over to the rack of dried herbs, carefully smelling everything. After that he opened the pots of spices and began smelling those as well, earning him hearty laughs and words of encouragement from the other contestants. Diana could tell that nobody was taking it all that seriously and that everyone seemed intent on having a good time. She was not usually one for social gatherings, but she had to admit that she was having a lot of fun and that she was enjoying Lorne's company. It was nice to be around him when he didn't feel the need to protect her. When he was just being... well... normal.

With a look of triumph on his face, he brought over a small

brown pot and set it on the table in front of her. She looked from the pot to him.

"And what is this then?" she asked.

"I'm nae sure what it is, but it smells like somethin' we tasted in those sweetcakes."

Diana picked up the pot and inhaled deeply. "'Tis ginger," she said thoughtfully. "And ye may be right. This may be what we need."

"Time tae get yer cakes intae the ovens," Helsa called.

Diana and Lorne laughed together as they finished putting their sweetcakes together and getting them onto a tray and then into the ovens.

"They're ugly little things," Lorne said.

"The taste is what matters most," she replied with a laugh.

"I hope the shape of them daesnae put anybody off their feed."

Diana laughed and slapped him playfully on the arm. Once everybody was done assembling their pastries, Helsa and the staff ushered them all out into the reception hall where the cakes would be brought out and judged once they had finished baking. A great feast had already been laid out for them. Still laughing together over their slightly misshapen sweetcakes, Diana and Lorne piled food onto their plates then found a spot at the table across from Gavin and Beatrix. They too were laughing at their misadventures in the kitchens. They both laughed and leaned together. "I'm nae sure what we made is goin' tae turn out tae be edible," Gavin said.

"It certainly will be naethin' like Maither's sweetcakes, that much I can tell ye," Beatrix said.

"But we had fun makin' them," Gavin added.

"Aye, I can tell by the flour in yer hair," Diana said.

Gavin offered her a cockeyed grin and a shrug. "I'm dedicated tae me craft."

Beatrix gazed at him adoringly then turned to Diana. "And how'd ye get on with it then?"

"They're ugly as sin," Lorne admitted. "It was hard tryin' tae form those little cake shapes."

"I think we did all right," Diana said with a firm nod and a giggle. "I think we recreated those bleedin' sweetcakes."

They talked and laughed together as they ate. The hall rang with laughter and good conversation. Diana looked around and smiled. For the first time perhaps in her entire life, she didn't feel the sort of pressure or strain that usually came with the social gatherings her parents threw. She was just having fun. She couldn't recall ever feeling so relaxed or unbothered by social norms and etiquette. She could just be, enjoy the day. It was a nice feeling.

A bell rang and Helsa came out through the doorway that led to the kitchens, a couple of the scullery maids behind her pushing wheeled carts. The crowd quieted down and everybody turned to watch as the trays of sweetcakes were laid out on a table at the front of the room. Helsa waited until the task was done then turned to the gathering, a smile on her face.

"All right," she said. "Some of ye made some sweetcakes that were neither sweet, nor cakes. I dinnae ken what ye were daein'."

This comment was directed straight at Gavin and Beatrix, who broke into an uncontrollable fit of laughter. That ignited an amused uproar among the crowd, who applauded them.

"We dae have winners," Helsa intoned once the laughter had died down.

Diana sat up straight, a look of pride already stretching across her face.

"And they are… Lady Elayne and Laird Dunn."

Diana frowned and felt a slight sting of disappointment, but when she turned and found Lorne laughing and applauding along with everybody else, that sting ebbed. She too found herself cheering on her parents, a wide smile on her face.

"Well done, Maither and Faither," she called.

Dunn grinned at them. "When ye've got the right one by yer side and the chemistry has been built over years, there is naethin' ye cannae dae," he said and tipped her a wink. "Ye should remember that. Ye all should."

Conversation returned to the hall as the crowd got up to inspect the cakes and try them out, more than a few people casting teasing remarks at Beatrix and Gavin's contribution. They took it in stride though, enjoying themselves thoroughly. It had been a good day. A really good day. Diana couldn't recall having had a better day in a very long time.

That all changed though, when the doors to the hall crashed open with a resounding bang that stopped all conversation dead in its tracks. Tomson, of the household guard, was half-carrying a bloodied, wounded man into the hall, a worried looking woman following them in.

"Me laird," he said. "There's been some trouble."

CHAPTER TWENTY-ONE

"What happened?" Laird Dunn asked.

The man Diana had called Tomson, who was one of Dunn's scouts, sat on one of the benches, his face red, sweat sheening his skin. He drank deeply from the cup of ale Dunn had given him. He looked as if he'd run a great distance while carrying the wounded man on his back. The wounded man, another scout named Errol, sat on a bench on the other side of the room while Diana tended to his wounds. The crowd stood around watching, murmuring quietly to one another, the festive atmosphere gone like a puff of smoke in a breeze.

And standing to the side of the room was the woman who had come in with them. She wrung her hands together, her face etched with worry and with fear. She was young. Not much older than Diana, if he had to guess. She was petite, with rich auburn locks that fell past her shoulders, cream-colored skin, and eyes as blue as the sky overhead. She had not said a word since they'd arrived and nobody had spoken to her just yet.

"Tomson," Dunn repeated. "What happened out there?"

"We were out on patrol, me laird. And we saw a couple of men we had never seen around here before. They were havin' a go at that one," Tomson said as he gestured to the auburn-haired woman. "Errol and I rushed over tae put a stop tae it, but they had a couple more lads we didnae see at first. They got the drop on us and thrashed Errol pretty good."

As the scout was talking to Dunn, Lorne watched Diana tending to the wounded man. She spoke reassuringly to him as she cleaned and bandaged his wounds. Her touch was light and delicate, but at the same time, she moved as if she was very sure of herself and in total control of the situation. She had such an easy manner about her and seemed able to comfort the wounded man without trying too hard. That was just her way and Lorne found himself coming to appreciate that about her more and more.

"And what is yer name, lass?" Dunn called to the woman. "Please, step closer."

The woman's movements were tentative, and her demeanor was shy. Her cheeks flushed and she ducked her head when all eyes in the hall turned to her. But she stepped over to Dunn and gave him a polite curtsey.

"Me name is Rhona, me laird," she said.

"And how'd ye find yerself in this spot of trouble?" Dunn asked.

"I was simply passin' through on me way north," she replied. "These men set on me. I'm nae sure if they was wantin' fer me purse or... or... somethin' else."

She shuddered at the last bit, an expression of revulsion

crossing her face. Lady Elayne's expression mirrored Rhona's, though hers was tinged with anger as well.

"I'm sorry fer yer troubles, Rhona," Elayne said with genuine regret in her voice. "Our lands are normally nae so... inhospitable."

"'Tis nae yer fault, me lady. Bad people are everywhere these days, I'm afraid."

"And what's in the north fer ye, lass?" Dunn asked.

"Kin, me laird," she said. "Me parents... well... they died, me laird. The only kin I've got left is in the north so I was headin' tae them."

"I'm sorry about yer parents, lass. What did they die of?"

"Dunn, stop interrogatin' the girl. She's had enough of an ordeal as it is," Elayne said. "Rhona, ye'll be stayin' here a day or two. Just enough tae get ye a couple of good meals and a hot bath. I think that'll dae wonders fer ye."

"I'm grateful, me lady, but ye dinnae—"

"Ye'll stay. At least a night," Elayne commanded. "But ye're welcome tae stay as long as ye need tae until ye feel safe and strong enough tae travel."

The girl gave Elayne a small smile and a grateful bow of her head. "Thank ye, me lady. I'm truly grateful fer yer hospitality."

"Of course," Elayne said. "Vera, please see Rhona tae one of the maid's rooms. See that she has a bath and some fresh clothes."

"Aye, me lady," said Vera, one of the chambermaids, with a curtsy.

"Oh, and Rhona, when ye feel up tae it," she said, "please come and indulge. Maybe some food, wine, and laughs will get ye feelin' right as rain again."

"Thank ye again, Lady Elayne."

Vera led Rhona away and Diana directed a couple of the chambermaids to take Tomson and Errol to the healer's chambers.

"Their wounds are nae serious, but the healer can give them some ointments tae soothe their pain," she said.

"Very good," Dunn said gruffly. "I still cannae believe this happened in our lands."

"Like the girl said, there are bad people everywhere," Elayne said.

"Given what's happened, I dinnae think we should go on with the banquet tonight," Dunn said, his tone sober.

"Nonsense. Everybody needs a lift after what just happened," Elayne replied. "A banquet is just what we need tae lift our spirits, eh?"

"Maybe Faither has a point," Diana said.

"I say rubbish," Elayne said. "The banquet will go on as planned."

Dunn smiled and shook his head. "As me lady commands, so shall it be."

"'Tis a good answer, husband."

They laughed together as Dunn pulled her into an embrace. As he watched them, Lorne found himself secretly longing for that kind of closeness with another person. No. Not exactly. He found himself longing for that kind of closeness with Diana. And the fact that this charade would soon be coming to an end put twin daggers of guilt and grief through his heart. Especially after having had such a good day.

"I guess we're goin' tae banquet tonight," Diana said.

"Kind of sounds that way," he replied with a chuckle.

The hall was filled with lively music, hearty laughter, and the aroma of the feast that had been laid out on the tables. The atmosphere was jubilant. It was as if the scene earlier in the day hadn't even happened. Elayne was right, everybody needed a little festivity to lift the dark cloud that had settled down over the castle.

Lorne drank from his cup of spiced wine and took in the scene around him. He couldn't recall the last time they'd had a party at home. His father was never one for celebrations or festivities when he did not have to. He certainly would never host a game day followed by a banquet celebrating the conclusion of the day.

His father's way was the only way he'd ever known. Lorne had never considered the idea that there was another way of doing things. But having spent this time with the Macgillivrays and seeing how they did things, how they treated not just their family, but their household staff, had showed him another way. A better way. Dunn and Elayne Macgillivray were kind to all. They were firm when they needed to be, but they were even handed with their daughters and treated their staff well.

It wasn't that his father was cruel or unkind to their household staff. But one thing he noticed about the Macgillivrays was that they knew the names of everybody working in their household. Lorne doubted his father knew many people in theirs by name. He decided then and there he would be that sort of laird. He would know his staff, but more than that, he would treat his children the way he wished his father had treated him.

"Ye look like a man with heavy things on yer mind."

He turned and offered Diana a smile. "I'm just tryin' tae figure out how the sweetcakes yer parents made beat the ones we made."

Her laughter rang in his ears. It was a high, sweet, musical sound he had grown very fond of. It was a laugh he knew he could never grow tired of hearing. They stood to the side of the hall watching the festivities. Beatrix and Gavin stood nearby, lost in conversation and absorbed in each other, as usual. Lorne wanted to be happy for his cousin that he'd found a love so true. But all he felt was a dull ache in his heart knowing it would not last. Could not last.

"She came down," Diana said.

"Who?"

"Rhona," she replied. "The girl Tomson and Errol saved."

She pointed to where the girl was standing. She seemed to be having an animated conversation with one of the serving women.

"She's an odd lass," Diana said.

"How so?"

"I tried talkin' tae her earlier and she seemed like she didnae want tae be in the same room with me," she replied.

"Maybe she's shy."

"Maybe. She's just... odd."

Diana watched as Rhona and the serving girl, Maribel, huddled close together, talking intently. It was almost as if they knew each other. She wasn't sure, but something about the stranger just seemed... off. The music slowed down, and Lorne looked around, watching the people moving closer together as they danced. He turned to Diana and held out his hand and gave her a bow.

"Would ye dae me the honor of dancin' with me, Lady Diana?"

She laughed. "Ye cannae be serious."

"I'm very serious. Dance with me."

"I wasnae aware ye could dance."

The corner of his mouth quirked upward mischievously. "I've got a great many talents ye dinnae ken about just yet."

Her laughter set his soul on fire, but she gave him her hand, surprising him, and gave him a slight curtsy in return.

"Well then, let us see if ye truly dae have a hidden talent for dance," she said.

Grinning, Lorne led her out onto the dance floor. He was immediately aware of her soft, yet firm body close to his. She leaned forward, her breath warm and smelling of berries. He closed his eyes as they spun slowly around the dance floor, their bodies moving in a slow rhythm.

Her breath quickened and he looked down at her. Diana turned her face up to him, her dark brown eyes smoldering and filled with the same desire that coursed through him Lorne felt himself warm from the inside. It took everything in him to not close that gap and press his mouth to hers.

Blessedly, the song ended and they took a step back, though their gazes remain fixed on each other, anticipation and desire filling the space between them. Lorne's eyes drifted to her lips, so full and pillowy soft, and the urge to feel them pressed to his was overwhelming.

"Drinks, Maister Davidson? Lady Macgillivray?"

They turned to see Maribel standing with a tray in her hand. She looked at them with wide eyes and a strange look on her face, as if she wanted to be anywhere but there, serving drinks at a party.

Diana took a cup of wine from the tray. "Thank ye, Maribel."

"Of course, me lady," she said. "Maister Davidson?"

He reached for a cup but Laird Dunn waving at him caught Lorne's attention. Standing on the other side of the room, the man held up a cup with an amber liquid in it, offering him what Lorne knew would be excellent whisky. He took his hand back and turned to Diana.

"Yer Faither would like a word with me, it seems," he said.

She scoffed. "He'd like tae share a cup with ye."

"But mostly a word."

She laughed. "Go. I'll go and butt in on me sister and Gavin."

"I'll be back," he said. "Save me another dance."

She took a drink of her wine and shrugged. "I might," she said. "I'm just nae sure ye've got the talent ye think ye dae."

He put his hand over his heart, mimicking a look of pain. "Madame, ye wound me so."

With a laugh, Lorne turned and walked over to where Laird Dunn was standing. He accepted the cup of whisky with a grateful nod.

"Thank ye, me laird."

"Please. Just call me Dunn."

Lorne gave him a polite bow of the head. "Thank ye, Dunn."

"So, how dae ye find things, Lorne? How are ye and Diana gettin' along?"

The expectant way he asked the question told Lorne he was asking about the state of their courtship, which only reminded him of the lie that had brought them there in the first place. A shadow crossed his heart, and he had to fight to keep the frown off his lips.

"Diana is… remarkable," he said. It wasn't a lie.

"Aye. That she is."

As Lorne watched Diana, he felt his heart swelling in his chest. She was everything he never even knew he wanted. She was exceptional in every way and Lorne felt himself falling hard for her. That emotion though, was tempered by the fact that he knew he would never have her.

He took another sip of the whisky and complimented Dunn on how exceptionally good it was.

When he turned back to look for Diana, he couldn't find her among the guests. Then he saw the arm of that girl, Rhonda, was around her shoulders, and she was taking her somewhere. At that exact moment Diana turned to look at him, sickly pale and with pleading eyes.

CHAPTER TWENTY-TWO

Diana laughed heartily at something Gavin had just said to Beatrix. His humor was a bit off color—bawdy at times—but she couldn't keep herself from laughing. As she drank her wine, she cut a glance at Lorne who stood on the other side of the hall with her father. They were talking and laughing like old friends. Her father seemed to really be getting on well with him. Watching them together made Diana smile.

As she took another drink, Diana felt a strange sensation churning in the pit of her stomach. She suddenly felt warm—unnaturally warm. Admittedly, she didn't drink much, but she indulged in wine now and again and she had never felt like this before. Her vision wavered and she felt a wave of nausea wash over her.

"Are ye all right?" Beatrix asked.

"I dinnae—somethin's wrong," she said, her voice thick in her mouth.

Diana stared into her cup of wine as if searching for the answers in the red liquid. She caught sight of Maribel. The young woman's eyes were wide, and she wore a strange expression. When their eyes met though, she turned and hurried away. She felt like she was floating. As if she had somehow become lighter than air and was drifting away on the breeze.

A hand fell on her shoulder, making her jump and she turned to see Gavin and Beatrix both staring at her, concern on their faces. She swayed on her feet and felt herself growing pale even as the heat within her grew, becoming almost intolerable. Beads of sweat dotted her brow, then rolled down her face.

"Diana," Beatrix said. "What's wrong with ye?"

She shook her head. "I—I dinnae ken. I just… I…"

Her voice tapered off as the sway in her body grew. Diana's legs trembled and she felt like they might give out beneath her, sending her toppling to the hard stone floor. But then another hand grasped her arm, and she turned to see Rhona's face, her startling blue eyes fixed on her. Diana's gaze fell to the woman's full, plump lips for some reason, finding herself curiously fascinated with them.

"Looks like somebody's had a wee bit too much tae drink, eh?" Rhona said with a smile, her voice low and husky.

"I dinnae think that's what it is," Beatrix said. "Me sister daesnae drink—"

"Nonsense," Rhona cut her off. "I've seen more than me share of people in their cups."

"I'm nae sure either," Gavin said. "She looks ill tae me."

"Naethin' a little fresh air willnae fix right up," Rhona said. "Ye'll see. A few deep breaths of that cool night air and she'll be right as rain in nay time."

Diana shook her head, trying desperately to gather her wits. "'Tis all right, Beatrix," she said. "Maybe she's right. I've had a couple of cups and 'tis very warm in here. Maybe some fresh air 'tis all I need right now."

"I shall come with ye—" Beatrix said, but Rhona smiled and waved her hand.

"Nay need. We will be out on the balcony, ye will see us from here. Enjoy yer conversation, I will call if I need any help."

"'Tis all right, Sister," Diana said. "I'll get some air and come right back."

"Are ye certain?" Gavin asked, his voice uneasy.

"Aye. I'll be back straight away," she replied. "Just need some air."

"See?" Rhona chirped. "All will be well."

Rhona slipped her arm around Diana's shoulders and turned her around. Suddenly feeling so weak and suddenly spent, Diana couldn't put up a fight and leaned heavily on the woman. It was as if she was no longer in control of her own body as the woman—the stranger—walked her toward the doors that would lead them outside. Fear seized her heart and though she tried to arrest her movement, she was powerless to do so.

Diana turned her head—the only thing she seemed capable of doing—and locked eyes with Lorne. Concern etched his features already and when she looked at him, silently pleading with him for help, he dropped his cup and tried to cut through the crowd. Her heart raced and her stomach churned as they drew near the doors and Lorne was still caught amongst the people. Diana had no idea what would happen to her if Rhona got her outside. She knew it was irrational, that they could be seen from the inside, but she felt fear grip her heart.

They were mere feet from the doorway when she felt a strong, powerful hand clamp onto her arm. She rolled her head and felt a wave of relief crash down over her when she found herself staring into Lorne's blue eyes. Rhona turned, a sneer on her lips. Just as soon as Diana had seen it though, it was gone, replaced by a sweet, toothy smile.

"She seems a little the worse fer wear, Maister Davidson," Rhona smiled. "I thought some fresh air might dae her some good."

"And how dae ye ken me name?" he asked.

"I've asked around," she replied pleasantly. "Just tryin' tae remember the names of everybody who's been so kind tae me."

"Uh huh."

As Diana listened to them speaking, her stomach churned, growing more sour by the second. She was sure she was going to be sick. She opened her mouth to speak, to tell them to let her lie down, but her tongue felt thick and there was a bitter taste in the back of her throat. Diana tried, but wasn't able to get a sound out, let alone a coherent sentence. Something was wrong. Something was very, very wrong. Fear flowed through her veins like fire and tears spilled from the corners of her eyes.

"I'll just get her some air," Rhona said agreeably.

"She'll nae be goin' anywhere alone," he said, his voice harder than stone. "If she needs air, I'll be takin' her out."

"Oh, 'tis nay bother. I'm just standin' around—"

"Let go of her, Rhona. Now," Lorne hissed, his eyes narrow, his jaw clenched.

"Really, Maister Davidson—"

"I said take yer hands off her."

A commotion followed by the sound of screaming echoed through the hall. Diana was able to turn her head enough to see several men in black emerge from doorways, swords drawn. Their arrival sent the crowd in the hall scrambling out of the way. Her father's guards rushed in and moved to intercept, sending the crowd into a panicked frenzy as they stampeded for the doors. Shrieks and cries of agony sounded throughout the banquet hall as chaos reigned.

The clash of steel on steel rang out and Diana saw Lorne's hand moving for the dagger on his belt. With a vicious sneer on her lips, Rhona gave her a two-handed shove in the chest that sent her falling into Lorne. He caught her and managed to keep them both upright, but Rhona turned and fled through the open door. As if she weighed nothing at all, Lorne scooped her up and carried her to her father's dais. He sat her down gently in his chair, then turned to a trio of guards that were rushing past to join the fray.

"Ye three!" he shouted above the din.

The three guards stopped and dashed over. A stern look on his face, Lorne pointed to them then to her. Diana searched the chaos in the room, looking for her parents and her sister. Amid the tumult, she spotted a group of men rushing her mother out of the room. Gavin stood protectively in front of

Beatrix in a corner, a blade in his hand. But she saw no sign of her father. Fear blossomed in her chest when she saw blood—so much blood—and bodies all over the stone floor of the banquet hall and she was terrified her father was among the fallen.

"Ye three get her tae the healer. And protect her with yer bleedin' lives," he commanded. "Dae ye understand me? With yer very bleedin' lives."

It was a crazy time to be thinking about it, but she watched how smoothly and firmly he took command of the men—her father's men—and she saw how quickly they responded to him. Lorne was a natural leader. The sort of man people would follow into battle without a moment's hesitation. He was the sort of man others would fight and die for.

"With yer bleedin' lives," he said one final time.

As the three armored guards lifted her up to get her to the healer, she watched as Lorne leaped off the dais and picked up a sword from one of the fallen and rushed into the fray. She feared for him. Feared for his life. She wasn't sure what it was between them, but it seemed to be growing, to be taking root.

And she found herself wanting to see what blossomed.

CHAPTER TWENTY-THREE

Lorne stood on the dais, surveying the chaos and the carnage. He had no idea who these men in black were, but he knew that woman—Rhona—was involved with them. The fact that she had been trying to get away with Diana told him as much. His eyes roving the hall, he spotted Gavin across the room. He stood in front of Beatrix, sword in hand, protecting her from the onslaught of black-clad attackers.

Lorne cast one last glance back at Diana, ensuring the men he'd left her with were getting her to the healer. Two men formed a protective wall while the third was picking her up. Satisfied, he jumped off the dais and picked up a sword from the ground. From the corner of his eye, he spotted a figure in black making a dash for Diana. He swung around and ran, slamming his shoulder into the man's back.

The soldier went sprawling, hitting the ground with a loud grunt. Before he was able to rise, Lorne drove the point of the sword through him. A splash of crimson painted the stone floor and when Lorne yanked his blade free of the man's body, he slumped forward and fell, dead before he hit the ground. Lorne took one last look, making sure they were getting Diana out of the hall before turning and plunging into the melee.

He fought his way over to his cousin but the men in black seemed to be coming from everywhere. It was like they'd kicked an anthill. The song of steel ringing on steel filled his ears, blending with the shrieks and cries of the wounded, creating a symphony of battle. His blood flowed with fire and rage as he struck down attackers on his left and right, dancing and parrying like the most graceful dancer in the world.

He slipped into a clearing in the fighting. Ahead of him he saw Gavin trading blows with one of the attackers. Lorne's heart dropped into his stomach when he saw the attacker drive his cousin's blade high then deliver a vicious slash along his ribs. Blood spilled down his side and Beatrix shrieked. Gavin though, grimaced and fought through the pain, parrying the man's next thrust before driving his foot into his knee. The man screamed as his leg buckled and his cousin drove his sword through the man's chest.

Lorne rushed to him. "Gavin—"

"I'm fine. Get Beatrix out of here," he grunted.

"I'm nae goin' anywhere without ye," she screamed.

"Ye get her out of here," Lorne said. "I'll cover yer retreat."

"I'm nae retreatin'!" Gavin growled.

"Dinnae be a fool," Lorne said. "There's too many of 'em and ye're hurt."

"I'm nae goin' anywhere."

A pair of black-clad soldiers charged at them, ending the discussion as Lorne and Gavin defended against them. Sparks flew through the air as Lorne's sword clashed with his attacker's. The two men circled each other, changing thrust and slashes, parrying each of their blows. From the corner of his eye, he kept watch on Gavin. His cousin's face was pale, sweat slicked his brow, and he wore a grimace of agony as blood continued to flow from the wound in his side.

Lorne's attacker, seeing his momentary distraction, charged in. Snapping back to the moment, Lorne deflected the man's thrust, but not quickly enough as the edge of his blade slid along his upper arm, opening a gash that bled freely. Wincing in pain, Lorne spun to his left and drove a backward kick into the back of the man's knee. He buckled and went down, but was fast and avoided the worst of Lorne's follow up, suffering only a slice along his shoulder.

Gavin danced with his man, his movements sluggish, his face racked with pain. They circled around each other, trading blows. Lorne knew the man was simply waiting his cousin out. Lorne needed to end his fight quickly and aid Gavin.

His man grinned darkly at him, as if reading his thoughts. His intention was clear. He was going to delay their fight as long as possible and keep him occupied so he could not help Gavin.

Lorne could hear Beatrix crying softly in the corner of the hall. Gavin stayed in front of her, not letting his attacker near her. But Lorne could see more and more crimson droplets spattering to the stone beneath him. Time was running out. He was, by nature, a cautious fighter. It was how he'd been taught. He believed in letting the fight come to him rather than forcing the issue, he let other people tire out first. Tired people made mistakes. But he didn't have the luxury of time. He had to end this and tend to Gavin.

Throwing caution to the wind, Lorne waded in, slicing, thrusting, and slashing with his sword in a frenzied attack. The man stepped forward and drove a powerful thrust toward Lorne, but he quickly countered, deflecting his blade harmlessly, before delivering a vicious slash across the man's arm.

Lorne pressed his attack. The man's face darkened as he struggled to keep up with the speed of his strikes. He was breathing heavily and sweat slicked his brow now, but he kept managing to deflect the worst of Lorne's blows. Gritting his teeth in frustration, Lorne drove himself forward, the clang of their swords clashing ringing in his ears. He deflected a blow from the man that would have pierced his neck but the tip of his blade still managed to open a shallow cut along Lorne's cheek.

The blood spilled down his cheek and Lorne winced, but he pressed on. It staggered his attacker just enough to give Lorne and advantage that he did not miss. Raising his sword, he drove it through the man's stomach, the tip of it bursting through his back.

His attacker's face paled, and his eyes widened as he stared into Lorne's eyes. He toppled over with a wordless grunt, crashing to the stone floor, and was still.

Feeling like time was running out, Lorne rushed toward Gavin. His attacker spotted Lorne coming and turned to defend, but it was too late. With an upward slice, he knocked the man's blade toward the ceiling, leaving his middle open. Lorne struck, driving the dagger in his other hand into the man's chest, burying it to the hilt.

The man's sword hit the stone floor with a sharp clang, and he pitched forward, falling onto his face, silent forevermore. Lorne turned to his cousin who had dropped to a knee, his breath ragged, his face as pale as the dead. Beatrix was on her knees beside him, stroking his hair and sobbing wildly. She pressed a kiss to his cheek, her entire body trembling.

Gavin's entire left side was slick with blood and his gaze was becoming unfocused. His cousin was dying. And unless they got him to a healer soon, it would be too late. All around them, the sounds of battle faded as the men in black were turned back, those not lying on the ground in pools of their own blood fleeing from the hall, Dunn's guard giving chase.

"Help!" Lorne called. "We need a healer!"

"Get the healers!"

Lorne turned to see Laird Dunn walking over to him. He hadn't seen the laird during the fighting, but the blood on his face and clothing, as well as the blade in his hand that dripped red told Lorne the man had seen plenty of action. He stood over Gavin; his expression grave but then his gaze shifted to Lorne.

"Is the Lady Elayne—"

Dunn nodded curtly. "She's fine. Safe," he said. "Me daughter?"

"I had a couple of yer guards take her tae the healer," he said. "I suspect she was poisoned and that that Rhona had somethin' tae dae with it—with all of this."

"Bleedin' hell," he muttered and looked around. "Where is she now?"

"Gone, me laird. She fled once the fightin' started."

Dunn shook his head. "What in the bleedin' hell was this all about?"

"I dinnae ken. Nae fer certain," Lorne replied. "But somebody was tryin' tae get their hands on Diana."

"It's got tae be that bleedin' bastard, Munro," Dunn muttered. "He said he would have his vengeance. This must be it. Thought he could steal me daughter out from under me nose."

Gavin mumbled under his breath and a choked sob burst from Beatrix's mouth. Lorne felt his insides churning and his heart leap into this throat as he watched the life draining away from his cousin. He put a hand to his head and tried to control his emotions.

"Where are the healers!" Dunn shouted.

"Here, me laird. Here."

A woman roughly Dunn's age stepped over to them and dropped to her knees. She made a quick survey of Gavin's wounds, her expression sober. Without saying a word, she set to work packing and bandaging his wound to stop the flow of blood. When she was done with that, she turned her face up to Dunn.

"I'll need tae get him back down tae me rooms," she said. "We'll need tae treat him—"

"What can ye tell us?" Dunn demanded.

She shook her head. "He's lost a lot of blood. There's nae much I can tell ye at the moment, me laird. But we need tae get him tae me rooms right away if he's tae have a chance."

She motioned for a pair of men who rushed over and loaded Gavin onto a litter. They picked him up and rushed him out of the hall. Lorne watched them go until they disappeared from sight, his stomach twisting and turning in knots so tight they were painful. With a cry, Beatrix jumped to her feet and chased after Gavin.

Lorne took a beat to collect his thoughts then turned to the healer. "Diana?"

"She's lucky. She took enough of whatever was in her wine tae make her dizzy and disoriented, but nae enough tae be fatal," she said. "She needs some rest, but she'll be fine."

Relief flooded Lorne's veins—the same powerful relief he saw etched into Dunn's features. Lorne got to his feet.

"Please," he said. "Help him."

"'Tis me plan."

The healer stood and hustled out of the hall to take care of Gavin and the number of others who had sustained wounds, some of them grievous, in the fighting. Dunn put a hand on his shoulder and gave it a gentle squeeze.

"Yer braither will be all right, Lorne," he said. "He's in the hands of the most capable healer I've ever kent."

"Thank ye, me laird."

Though his words were meant to be reassuring, they fell flat in Lorne's ears. In his mind's eye, all he could see was Gavin's face when the sword sliced him open, his agony and shock. And for the briefest of moments, as his blood flowed from his wound, Gavin had turned to Beatrix and Lorne could distinctly recall seeing a flash of guilt. Perhaps the guilt came from his cousin believing he would die without telling Beatrix the truth, or perhaps it was something else, but the guilt he saw on his cousin's face was now rampaging through Lorne's mind and soul as well.

And all he could wonder was whether their lie had brought this down on everybody. For if not for this false courtship, perhaps Laird Munro would have had no cause to have attacked Castle Macgillivray and possibly abduct Diana with a battle that had or could still claim far too many lives.

As he stood there among the carnage, Lorne was forced to wonder whether, if they had told the truth from the start, any of this would have happened at all.

CHAPTER TWENTY-FOUR

Her head was spinning and through a dull pounding, she heard voices, though it sounded as though she was hearing them from underwater. Diana's eyes fluttered open and she saw Lorne and Beatrix sitting beside her bed. She turned her head and saw that Gavin lay on a bed beside her, obviously unconscious. He had a large bandage wrapped around his midsection, his skin was pale, and even though her vision was still a bit hazy, she could tell he didn't look good.

She lay there a moment, watching Beatrix wiping Gavin's head with a cool cloth and listened to her talking to Lorne. They spoke in low tones, apparently trying to keep from disturbing her, sharing stories about her and Gavin.

Her throat was bone dry, and she had trouble getting a single word out, so she cleared her throat. Lorne turned to her instantly and his face was flooded with relief. He and Beatrix crowded around her, smiling wide and laughing ruefully together.

"Ye're awake," Beatrix cried.

"Water," she rasped. "Please."

Beatrix jumped and quickly retrieved a cup of water, bringing it back and holding it so Diana could drink. The water was cool and soothing on her aching throat. She drank down two glasses before she'd had her fill and sat up. She put her hands to her temples, feeling her head throbbing.

"How is he?" she asked, her voice still raspy. "How is Gavin?"

Lorne's face tightened and he shook his head. "We dinnae ken. The healer says he might be all right, or he might take an infection and get worse. We have tae wait and see."

"I'm sorry, Lorne."

He nodded. "Gavin's a fighter. Always been one. He'll fight through this too."

"He will," Beatrix agreed with a hitch in her voice. "He has tae."

"In better news, the healer says ye're goin' tae be fine," Lorne said. "She said ye were poisoned, but ye didnae drink enough tae dae any real damage. But ye're nae goin' tae feel right fer a couple of days, probably."

"Aye," Beatrix said. "She said ye'd be wrung out and exhausted. Because of what ye were given by that horrid shrew."

Diana racked her mind for a moment, but then the memories began falling into place in her mind. Of course. Rhona. The wayward traveler who was supposedly set upon by bandits.

"Where is she?" Diana said, her voice pinched with anger. "Rhona. Where is she?"

"She got away. Slipped out when all the fightin' started," Lorne told her. "We've nae been able tae find her yet. But yer faither has men out lookin'."

"Dae we ken who she is or why she did this?"

Lorne shrugged. "We dinnae ken for sure, but our best guess is she's Munro's creature. Sent here tae abduct ye and take ye back tae him."

A cold chill crept through Diana's body, sending goosebumps marching across her skin. She shuddered and shook her head, equal parts repulsed and terrified by the idea that Munro would send somebody to abduct her. She pushed it all away and tried to focus on the here and now. She was safe. They had protected her and fought off the attackers. That was good. Rhona would be caught in time.

Right now, all that mattered was there in that room with her and they needed to be putting their attention on Gavin and his recovery. She thought she might be able to use her skills to help with that. But she was having a hard time thinking straight and still felt weak. Maybe after she slept a bit and was able to clear her head—or at least, stop it from throbbing quite so hard—she would be able to figure something out that might speed his healing along.

"How long have ye two been here? And how are Maither and Faither?" she asked.

"All night," Beatrix replied. "Neither of us were goin' tae leave. Maither and Faither were here earlier. They sat fer a while, but then had tae meet with the council."

Diana felt a surge of emotion in her chest at her sister's words. She bit her bottom lip, doing her best to control herself and keep the tears welling in her eyes from falling.

Perhaps it was silly, but in that moment, she felt genuinely cared for.

"Ye should rest," Lorne said.

She nodded. "Aye. But I'd like tae rest in me own bed."

"All right, let me help ye up then."

Lorne was gentle as he helped her off the cot she laid on and got her on her feet. Diana felt queasy and her legs trembled. He slipped a hand around her waist to steady her.

"I'll walk ye back tae yer chamber," he said.

"Thank ye," she said.

"I'll be back," Lorne said to Beatrix.

She looked at him. "Actually, if ye dinnae mind, I'd like a little time alone with Gavin," she said. "Besides, ye look like ye could use a little rest too, since ye were wounded too. Why dinnae ye come later and we can take turns watchin' over him."

Lorne nodded. "All right. I'll be back later then tae relieve ye."

"Thank ye, Lorne."

"Of course."

Leaning on him heavily, Diana let Lorne lead her out of the healer's chambers and through the corridors to her room.

"Ye were hurt? Are ye well? How many of ours were lost?" she asked.

"I am fine, the healer cleaned up and bandaged me wounds. They were superficial. Tae answer yer other question, eight," he replied. "But we took out more than a dozen of theirs."

She was relieved that Lorne was well, but her heart ached for the eight souls lost in the banquet hall and couldn't help but feel that, in some small way, this was her fault. She knew it was silly. This was because of one man's jealousy and inability to take her refusal of his offer of courtship and marriage with dignity and grace. And perhaps triggered even more by that fight in the inn, which was her fault as well. If not for her refusal, those eight men would be still be alive. They had given their life for hers.

"Are ye all right?" Lorne asked gently.

"Aye. It's just…"

Her voice tapered off and Lorne turned to her. His eyes were piercing and her breath caught in her throat as he looked at her. It felt almost as if he was seeing through her. His expression softened and he shook his head.

"'Tis nae yer fault," he said.

"How did ye ken—"

"I can see the guilt on yer face," he replied. "This is nae yer fault, so get that thought out of yer head. Ye are nae responsible fer one man's greed and vanity. That's all this was—aggression tae appease Munro's greed and vanity. Period."

"What if he's nae done? What if he comes back?"

"He very well might," Lorne said. "But he's lost the element of surprise. We will be ready fer him and when he comes, he's goin' tae have a nasty surprise waitin' fer him."

He stopped her in the hall and turned her to face him, still holding onto her arms to keep her steady. His gaze was firm, his face etched with earnestness.

"He'll never get anywhere near ye, Diana," he said. "I will cut him down meself or die tryin' before I let him get one hand on ye."

His words heartened her and for the first time since she'd awoken, she felt better. He slipped his arm around her waist again and walked her to her chambers, opening the door and all but carried her over to her bed. She sat on the edge of it while he knelt down and took off her shoes and stockings, tossing them to the side of the room before standing up.

"I'll let ye get some rest," he said.

Diana nodded and began fumbling with her dress. Her fingers felt thick and clumsy, and she was having a hard time with the laces. Frustrated, she was about to give up and just lie down when Lorne walked over and offered her a gentle smile.

"Let me," he said.

With surprisingly delicate fingers, he unlaced her dress in short order. She felt the tips of his fingers brush her skin, leaving trails of fire across her back as he pulled it off, leaving her in just her shift. His eyes lingered on hers and Diana saw the desire raging through her reflected back in his eyes. He cleared his throat and turned away, carrying her dress over to a chair and carefully laid it over the back of it, taking care to smooth it out.

Lorne returned and helped Diana crawl into bed then pulled the bedding over her. His face lingered over hers for a long moment, his blue eyes boring into hers. Diana's breath caught in her throat and her heart raced wildly as she felt butterflies inside of her belly. Slowly, as if drawn together by some inexorable force, the distance between them shrank, then disappeared altogether and when Lorne's lips touched hers, Diana's entire body exploded in sensation.

His tongue slipped past her teeth, rolling languidly around hers and Diana felt as if she couldn't breathe. She thought her heart had stopped dead in her chest. Then, her entire body vibrated with sensation as she felt warmed from the inside and goosebumps rose on every part of her. She leaned into him, the feeling of his mouth on hers unlike anything she'd ever experienced before.

Diana ran her fingers through his hair as their kiss deepened and grew more insistent. The heat inside of her spread through her veins, moving through her entire body, then seemed to grow impossibly warm between her thighs. She quivered and pulsed, groaning into his mouth. She wanted that moment to last forever and when Lorne finally pulled back, she touched her lips, which still burned with his kiss.

"I'm sorry," he said. "I shouldnae have."

"'Tis all right. 'Twas nice," she said.

"I should go. Let ye get some rest."

He kissed her forehead, and then turned quickly and fled the room, softly closing the door behind him. Diana's stomach still churned and she had a smile on her lips she knew would not be going away any time soon. She stared up at the ceiling as a thousand different emotions and sensations coursed through her body, the insides of her thighs strangely warm and slick. That had been her first kiss and as tightly as she had held onto it, she did not regret giving it to Lorne. In fact, in his absence, she found herself longing for more.

She needed rest but Diana knew sleep would not be coming for her any time soon.

CHAPTER TWENTY-FIVE

Lorne lay in bed, staring up at the ceiling, his mind still spinning with worry about Gavin. He didn't look good and the healer hadn't been entirely encouraging about his recovery. But Gavin was a fighter, he'd taken wounds before and had always found a way through them. Lorne expected this wouldn't be any different. At least, he hoped. Lorne said a silent prayer for his cousin's recovery.

As he finished his prayer for Gavin, his thoughts drifted to Diana. Even though she was fine and would fully recover, the sight of her collapsing had stayed with him. The fear that had gripped him when he had thought she was going to die was unlike anything he'd ever felt. It was visceral and raw, and even though she was fine, it continued to echo through his heart as he continued to see the moment over and over again in his mind.

Diana had gotten deeper beneath his skin than anybody ever had, more than he thought anybody could. He bore a tremendous sense of guilt for how he had gotten to know her, but his feelings for her had nothing to do with that. His feelings for her were genuine, powerful and all very real.

Lorne didn't know what he was going to do. Once Diana and her family found out that Gavin—and he—had lied to them, he was going to lose her. The mere thought of losing her hurt every bit as deeply as it had to watch her collapse.

He shook his head, trying to figure some way to get out from under his lie. There had to be a way to make her forgive him.

From there, his mind turned to thoughts of the kiss they'd shared in her chambers. He closed his eyes and thought about her pillow soft lips, the feel of her breath, warm and sweet that had filled his mouth, and the sound of her soft whimpers as his mouth had lingered on hers. The memories sent a rush of tingles across his skin and put a pleasant flutter in his belly. Their kiss had been passionate but tender.

As a thousand thoughts, fears, and memories raced through his brain and his body, the door to his bedchamber opened with a soft squeal. Fearing it was somebody bringing bad tidings about Gavin, he sat up quickly, his heart racing, his stomach churning. But when he saw Diana step into his room and close the door behind her, he swallowed hard and blinked at her, saying nothing for a long moment. Not sure what to say.

Diana stood in naught but her shift and a thin robe, shifting on her feet, wringing her hands together, an expression of uncertainty etched into her features. She licked her lips and cleared her throat, the silence between them dragging out, filling the air with a tense and awkward air. Lorne sat up a little straighter and ran a hand over his face.

"What are ye daein' here, Diana?" he asked hesitantly. "Are ye bringin' news about Gavin?"

She shook her head. "Nay. I've nay news about Gavin."

He stared at her for a moment, expecting her to say something more. But she didn't she continued wringing her hands, her face blanching as she stood there.

"What is it?" he finally asked. "Are ye all right?"

"Aye. I'm fine. I just…"

Her voice trailed off and she lowered her gaze. Lorne's curiosity was piqued. What could she possibly be doing in his chambers in the small hours of the night?

"Diana?"

"I just… I dinnae want tae be alone tonight," she said, her words slow and halting. "Would ye mind if I stayed here? With ye?"

"Uh, of course nae," he said.

She walked over to the bed and slipped out of her robe, leaving herself in nothing but her shift, before she slid under the covers beside him. Lorne was keenly aware of the warmth of her body, of her soft curves as she nuzzled against him. His stomach churned and his heart began to race. Lorne gritted his teeth, swallowed hard, and tried to control his arousal.

They lay with her back pressed to his chest and his arm draped around her waist for a long moment, neither of them speaking. Lorne savored the soft, floral aroma that drifted from her body. She rolled over with a sigh and faced him. He stared deep into her dark eyes, feeling his breath catch in his throat. He swallowed the lump that had risen in his throat.

"Are ye all right, Diana?"

"I just… what happened tae me… I mean, 'tis naethin' compared tae what happened tae yer braither and the others, but it scared me. Still scares me," she says, her voice barely more than a whisper. "I'm afraid Munro is goin' tae keep comin' fer me."

"I'll nae let anythin' happen tae ye," he replied firmly.

"I believe ye," she said, her full lips curling upward in a smile.

They lay facing one another, staring into each other's eyes in silence for a long moment. The awkward energy faded, replaced by a growing sense of expectation. Anticipation.

"Dae ye ken what I keep thinkin' about?" she asked, her voice a whisper.

"What's that?"

"Ye kissin' me," she said.

Lorne's heart lurched and the desire within him grew, but he tried to temper it. "I'm sorry about that," he said. "If I was out of line—"

"Nay. I… I liked it."

"Aye?"

She nodded. "Aye."

"I did too."

A faint smile curled her lips and even in the dim light of his chamber, he could see the uncertainty in her eyes along with a gleaming light of desire. But he tried to tamp it down, knowing it was a line that if crossed, they could not come back from. And with his deception hanging over his head like a dark, angry cloud, Lorne knew he should not, could not, indulge his desires.

And yet, that longing inside of him stirred. Not just to have her physically, but to be with her on a far deeper level. He wanted Diana, but not just her body. He wanted her mind, spirit, and soul as well. He wanted everything. And he wanted it—wanted her—more than he'd ever wanted anything in his entire life.

Diana reached out and laid a gentle hand against his cheek. "What is it?" she asked softly. "Are ye all right?"

"Aye," he said, his voice faltering.

"Dae ye nae want tae kiss me again?"

"More than anythin'," he said. "I just... I dinnae ken if I should."

"Why nae?"

Lorne's body was screaming out to kiss her, to taste her, to feel her body pressed to his. But still, he hesitated.

"I'm nae sure... I mean, I think—"

A smile on her lips made him swallow down the rest of his words.

"What?" he asked.

"Fer the first time in me life, I dinnae want tae think," she said. "I just want tae feel."

"But—"

"I've lived me life so tightly controlled, always worried about daein' the right thing and never daein' anythin' I wanted tae dae. Never daein' anythin' fer meself," she said.

"Diana—"

She leaned forward and pressed her mouth to his, cutting him off. Her kiss was so sudden and unexpected that it took his breath away for a moment. But then his instincts took over, his passion and desire ignited, and he leaned into her, any thought of propriety or right and wrong fleeing from his mind in the blink of an eye.

Diana raked her fingers through his hair, pulling his face closer to him. Lorne's hands roamed her back, her arms, caressed the back of her neck as he devoured her. Their tongues rolled languidly around one another and he swallowed the soft whimpers that drifted out of her throat. Lorne pulled back and stared into her eyes.

"What is it?" she asked.

"Are ye certain of this?" he asked. "Are ye certain about… about me?"

"More than certain."

Their mouths found each other again and he slipped his tongue passed her teeth as he slid his hand down to her waist and pulled her to him. He felt his arousal growing, warming his skin from the inside. Diana's velvety tongue darted into his mouth, her hands sliding down his back. He tugged and pulled at her shift.

Biting her bottom lip, she sat up and raised her arms, allowing him to slide the shift off her body. Lorne drew in a sharp breath as he gazed upon her naked body for the first time. He admired her smooth, creamy skin and the swell of her full breasts and hips. His gaze slid along the curve of her thighs and the thatch of golden hair between her legs. He felt himself growing impossibly hard and when his eyes met hers, the gleam of passion that lit up her face made his heart stutter drunkenly in his chest.

"Ye're as beautiful as the angels above," he said, his voice thick.

She slid her hand behind his neck and pulled him down into another kiss. She grabbed at his nightshirt and tugged it upward. Lorne quickly stripped it off and threw it to the floor with hers, then planted a line of kisses down her neck as he cupped her breasts. Diana moaned softly as he lowered his face, circling her stiff nipples with the tip of his tongue.

Diana lay back, pulling him down on top of her. She parted her thighs as Lorne braced himself above her on his arms. He stared down into her warm, brown eyes. Her pale cheeks were flushed, and she bit her bottom lip, nervous. He seemed nervous as he leaned down to kiss her. Diana felt a sudden rush of warmth flow through her.

"A woman's first time is painful," he said, kissing her. "Yet I can promise I will be gentle if ye wish tae continue."

"'Tis all right. I trust ye."

"Are ye certain about this? I dinnae mind stealin' yer kisses only, me bonnie."

"More certain than I've ever been about anythin'."

Their mouths found each other again, their kiss slow and gentle. Diana's entire body tingled as his tongue rolled languidly around hers. She caressed his body, marveling at the toned, corded muscles, amazed that he felt so hard and yet so soft at the same time. Lorne's caresses were tender, gentle. And they filled her with a fire only he could quench. He entered her with a finger, then a second one and she could feel easing around him. He kept the rhythm of his members trusting inside and then he stroke the apex of her sex slowly and teasingly a few times. She all but melted against his touch, desperate to reach a peak she didn't know existed.

"Are ye ready?" he asked softly.

She nodded, encouraging him to continue. Lorne leaned down and kissed her again as he nestled the head of his manhood between her wet, warm folds. With a gentle roll of his hips, he buried himself inside of her. She grimaced in pain.

"Are ye all right?" he asked. "Dae ye want—"

"Dinnae stop," she gasped.

Her teeth were gritted and her face contorted with pain as her body tensed up around him. She gripped his shoulders, her nails digging into his flesh. Lorne paused for a long moment, giving her time to adjust to having him inside of her. The fit was incredibly tight, but she was warm and wet. Countless sensations prickled his flesh, and his head spun. Diana's body slowly began to relax, and a wavering smile crossed her lips as the look of pain faded.

"Oh, me God," she whispered, a tone of awe in her voice.

Lorne started to move within her, his thick staff sliding along her slick inner walls. She gazed into his eyes as their bodies moved in a slow, sinuous rhythm. He trembled as they moved together, her eye contact making the heat between them burn brighter and hotter. He rolled his hips, sliding deeper into her molten core, both of them shuddering with pleasure.

"Ye feel so good," he said.

"Aye. So dae ye."

She writhed and squirmed beneath him, their movements slow and tender. And through it all, they never broke eye contact, making the sensations coursing through him all the more intense, making their coupling all the more intimate. Lorne felt the pressure building up deep inside of him, felt his staff growing thicker and harder. Diana's body tensed, her sex tightening around his staff, making the fit inside of her even tighter.

Diana's eyes widened and her full lips parted, a slow, sensuous moan passing her lips as she began to tremble. She shook harder, digging her nails so hard into his shoulders he was sure she was drawing blood. He drew in a sharp breath and felt his staff pulse. As Diana's moans grew into cries of passion, Lorne's arousal reached a pinnacle and he threw his head back, a loud, sultry cry issuing from his throat as his manhood twitched and a moment later, he erupted within her.

Their eyes still locked onto each other, their cries blended together, creating an erotic melody that made Lorne's heart skip a beat. As she pulsed around his thick staff, he pumped his warm, sticky seed into her, filling her up entirely. She clung to him, their bodies warm, their skin slick with a thin sheen of sweat. Their breath was ragged as they were buffeted along on a powerful current of pleasure.

As she milked the last of his seed out of him and he felt himself soften, Lorne rolled off her and flopped onto his back, trying to catch his breath. Diana laid her head on his chest and nuzzled up next to him. He caressed her back with his fingertips, making her shudder with pleasure.

"That was amazin'," she said dreamily.

"Aye," he replied softly. "That it was."

They lay together in silence, wrapped in the afterglow of their coupling. It wasn't long before her breath turned even and regular as she drifted away on a tide of sleep, a small smile curling the corners of her mouth. She slept peacefully. And as she did, Loren felt the bitter sting of guilt. But he also felt a steely determination rise within him to fight for Diana... to fight to keep what they have been building. Together.

CHAPTER TWENTY-SIX

Diana stirred and woke up, a small smile playing across her lips as she thought about what happened the night before.

At the first lights of dawn they had awoken and she had dressed and snuck back into her room before anybody could find her in Lorne's chambers.

Now she saw that a piece parchment had been slipped under her door, so she went to get it. It was from Lorne. He was letting her know that he had been called to participate in a council meeting. He was always so thoughtful. As she was reading it, a chamber maid came in and brought her some tea.

Diana poured herself a cup of tea and sat down at the table, looking out the window, her mind spinning with a myriad of thoughts. As she replayed the previous night over and over in her head, her smile warred with a frown upon her lips. What she'd done with Lorne had been amazing. More than amazing. At the same time though, it had been dangerous. If her father knew she had given her maidenhead to Lorne... he would not be happy.

Why had she acted so rashly and impulsively? Perhaps the trauma of being poisoned had triggered something in her brain, like some part of her didn't want to die without knowing the touch of a man. And with Munro apparently still coming for her, there was a possibility it could happen. Had that been all it was? Fear? Had she gone to Lorne because she was afraid? Or was it something deeper?

A tremor of concern passed through her—there was still some part of her that did not trust the feelings she had for him, for she'd never felt that way about anybody before. He inspired emotions she'd never experienced. Emotions she didn't understand.

Pushing all her uncertainty away, she took a sip of her tea and relived the night again. Her body tingled as she recalled the way he'd felt inside of her. It had been painful at the start but that quickly ebbed, and Diana had been awash with a sense of pleasure she didn't know even existed, which then reached a pinnacle that had been mind-blowing.

The memory of those pleasurable moments they'd shared gave way to other thoughts. She wouldn't have given herself to a man she did not care for. Diana knew herself well enough to know her virtue was something she'd protected all her life and would not have simply given away to just anybody.

Lorne was different. He hadn't tried to take her virtue. In fact, he had gone out of his way to make sure that was what she wanted. He was kind. Compassionate. And as this morning he had proven how thoughtful he was too. Lorne evoked feelings in her that had knocked her for a loop and muddied her thoughts. Look what she had given him.

Did she love Lorne?

She shook her head and tried to push away that question and the many thoughts that rampaged through her brain. She ran a hand across her face and sipped her tea. But the questions did not relent. If anything, they became more insistent.

As Diana sat at the table, trying to clear her mind, another thought, a darker one, slipped into her mind. She could still taste the bitterness of whatever had been slipped into her wine on her tongue, felt the burn of it sliding down her throat and filling her belly. She remembered the queasiness that had gripped her. Recalled the feeling of being so out of control. Her mind was filled with the memory of feeling like she was slipping below the surface of some dark pool of water, unable to swim her way out.

And then she remembered Lorne being there. His face had been the only thing she had seen clearly through her wavering vision. He'd pulled her out of the water and had gotten her to safety. It was because of him that she'd survived the poisoning and hadn't been taken by Munro.

Those thoughts gave way to a numbing cold in the pit of her stomach. In a bright flash, she realized just how powerless and weak she'd felt. Diana had always thought she'd able to protect herself. But that was not true.

She thought back to how badly she had spoken to Lorne at the village. She'd come close to being taken and perhaps either killed or forced into a life she did not want then too. Just thinking about it sent a cold ripple through her heart.

Diana did not like feeling weak nor powerless.

"'Tis goin' tae change," she said.

She finished her tea and got to her feet. She took a moment to get herself dressed, putting on a pair of breeches, boots, and a shirt she had from when she was younger and often played outdoors with the children of the castle. Diana stared at her reflection in the looking glass and had to stifle a giggle. She looked like a lad. But that was all right. It was practical and she couldn't do the work she was about to do in a dress.

Satisfied, she turned and headed through the castle, drawing curious looks from the household staff. She laughed to herself as she traversed the winding corridors. The ring of steel on steel echoed down the hall and Diana felt the first twinge of apprehension, doubt. But she gritted her teeth and marched on, silently renewing her sense of purpose.

She stepped through the archway and into the walled courtyard. Half a dozen men, shirtless, sweat glistening off their naked torsos were sparring together. All activity stopped when she was spotted standing there. The men inclined their heads respectfully. Arn, one of her father's personal guardsmen, stepped forward.

"Lady Diana," he said, his voice gruff. "What can we dae fer ye?"

She picked up one of the practice blades from the table and held it up. She had never picked up a blade in her life and it was heavier than she expected, but watching the way the sunlight glinted off it, she smiled. Just holding the sword made her feel more powerful and less helpless than ever before. She turned to Arn.

Her smile grew wider. "Teach me tae use this?"

CHAPTER TWENTY-SEVEN

The council meeting had been grim and tense, but Lorne had felt honored and privileged to have been asked to attend. The conversation centered on Munro and preparing for what was to come. The problem was, they didn't know what that was. They were all in agreement that he would try for Diana again. The only question was where and how. And whether he would bring his whole force to bear in an effort to get her.

They had asked his opinion on a number of things regarding his approach to battle and war. He told them what he could, shared what he'd learned, but the truth was, Lorne didn't have much to offer. He didn't know the lands and didn't know the players. More than that, he was a guest in the castle and thought it would be poor form to inject his opinion into Laird Macgillivray's clan matters. To his credit though, Dunn hadn't acted as if he was an outsider and at least pretended to give his words weight and due consideration.

The more he listened to Macgillivray conduct his meeting and watched the way he interacted with his men, the more he believed his initial assessment of the man was correct. He was a good man who cared about his people and wanted to keep them all as safe as he possibly could. He didn't approach the subject of war lightly, nor did he seem to have a particular taste for it. He seemed to want to avoid it all cost if he could.

But he was realistic enough to know that might not be possible. He knew that because of men like Munro, conflict sometimes could not be avoided. Lorne had suggested that he start preparing and training his men as if war was inevitable, arguing that it was better to be overprepared and ready to fight and not have to, than to have the fight come to them and not be ready for it. Laird Dunn had fully and had instructed his men to begin preparations for war.

After the meeting had broken, Lorne stalked the castle looking for Diana, eager to revel in the glow of their night spent together. He just wanted to be near her. She made him feel things he had never considered possible before. She filled him with a warmth and care he'd never known. She was intoxicating and he could not get enough of simply being in her presence.

When he wasn't able to find her, he spent some time sitting with Gavin. His cousin had still not awaken, but the healer was encouraged by the fact that he had not taken a fever and that his color seemed to be improving. She was cautiously optimistic, which gladdened his heart. Beatrix had come in a short time after he'd arrived to sit vigil, fresh from having gotten a bit of sleep and some food in her belly, her demeanor somewhat subdued but hopeful, so shortly thereafter, Lorne had taken his leave.

Now, he stalked the halls of the castle, trying to figure out what to do with himself. He was filled with a tense energy and had no idea what to do with it. As he rounded a corner, the sound of steel clashing rang in his ears. The sparring yard was exactly what he needed to burn off that nervous energy that was coursing through him.

Lorne stepped into the yard and stopped short, his eyes fixed on the sight before him. Diana was standing with a tall, muscular man in the middle of the yard, taking instruction from him. Lorne gritted his teeth, a powerful surge of jealousy flashing through him as he watched the man put his hands on Diana, positioning her. He swallowed down the caustic words that sprang to his tongue as he watched him moving her about like she was a doll. The man looked at her then nodded and stepped back, taking up a position in front of her.

"All right," he said. "Deflect me blow."

The man lunged forward, the tip of his practice blade clanging against Diana's. She yelped though and her blade went spinning away, landing in the dirt with a thud. She looked frustrated and the man put a calming hand on her shoulder, stoking those flames of jealousy burning inside of him.

"'Tis all right, Diana," he said. "Ye did good, ye blocked me thrust this time."

Lorne walked into the yard and picked up the fallen blade. He stepped behind her and put a hand on her hip and stepped close, drawing a soft gasp from her lips. Lorne felt her body tighten and she turned her head, looking at him over her shoulder. Her full lips parted slightly, and her eyes were wide, filled with the same glimmering desire he'd seen last night. But then she tore her eyes away and cleared her throat.

"Arn, this Lorne... Lorne Davidson," she said. "Lorne, this is

Arn, he's one of me faither's personal guards. He's teachin' me tae swing a blade."

"And why would ye want tae learn that?" Lorne asked.

"Because I want tae learn tae protect meself better," she said.

"She obviously has some room tae learn, but the lady is a quick study," Arn said.

A page ran into the yard. "Maister Arn, Laird Macgillivray is askin' fer ye and yer men. Says he needs tae see ye all in thae main hall right away."

"Aye," Arn replied and turned to Diana. "Sorry, me lady. We'll have tae pick this up later."

"Dinnae worry, I've got her,' Lorne said.

"As ye wish," Arn replied with a curt nod.

After the guardsmen had left the sparring yard, leaving them alone, Diana turned to him, her cheeks flushed and her eyes glimmering with mischief. Lorne was suddenly awash in memories of the night before. His skin tingled and his belly churned with delight as he imagined her skin, her mouth, and her warm, wet center. Being inside of her had felt unlike anything he'd ever experienced, better than anything he'd ever imagined.

"So," she said. "Ye're goin' tae teach me, eh?"

"Aye. If ye'd like."

"Aye."

He stepped behind her again and put his hands on her hips. Diana leaned back against him, stirring his arousal as memories of their time together the previous night flooded his mind once more. He put his hands over hers, feeling how warm her skin was, as he taught her how to properly grip the sword. Swallowing hard, he slid his hands up her arms, putting them in the correct position from which she could both strike and defend.

Once he had her in the proper position, he moved them, showing her the proper way to swing that would allowed her to parry thrusts, block slashes, then counter with a strike of her own. All the while, their bodies were pressed together, and Lorne was keenly aware of the heat and tension that radiated from her body. His cheek was pressed to hers, his nose filled with Diana's floral scent, his arousal growing by the moment as memories of their lovemaking flashed through his head.

"Are ye ready?" he asked.

"Aye."

Reluctantly, he stepped away and picked up one of the practice blades before taking his position in front of her. He raised the blade.

"All right," he said. "We'll start slow, just tae make sure ye've got the movements."

She nodded. "All right then."

Lorne moved at half-speed, thrusting and slashing, while watching her form as she defended. He did this a few times until it looked like she was something akin to comfortable with that most basic form. He nodded.

"All right," he said. "Faster this time."

They moved through the progression faster and indeed, Diana was a speedy learner. She successfully defended against him and when he banged his blade against hers, she managed to keep hold of it. He nodded, impressed.

"Very good, Diana. Very good indeed," he said.

"Teach me more."

He laughed but showed her some basic strikes. Nothing too fancy. Not until he was sure she had those most fundamental forms down. But she attacked them with a fervor that bordered on frenzied. She thrust and slashed, parried and thrusted until their faces were red, they were out of breath, and they were both slicked with sweat.

"Are ye always this intense?" he asked.

A frown touched her lips. "I want tae learn tae fight. I need tae learn tae fight."

"Why?"

"Because… I feel responsible fer the attack. And when it was all happenin', I felt useless. I want tae be able tae protect others… and meself."

Her demeanor changed as she walked over and got a drink of water. She set the sword down and picked up a cloth, wiping her face. In her face, Lorne saw real pain, frustration. She sat down on the bench and looked at him, her dark eyes clouded over with emotion. But he got the sense there was much more to her frustration than simply being unable to swing a sword. Something told him it ran much deeper than that.

"What is it, Diana?"

"All me life I've been the responsible one. I always dae the right thing," she said. "I've never done anythin' without first worryin' about how it was goin' tae look, or what the consequences of me action might be. Me sister lives free of those cares and… I suppose part of me has always envied her that."

Lorne listened to her words, hearing what lay between them in the unspoken silences. Being the responsible and dutiful daughter, so concerned with doing the right thing and being perceived a certain way, was how she lived her life. Recklessness and spontaneity were concepts as foreign to her as swinging a sword. She had been so concerned about others that she had never been concerned for herself. She had existed, but she'd never truly lived.

He gave her a sly grin. "Tell me, if ye could dae somethin' that was totally crazy and out of character fer ye, what might that be?"

She giggled and he watched as the color rose in her neck then spread to her cheeks. Though a shy, demure expression crossed her face, Lorne could see the mischievous glint that sparkled in her eyes. Diana bit her bottom lip and turned away.

"I cannae say," she said.

"Of course, ye can."

"Nay, I cannae."

"Come on, lass. Tell me."

"'Tis too embarassin'."

"Come on, it will stay between us."

She sighed and turned back to him, a smile on her lips. "I want tae swim in the loch behind the rear grounds naked."

"Aye?"

She giggled and covered her mouth with her hand, her face bright red. "I just think it'd be so freein'."

Lorne laughed and nodded. "I imagine it might be that."

Diana jumped to her feet and picked up her sword. "Now, then. Teach me more."

An amused expression on his face, Lorne picked up his blade and continued the lessons with her as an idea began taking shape in his mind. He would teach Diana how to swing a sword, and then he would teach her how to be free.

CHAPTER TWENTY-EIGHT

"Has she been found yet?" Diana asked. "The woman who poisoned me?"

Her mother shook her head. "Nay. She's vanished like she never existed at all."

Diana muttered under her breath, her heart heavy, her thoughts dark. What had happened in the banquet hall and the loss of all those men weighed on her, the guilt pressing down on her so hard, she felt like she couldn't breathe.

"Ease yer mind, lass," her mother said as if reading her mind. "None of this is yer fault."

Diana sat in her mother's salon with her. She was wrapped in a fur sitting before a roaring fire, a cup of mulled wine in hand. It seemed a long time she and her mother had sat together, talking long into the night. It was something she had always loved. Diana felt like she could always talk with her mother about anything. That night, it was the burden of guilt she carried.

"I cannae help but feel like it is," she said softly. "If I'd nae rebuffed Laird Munro—"

"Laird Munro has shown us the kind of man he truly us," her mother cut her off. "And speakin' fer meself, I'm glad ye'll nae be marryin' a man like that."

"But our men who were killed—"

"'Tis nae yer fault."

"I feel like they died fer me."

"They died protectin' this family. Every man who swears their allegiance tae yer faither kens what that entails," Elayne said. "And yet, they make that choice willingly."

"And yet—"

"They fight fer the clan, nae fer ye, Diana," Elayne said softly. "I understand the guilt ye're feelin', but those men died with honor, defendin' the clan. And if they were able tae tell ye themselves, they'd tell ye it was a sacrifice they'd make a hundred more times."

Diana took a sip of her wine and stared into the flames. The wood in the fireplace cracked, sending a shower of sparks up the chimney like a swarm of fireflies. She felt the weight of her mother's gaze and turned to see the woman staring at her, the fire glittering in her eyes and her lips curled in a gentle smile. She was once again reminded of just how much she didn't look like her mother the way Beatrix did.

"What is it then?" Diana asked softly.

"Ye've always been one tae take everythin' tae heart. 'Tis a good quality tae have that kind of compassion fer others. And 'tis why ye make such a fine healer," she replied. "But what happened in the banquet hall had naethin' tae dae with ye.

'Twas all about the vanity and ego of one man. 'Tis all. Ease yer heart and mind, child."

The corners of Diana's mouth flickered upward. "Thank ye, Maither."

Before Elayne could respond, the door to the salon flew open, slamming into the wall behind it with a resounding crash. Auburn locks flying and eyes wild, Beatrix came storming in. She fell to her knees before their mother, eyes shimmering with tears.

"He's alive. He woke up," Beatrix cried.

"'Tis wonderful news," Elayne said as she stroked Beatrix's hair.

"Aye. 'Tis wonderful news indeed," Beatrix cried, sniffing back tears of joy. "I love him, Maither. Bein' so close tae losin' him made me realize I only ever want tae be with him. Please, Maither, I love him with everythin' in me."

Elayne and Beatrix turned to Diana as one and she knew what they were thinking: she was the only thing standing in the way of her sister's eternal love and happiness. All that had to happen for Beatrix to be with Gavin forever was for her to marry Lorne. And as strong as her feelings for him were, she wasn't sure where things stood with him. She knew he returned her feelings to some degree, she just wasn't sure how deeply they ran or if he was truly thinking about marriage.

Her stomach churning, Diana stood up and offered them both an awkward smile, letting the fur fall to the chair.

"I think I'll go tae bed and give ye two some time tae talk," Diana said.

Before either of them could respond and draw her into that sticky conversation, Diana turned and bolted, closing the door to the salon behind her firmly. Her emotions churning wildly, she closed her chamber door behind her and took a moment to gather herself. She was glad Beatrix had found a true love. But she had no idea what that meant for her. Or more specifically, what that portended for she and Lorne, if anything at all.

She had given him her virtue. But that had been her choice to make and did not require him to ask for her hand in marriage. Wanting to push all those thoughts from her mind, she readies herself for bed. Only in the darkness of sleep would she be able to escape from all the questions, all the doubts, and all the uncertainty she was feeling. Diana slipped beneath the covers and closed her eyes, falling quickly into the welcome embrace of sleep.

She had no idea how long she'd been asleep when her eyes flew open. A hand was on her shoulder, giving her a gentle shake. She quickly sat up, eyes wide, heart racing to find herself staring into Lorne's smiling face. Diana opened her mouth to speak, but Lorne put a finger to her lips, cutting off her words before she could utter them.

"Get dressed, lass," he whispers. "Hurry."

"What are ye—"

He pulls her out of bed with a low chuckle. "Dress."

"What time is it?"

"Late," he said. "Now, dress."

"What are ye daein' here—"

"Waitin' fer ye tae dress. Now, come on."

Against her better judgment, but her curiosity piqued, Diana quickly got dressed. She had just finished putting her shoes on when Lorne thrust a cloak into her hands. She slipped it around her shoulders, and he took her by the hand. Without a word, he led her out of her chamber and through the deserted hallways of the castle. It must have been very late, for the corridors were silent and Diana did not see a single soul around.

Lorne led her through a door that led outside. There, two horses stood saddled and waiting for them. She turned to him to find a mischievous grin on his face.

"And what are we daein' then, eh?" she asked.

"Ye'll see."

Uncertain, but curious, Diana let him help her onto the back of the mount. Once she was settled, he climbed onto the back of his horse and together, they rode out. He led her through the gate in the wall that surrounded the rear grounds and into the open fields behind them. They rode for a little while in silence, her heart racing and her belly churning.

The cool wind caressed her skin as they rode and despite her unease, Diana found herself smiling. This was crazy. She had never slipped out of the castle in the small hours before. It just wasn't proper. And yet, despite the inappropriateness of being out at that hour, she felt a small flash of wonder, almost of triumph.

"This is crazy," she said.

Lorne smiled at her. "Maybe a wee bit."

She laughed and followed him along a path that cut through the dense forest well beyond the castle walls. Overhead, the sky was like black velvet, the stars glimmering like jewels. It was breathtaking. Exhilarating.

"Are ye goin' tae tell me where we're goin'?" she asked.

"How about I show ye?"

They crested a small rise and below them, the loch stretched out before them. It was dark, the gibbous moon reflecting off the still surface of the water and casting the world around them in a monochromatic, silvery light. The loch was like glass, and she could even see the stars reflected off the water, bringing an awestruck smile to her lips.

"'Tis beautiful," she said.

"Come."

She followed Lorne down to the shore of the loch where he helped her off the back of her horse. Together, they stood at the edge of the water, admiring the beauty in silence. But then he turned to her, a mischievous smirk playing across his lips.

"What is it?" she asked.

Without answering, Lorne quickly stripped out of his clothing. She swallowed hard, gaping at his naked, muscular form in the moonlight. Even the night they'd coupled, she hadn't truly gotten a look at his body, but now, by the light of the moon, she saw every angle and plane of his body. Bathed in that silvery light, he looked like he'd been chiseled from marble in the image of the ancient gods themselves.

"Wh—what are ye daein' then?" she asked, finally managing to find her voice.

"Goin' fer a swim," he said. "Ye comin'?"

A laugh bursting from his lips, he turned and dashed into the water, sending ripples and waves across the surface. Diana stood on the shore staring at him. Her stomach was turning over on itself, her veins flowing with liquid fire, and she was quite sure, even in the darkness, her face glowed like a bright red beacon.

"Come on, Diana," he called, his voice echoing through the trees that ringed the lock. "The water is brisk but feels nice!"

Her mind spun wildly, and a giggle burst from her mouth. This was insane, reckless. But it was also something she'd always wanted to do, simply for the sense of freedom she thought it might give her. Diana bit her bottom lip, a thousand voices echoing in her mind. Without stopping to think about what she was doing, Diana felt herself stripping. Lorne's applause and laughter rang in her ears and before she knew it, she plunged into the waters of the loch, completely naked.

She burst through the surface of the water with a shriek. "Brisk? This is bleedin' freezin'!"

He laughed. "Ye'll get used tae it."

And he was right. It only took a moment for her body to adjust and for the cold water to feel nice against her skin. She floated on her back, staring up at the stars above, filled with awe and wonder at what she was doing. Lorne paddled over to her and laughed.

"And how daes it feel, lass?"

"Like freedom," she said softly.

Diana turned to Lorne and grinned mischievously, then splashed him in the face. He howled with laughter as he splashed her back and together, they engaged in a water fight like a couple of children. Their cries and giggling rang in Diana's ears, and she felt a sense of joy and liberation she'd never felt before blooming in her chest. She splashed him again.

They played in the water for a long while but eventually made it back to the shore. Lorne stretched a blanket down on the shoreline and together, still naked, they flopped onto it. Diana stared at the velvety blackness above, a wide smile still fixed on her lips. She turned her head. Lorne too, was staring at the stars, a look of peace and contentment on his face.

"Thank ye fer this," she said. "It's by far, the most reckless and impulsive thing I've ever done in me life, but..."

"But ye enjoyed it, didnae ye?"

She laughed. "Aye, I enjoyed it."

"Good. 'Tis what life is about... enjoyin' the simple things."

Lorne rolled over and stared down into her eyes, the intensity of his gaze burning into hers taking her breath away. He leaned down and kissed her and trailed the tips of his fingers up her flat, taut stomach. Diana shuddered and sighed softly into his mouth as goosebumps of pleasure prickled her skin. Their kiss deepened as did her need. She wanted him more than anything. And as if sensing the desire building within her, Lorne pulled her over on top of him.

She squealed and giggled as she sat astride him, looking down into his stormy blue eyes. Leaning down, she pressed her mouth to his, whimpering softly as his tongue slipped past her teeth and dashed against hers. Lorne cupped the back of her head, pulling her down into the kiss, making her entire body tingle.

His lips brushed her ear softly, making her shudder. "I need ye," he whispered. "I need tae be inside of ye."

Diana rolled her hips, relishing the feeling of him lengthening and growing hard beneath her. She moaned softly as she rubbed herself along his shaft, growing hotter and slicker by the moment. Diana reached down and took hold of his staff, gripping it tightly and giving it a couple of firm strokes that pulled a low groan from his lips. He was harder than iron and as she stroked him, a wave of lust washed over her.

Diana nestled the tip of his staff between her folds, now dripping wet and burning hot. Never taking her gaze from his, she lowered herself down onto him. She took him into her slowly, inch by inch. The length and girth of his staff was painful at first, but it quickly faded, giving way to the intense sense of pleasure she'd felt the night before. And when he was fully sheathed inside of her, Diana put her hands on his chest and stared down at him, giving herself a moment to adjust to being filled up so completely.

Lorne stared up at her with something like wonder on his face as she began to slide up and down on his hardness, taking him deeper into her with every stroke. She bit her bottom lip, wincing at the brief flash of pain that came with sinking down on him. It wasn't long though, before the pain faded entirely, leaving her with nothing but the feeling of rapture and bliss that coursed through her.

Squeezing her eyes shut, Diana threw her head back as she rose and fell on him, taking him deep into her sex. She shuddered as his hands roamed her body, cupping and kneading her breasts. He pinched her stiff nipples, drawing a moan of pleasure from her lips. She fell forward on him, hands still braced on his chest, her long blond hair falling forward, forming a curtain around both their faces, shutting the world around them out.

Their gazes locked and their bodies moved in a sensual rhythm, Diana smiled. She leaned down and kissed him, reveling in the feeling of his tongue in her mouth and his hands traversing her body. As his fingers trailed up her thighs, leaving furrows of heat along her skin, Diana shivered and moaned. He grabbed her hips as if he was about to turn her over, but she slapped his hands away, her lips curling in a smile.

"Nay," she said. "'Tis me turn."

"So, ye're the commander tonight, eh?"

"Aye. That I am."

He laughed as she started to roll her hips, moving up and down on him harder and faster. She sank down onto his shaft, burying him deep in her core, and let out a sharp gasp as she was battered by waves of pleasure. Lorne's large, rough hands continued to explore her body, trailing down her back, up her thighs, cupping her breasts, and firmly pinching of her pert, sensitive nipples. She continued driving herself onto his stalk, her body awash in a myriad of sensations.

Lorne's gaze remained fixed on hers as he thrust himself upward, driving his organ even deeper into her. Diana's mouth fell open and she gasped, pressure building up deep inside of her. Her body grew warm slick. The feeling of him sliding along her slippery inner walls made her tremble, her breath a stuttering gasp. Diana dug her nails into his chest, as if holding onto him as they moved together, thrusting and counterthrusting, driving each other to the heights of pleasure.

She thrust herself downward just as he thrust himself up, hitting that spot deep within her that touched off an explosion of ecstasy. She threw her head back and for a moment, felt completely weightless. Her body tensed and a moment after that, she felt a powerful wave crashing down over her. She cried out, shaking wildly as she climaxed. Diana felt her sex pulsing as she writhed on top of Lorne, unable to control her movements as she slid up and down on him.

Lorne let out a low grunt and as she pulsed around his manhood, she felt him swelling inside of her. His fingers dug into her hips and he pulled her down on top of him, thrusting himself upward again, as if seeking her very center. Diana quivered and when she met his gaze, her full lips parted and as she gasped, he erupted. She felt him throbbing in her sex, shooting his warm, thick seed deep into her. He grabbed her hands, their fingers interlocked, and they both shook and cried out, their gazes locked as firmly together as their bodies.

Joined together, they moved as one as he filled her with his seed. Diana leaned down and kissed him, their tongues lashing each other as they climaxed together. Slowly, their orgasms ebbed and she felt him growing softer within her. She stayed astride him, looking into his eyes as a trembling smile touched her lips. As she looked, she felt as if the world around them had fallen away, leaving just the two of them in that moment—a moment she didn't want to end.

Eventually, she slid off him, her heart still racing, her entire body tingling. He wrapped his arm around her and pulled her to him. She laid her head on his chest and traced small circles on his taut stomach as she listened to the steady rhythm of his heart. Wrapped in the warm glow of their coupling and the emotions that came with it, she raised her head and met his eyes.

"Thank ye," she said. "Fer tonight."

He chuckled. "I feel like I should be thankin' ye fer tonight."

She playfully slapped his chest and giggled. "Ye ken what I mean," she said. "I've never felt more alive than I did tonight."

He held her gaze and she could see the breadth and depth of emotions that scrolled across his face. Lorne pulled her to him and gave her a gentle kiss.

"Ye're welcome. Life is meant tae be lived, lass," he said. "I want ye tae feel like ye did tonight fer all the rest of yer days."

"I'd like that too," she replied softly.

Diana laid back down and nuzzled close to him. She too, wanted to feel like she did tonight for the rest of her days. More than anything, she knew without a single doubt, that she wanted the rest of her days to include Lorne. It was a realization tinged with uncertainty that filled her with a profound sense of joy, but at the same time, terrified her to no end.

CHAPTER TWENTY-NINE

"Wait," he said. "Just a second, lass."

They stood outside the curtain wall of the castle with the sun shining high overhead. They hadn't meant to, but they'd fallen asleep beside the loch. Despite how grave the situation was, Lorne couldn't help but smile as he thought back to the night before. Diana, on the other hand, was terrified. And he supposed he couldn't blame her. Being out all night, with a man no less, would surely not be looked upon favorably by her father.

He cracked open the hidden door in the curtain wall and peered through. Seeing nobody around, he led her through the rear grounds of the castle, taking care to move as quickly and quietly as they could, doing their best to remain unseen. They led the horsed back to the stables, where they took off their saddles and brushed them down. They figured that if anyone saw them, they would say they had gone for an early morning ride. He was just about to lead her across the open stretch of ground that led to the door to the kitchens when he pulled up short. His heart thundered in his chest and adrenaline made the blood in his veins flow warm.

"Down," he said.

Lorne pulled Diana behind a large, flowering bush. Peering between the lush leaves and flowers that adorned it, he watched as Laird Dunn and Lady Elayne strolled across the grass, hand in hand. They were lost in conversation, smiling and laughing at one another. They looked to be a couple deeply in love and Lorne felt a stitch in his heart knowing now that he wanted that himself.

"What is it?" Diana hissed.

"Yer parents," he replied.

She grew rigid beside him, her face flushing. "Weren't we going tae say that we had gone fer an early morning ride if we got caught?"

"True, but of all people, we dinnae necessarily bump intae them. They're movin' away."

"How can ye be sure?"

"Because I'm watchin' them move away," he said and flashed her a grin.

The flush in her cheeks deepened and Lorne had to stop himself from laughing. She had every right to worry and he knew he should not be making fun of her for it. Once Dunn and Elayne rounded a corner and disappeared from view, Lorne silently counted to ten, making sure they were not coming back, before he grabbed Diana by the hand, kissed it and pulled her to her feet.

"Come on, let's go," he said.

Hand in hand, they ran through the grass and Lorne couldn't keep himself from laughing at the absurdity of it all. They were behaving like besotted children. He glanced at Diana who was smiling and a moment later, a laugh burst from her mouth as well, perhaps seeing the silliness in it all as well. Or perhaps they were both just feeling good after their night together. Things fell into place in Lorne's mind while they had been together, and he found himself indulging in thoughts he never thought he would have. Thoughts that filled his heart with a lightness he never thought he would feel. And it was all because of the woman running beside him.

They burst through the main door of the castle and dashed into the dining hall, taking a seat at a long table that was set for breakfast. The hall was empty save for them, and after a long night out, they were both ravenous. Lorne chewed a piece of bread and cheese, watching as Diana popped a strawberry pastry into her mouth. The sunlight streaming through the window set high in the wall cast her in a sparkling nimbus, making her skin glow as if from within. She looked ethereal.

"What are ye starin' at me like that fer?" she asked.

"Because ye're the most beautiful woman I've ever laid eyes upon."

She swallowed her pastry then washed it down with a sip from the bottle of mead Lorne had pilfered. A shadow crossed her face, and the corners of her mouth turned down.

"What is it?" he asked, suddenly worried. "Did I say somethin' wrong?"

"Nay," she said as her eyes shimmered with unspent tears. "I just... I've been so caught up in the moment with ye that I didnae stop tae think about what this all means."

Lorne cocked his head. "What dae ye mean?"

"It's just... I enjoyed spendin' the night with ye, Lorne."

"And I enjoyed bein' with ye too."

"I was so caught up in how I felt about ye and... well... everythin' else that felt so good... that I didnae stop tae think about it," she said, her voice thick with emotion. "But the truth of it is that I'm ruined, Lorne. And when me parents find out..."

"Ruined? What are ye talkin' about?"

She wiped away the tears that raced down her soft, pale cheeks, the agony on her face twisting Lorne's insides. He never wanted her to feel pain or hurt of any kind. And knowing he was the cause of her suffering was tearing him to pieces.

"I gave ye me virtue, Lorne. I'm ruined," she explained. "And once me parents find out I've lost me virtue...

"What are ye talkin' about?" he asked. "How can ye be ruined if I intend tae marry ye? If ye'll have me that is."

Diana raised her head and looked at him. The sunlight glinted off the tracks of her tears and glistened off the new drops that were forming in her eyes. He pulled her hand to him and placed a soft kiss on her knuckles. He could see the questions in her eyes but felt a swelling in his heart he'd been trying so hard to deny but could no longer stifle.

"What are ye sayin'?" she asked quietly.

"That ye're what I've been lookin' fer me whole life. Ye're everythin' I never even kent I wanted," he said. "I would have never taken yer innocence if I wasnae sure I wanted tae be yer husband, Diana."

Her lips quivered and disbelief warred with the glimmer of hope upon her face. She took a deep breath and let it out slowly.

"Are ye sayin' what I think ye're sayin'?" she asked.

"If ye're thinkin' that I want tae ask fer yer hand, then aye, 'tis what I'm sayin'."

Diana clapped her hands over her mouth, her eyes wider than saucers. More tears spilled from the corners of her eyes, and Lorne could tell they were tears of surprise and joy.

"When I first arrived here, I wasnae sure about anythin'. I didnae ken if marriage would be right fer either of us," he confessed. "But the more time I've spent with ye, the better I've gotten tae ken ye, I've come tae realize there's nobody I'd rather spend me life with."

Diana stood and came around the table and pulled Lorne to his feet. She leaned into him, wrapping her arms tightly around him and squeezed as tight as she could. Lorne melted into her, relishing the feeling of her body intertwined with his. They stood like that for several long moments, just enjoying each other. Finally, she turned her head up and looked into his eyes.

"What dae ye say?" he asked.

"There's nobody I'd rather marry than ye," she said. "Of course, I want tae be with ye."

Lorne's heart swelled so big, he thought it might burst from his chest. He stared into her eyes, feeling her emotion radiating from her like heat from a fire. Leaning down, he placed a gentle kiss upon her lips.

"I've got tae speak with yer Faither," he said. "And I suppose that I've also got tae write tae me faither as well."

Diana laid a gentle hand against his cheek. "Ye're a good man, Lorne Davidson. And it'd be me honor tae call ye me husband."

Lorne kissed her again, relishing the taste of her lips and her body pressed to his so tightly. In truth, he was terrified that she would find out about the secret. Yet, he had indeed laid with her already and there was no going back. Not that he wanted out, not by any means.

Once he had spoken with her father and hopefully received his permission, he would discuss with Gavin how would they tell the sisters the truth. And then, when everything was out in the open, Lorne could only pray that Diana would realize that his love had nothing to do with the lie, and everything to do with his feelings for her.

And hopefully she would make the same choice over again and become his bride.

CHAPTER THIRTY

After they'd eaten and Lorne had gone to clean up before searching out her father, Diana left the dining hall and dashed through the corridors, feeling as if she was dancing on air. Her heart was filled with sunshine and she felt light enough that she might float away on a breeze. Diana giggled to herself as she rounded the corner and reached her sister's bedroom. She didn't bother knocking, instead she simply threw the door open, slammed it closed behind her, then ran to the bed and jumped on the form beneath the bedcovers.

"Wake up, sister," she cried with a giggle.

Beatrix groaned and rolled over, opening one eye and stared at Diana, who was grinning madly. She rubbed a hand across her face and glowered at her.

"What are ye daein'? she mumbled, her voice still thick with exhaustion. "I was tryin' tae get some sleep."

"Get up," Diana replied. "We have tae talk."

Beatrix groaned. "Cannae it wait?"

"Nay. It cannae wait."

When Beatrix still did not move, Diana grabbed the bedcovers and yanked them off her sister, tossing them to the floor with a laugh. Beatrix sighed heavily but sat up. Diana ran to the other side of the room and grabbed a dress from the rack and threw it to her sister. Muttering darkly under her breath Beatrix stripped out of her nightclothes and into the dress as Diana brought back a pair of stockings and slippers. As if moving by rote, Beatrix put those on then walked over to the small table in the corner and splashed some water on her face.

"I would like tae have a bath, ye ken," Beatrix grumbled.

"Later."

As her sister washed her face, Diana quickly pulled Beatrix's hair back and tied it into a braid. Excitement flowed through her veins so wildly, her fingers trembled. Beatrix stared at her reflection in the looking glass and pursed her lips.

"What is wrong with ye?" she asked. "'Tis the sloppiest braid I've ever seen."

Diana sat back and stared at her work, frowning as she did. Strands of hair stood out everywhere and the braid was loose, rather than tight. She giggled.

"Sorry, Sister," Diana said.

She quickly redid her work, her quaking fingers somehow managing to pull the braid tight on her second effort. As she worked, Beatrix continued studying her in the looking glass, a quizzical expression on her face.

"Somethin's happened, eh?" Beatrix asked. "What is it then?"

"I'll tell ye while ye eat. Now, come."

Diana pulled Beatrix to her feet and led her out of the bedchamber and back to the dining hall. She waited until the kitchen staff had laid out a platter of food. Despite her exhaustion and grumpy mood, when Beatrix smelled the aroma of food wafting off the tray, she tucked into the meal, eating as greedily as if she hadn't had a bite in days.

"So?" Beartix asked around a mouthful of roasted ham. "What is this big news that's got ye so frazzled and flustered that ye had tae yank me out of bed then?"

"Tae be fair, 'tis long past daybreak. Ye should have been up already."

Beatrix rolled her eyes.

"The first thing I wanted tae say was that I'm sorry, Beatrix."

Her sister paused with a boiled egg halfway to her lips, her eyes widening, and a look of pure shock crossing her face. She set the egg back down and leaned forward.

"Sorry fer what then?"

"Fer always bein' so hard on ye," she said. "Fer callin' ye irresponsible. And fer condemin' ye fer it. I see now that ye're just a happy girl. And I suppose part of me has always envied that freedom and carefree disposition. So, I'm sorry if I was unkind tae ye. Nay. I'm sorry that I was unkind tae ye all these years."

Too stunned to speak for a moment, Beatrix ate a piece of meat then popped the egg into her mouth and chewed slowly, as if trying to wrap her mind around what Diana had just said. Diana knew she had not always been the best older sister. She had tried to set an example for Beatrix and when that example did not seem to be taking, she knew she could be overly harsh and judgmental. All Beatrix was doing was living her life and finding joy where she could.

If the time she spent with Lorne was teaching her anything, it was to do the same. To find joy. To bask in the glow of happiness. And to also reach for what ye truly wanted. Beatrix extended across the table and took Diana's hand, giving it a squeeze as her eyes shimmered with tears.

"What's gotten intae ye, sister?" she asked softly. "Are ye all right?"

"Aye. I'm fine."

"Are ye dyin'?" Beatrix asked with a sly grin.

A laugh burst from Diana's mouth. "Nay. I'm nae dyin'."

"Then what is it?"

Diana took a swallow of wine, fortifying herself. She set the cup back down on the table and drew in a long breath then let it out slowly. Telling her sister was proving to be more difficult than she'd anticipated. The words seemed stuck in her throat. She took a moment to steady her nerves and gather her thoughts. Diana finally raised her head and gave her sister a smile.

"Lorne has asked me tae marry him," she said. "We're goin' tae be wed… so long as Faither agrees tae give me hand tae him."

Beatrix sat back for a moment, eyes wide, mouth hanging open as she absorbed Diana's news. Giving herself a small shake, Beatrix grabbed her cup and drank deeply of her morning mead and when she set the cup back down, the smile on her face was wide and warm. Tears of joy rolled down her cheeks.

"'Tis wonderful news, Diana. I... I cannae even begin tae tell ye how happy I am fer ye," she squealed. "Lorne is a good man. I ken he'll dae right by ye."

"I believe so too."

Beatrix jumped up and rushed around the table, pulling Diana into a tight embrace. She leaned into her sister and together, they laughed, and cried, hugging each other warmly. Diana clung to her little sister, reveling in the feelings washing over her. She felt a joy she had never imagined she would have in her life and it made her heart swell until it felt too big for her chest.

Beatrix finally let go of Diana and sat down on the bench beside her, taking both her hands in hers and squeezing them tightly, the smile on her face wider than ever.

"I am so happy fer ye, Diana."

"Thank ye," she said, feeling the flush creeping into her face.

"And ye ken what this means, dinnae ye?"

"What's that?"

"With ye marryin' Lorne—"

"If Faither gives his approval."

Beatrix waved her away. "Of course, he's goin' tae give his approval. Lorne is here because of this. But more than that, he makes ye happy. 'Tis all Maither and Faither truly want fer us. They just want us tae be happy and with a man who will treat us well. Both of which, Lorne daes."

"I hope so."

"I ken so," she says, her voice crackling with excitement. "And when ye're married tae Lorne, they'll allow me tae be properly courted and married tae Gavin. Can ye imagine that? Who would have thought we'd be married tae braithers?"

Diana's heart skipped a beat as she thought about it. Now that her relationship with Beatrix seemed to be on the mend and they were growing closer, the thought of them marrying brothers, outlandish just a few weeks past, seemed comforting.

"Look at us," Diana said. "Who'd have thought, eh?"

"Nae I."

"Nor I."

"But I couldnae be happier, Sister."

Diana pulled Beatrix into another warm embrace, relishing the closeness of the bond they were forming. A bond she had longed for her entire life. Tears of joy spilled down her cheeks and she laughed softly to herself.

CHAPTER THIRTY-ONE

Freshly scrubbed and in the best clothing he'd brought with him, Lorne strode down the hall, trying to summon a courage that continued to elude him. His stomach churned and his heart raced wildly as he approached the door to Laird Dunn's study. The guard standing outside the door gave Lorne a curt nod and opened it for him. Lorne walked inside and the guard closed it behind him, sealing him inside with the man he sought to make his father-in-law.

Laird Dunn sat behind his desk studying the parchments in his hands. He was silent for a long moment and with every second that passed, Lorne's body grew tauter. Beads of sweat rolled down his back, the velvet doublet he wore growing uncomfortably warm. But he stood rigidly at attention before Laird Dunn, waiting for the man to invite him to speak.

Laird Dunn finally put down the parchments then picked up his cup of wine and took a drink, raising his gaze to Lorne. He could see the questions in his eyes but got the sense Laird Dunn knew why he was there. After all, asking for a private audience was unusual and typically could only mean a couple of things. Especially when the man asking for the audience was there courting his daughter. Dunn leaned back in his chair then motioned to the chair in front of his desk.

"Please," he said, "Have a seat, lad."

"Thank ye, me laird."

Lorne sat in the plush chair and squirmed around in it, trying to make himself comfortable. His heart was beating hard and his gut churning wildly. He gazed at the laird, offering what he hoped was a polite smile. In truth, he feared the expression on his face looked as sickly and awkward as it felt.

"So, what can I dae fer ye, Lorne?"

"Well, me laird, I was hopin' we could talk."

"'Tis what we're daein' isnae it?"

Lorne cleared his throat. "Aye, me laird. 'Tis so."

"All right," he said with a sly smile. "And what is it ye hoped we could talk about."

"Well, me laird, I was hopin' we could talk about... about... Diana."

Lorne was so certain in his conviction that he wanted to marry Diana and yet, in the face of her father, he was having trouble actually getting the words to come out.

"Are ye all right, lad?" Dunn asked. "Ye look a little green in the cheeks."

"Fine, me laird," he croaked. "Just a little somethin' in me throat, is all."

Dunn stood up and poured a cup of wine. He brought it around the desk and handed it to Lorne who took it with a grateful nod. As he drank deeply, trying to swallow down the lump in his throat, Laird Dunn sat down in the chair beside his and turned to him. The laird's green eyes sparkled in the light that slanted in through the windows, glittering with a mischievousness that matched the curl of his lips.

"Thank ye fer the wine, me laird."

Though the lump was gone from his throat, Lorne still felt sick to his stomach. Why was he having so much difficulty getting his words out? His heart and mind were both so certain. Why was it that his mouth didn't have that same sort of conviction?

"Ye said ye wanted tae talk about Diana?"

"Aye. Me laird."

"Wonderful lass, isnae she?"

Lorne nodded. "The most I've ever met."

He drew another deep breath and steadied himself. He was behaving like a child and gave himself a kick in the mental backside. Drawing upon all his strength and courage, he turned to Laird Dunn and set his jaw.

"Laird Dunn, as ye ken, I've been courtin' ye're daughter," he said. "And I believe the time has come tae ask ye fer her hand. I'd—I'd like tae wed Diana. That is, if 'tis all right with ye, of course. I'm hopin' tae have yer blessin'."

"I see," Dunn said, his voice low and tight.

The man stood and clasped his hands behind his back as he began to pace the room, his face blank and unyielding. Getting nothing from his face, Lorne tried to read the man's gestures and body language, trying to determine what he might be thinking. But he got nothing. He had to believe Laird Dunn would agree to the match. If he wasn't going to, why allow him to stay in his castle, courting his daughter for so long.

Laird Dunn finally stopped pacing and turned to Lorne. "So, ye want me daughter's hand."

"Aye, me laird. I dae."

"Which would make yer clan and mine allies then, eh?"

"Aye, I suppose so."

"And what dae ye want from this alliance? What is yer bride price?"

Lorne hadn't given that much thought. His father hadn't given him any specific demands to make of Larid Dunn if the match looked promising enough to ask for her hand. As he thought about it though, he found that he didn't care. Lorne returned his eyes to Laird Dunn's.

"Me laird, I would marry yer daughter without a bride price, if it was up tae me," he said. "Aye, we'll be allies if we are tae marry, but the details of who gets what can be hashed out by ye and me faither. I simply want tae marry Diana. And she wants tae marry me."

"Ye'd marry her without a bride price?"

"Aye. I dae nae care about men or money, land or titles. I only care about her."

A broad smile crossed Laird Dunn's face and he nodded before walking over and taking Lorne by the hand. He pulled him up and shook his hand fiercely.

"Ye're a good man, Lorne," he said. "I can see why me daughter fancies ye so."

Lorne felt an immediate wave of relief wash over him so powerful, he felt boneless for a moment, as if his legs might give out beneath him. But he managed to keep his feet. He shook Laird Dunn's hand and smiled gratefully.

"So, dae we have yer blessin' me laird?"

"Aye, ye've got me blessin'," he said. "I'd be proud tae have ye as me son-in-law."

Lorne cleared his throat. "I didnae come prepared tae discuss the terms, as I mentioned—"

He waved him off. "'Tis somethin' yer faither and I will work out taegether since we're goin' tae be allies and kin." he said. "All ye need tae worry about is takin' good care of me eldest daughter and doin' right by her."

"I'll treat her like a queen, me laird."

Dunn held his gaze firmly for a moment before nodding. "I believe ye'll dae just that. Now, go. I expect there's a certain bride tae be who's anxious tae hear whether I gave her hand or nae."

Lorne bounded to the door and threw it open, pausing at the threshold and turned back to Laird Dunn again.

"Thank ye again, me laird. Ye've truly made me the happiest man in the world."

Dunn chuckled. "Well, I hope me daughter makes ye even happier than that."

"I've nay doubts that she will."

With that, Lorne closed the door then dashed down the corridor in search of his cousin and Diana. First, he had something very important to do – discuss the plan of action with his cousin. And then find the love of his life and tell her everything.

And he could only pray she would forgive him.

CHAPTER THIRTY-TWO

*R*estless and nervous, Diana stalked the halls of the castle, waiting for Lorne. Diana had never truly been happy nor content in her life. And the feelings Lorne inspired within her were foreign. Uncomfortable. There was some small part of her that believed she was not destined to have the sort of joy she felt in her life and thus, her father would find some reason to declare Lorne an unsuitable match and refuse to give her hand. It was probably silly, she knew, but she had those fears all the same.

The sound of heavy boots on the stone floor behind her brought a smile to Diana's lips. They weren't even married yet, but she already knew the sound of his footsteps as well as she knew her own. Diana turned to see Lorne approaching her, a wide smile on his face.

"One of the people I was looking fer," he said.

"Who is the other one," Diana asked.

"Gavin," Lorne said and caressed her check. "But I guess he can wait a little bit. I have news fer ye."

Lorne looked around as if to make sure they were alone in the corridor, his eyes glittering mischievously. The look on his face told Diana all she needed to know. She squealed as Lorne swept her up in his arms. She wrapped her legs around his waist and locked her hands behind his neck. He carried her as if she weighed nothing at all and opened a door and stepped in, quickly closing it behind them.

Still holding her up, he pressed her against the door and kissed her. His lips burned against her, his tongue pushing past her teeth nearly stealing her breath. Diana raked her fingers through his hair as their kiss grew deep. Her stomach churned, her insides warmed. It wasn't long before that warmth became hot, and the insides of her thighs grew dewy and slick with her desire.

Lorne swallowed her moan as she ground herself against him, relishing the feel of his rigid length pressed to her center. Pulling back, his eyes bore into hers, the passion on his face making her belly turn somersaults inside of her. She opened her mouth to speak but Lorne put his finger to her lips, silencing her before she could. He carried her over to a table and set her down on top of it, leaning in to kiss her again.

Diana glanced around and realized they were in an old storeroom. Boxes and barrels were stacked in every corner and the top of the table was stacked with cloth of all kinds. Dried herbs hung from the ceiling but still dusted the air with their fragrance.

Their kiss grew frantic, their hands roaming each other's bodies with urgency. Diana's hands slid down his chest, trailing over the hard planes of his chest to his taut, flat stomach. She gripped him through his breeches, running her hand up and down the thick length of it. Lorne groaned as she stroked him through the fabric. He kissed a line down her neck, drawing a soft yelp from her as he nipped the skin on her collarbone.

Lorne slid his hands up her thighs, pushing her dress up around her waist. Growing impossibly hot and wet, Diana squeezed his manhood through his breeches, her body tingling with her need to feel him inside of her. She fumbled with the laces of his breeches, but she finally managed to get them undone. He pushed his breeches down and Diana took hold of his length, squeezing and stroking it firmly. Lorne rolled his head back and moaned, drawing a smile across her lips.

His face was flushed. She parted her thighs as she stepped forward, guiding the head of his hardness to her warm, slick opening. She bit her bottom lip, anticipating the pinch of pain she was going to feel. And as his length slid into her, she whimpered, gritting her teeth, her body clenching up around him.

Diana was so wet, he managed to slide in with relative ease. Lorne leaned forward and kissed her, swallowing her whimpers. As he began to roll his hips, the full length of him sliding along her slippery inner walls, Diana clung to him throwing her head back and sighed languidly.

She writhed against his body, taking him deep into her most intimate embrace, and felt her skin tingling from head to toe. Loren's eyes were locked on hers, the corners of his full lips upturned slightly, and a look of wonder upon his face. She clung to his body, writhing against him as he drove his staff deep into her sex. Diana gasped, her eyes widening as a torrent of white-hot pleasure flowed through her veins.

Lorne pushed her back onto the table and raised her legs, resting them on his shoulders. She watched him, her entire body alight with heat, as he wrapped his arms around her thighs and pounded himself into her. The sound of their bodies crashing together rang in her ears, blending with her cries of ecstasy and his groans of pure pleasure.

"Yes, Lorne. Me God, it feels so good. Dinnae stop."

With a low growl, his grip on her thighs tightened and Lorne thrusted into her even harder. The slap of their bodies crashing together grew louder, as did her cries. Diana felt her stomach tighten, quickly followed by the rest of her body. When she pressed her head back against the hard wooden table, her mouth fell open and her breath caught in her throat.

Diana felt weightless, as if she was falling from a great height. Her moan was a high-pitched wail which encouraged Lorne. He gripped her thighs tighter and drove his staff into her even harder. She shook wildly on the table beneath him, eyes squeezed shut tight as she relished the pleasure washing over her so thick, she felt like she couldn't breathe. The feeling of his staff plunging deep into her heightened the ecstasy that made her writhe.

She felt her sex pulsing and tightening around him and Lorne grunted, sliding himself as deep inside of her as he could and held himself there. Diana's eyes flew open, the slight hit of pain seeming to heighten the pleasure that gripped her. Lorne's groan was low and trembling, and she felt his rod twitch and swell. A moment later, he called her name as he erupted. Diana bit her bottom lip and shut her eyes, reveling in the sensation of him filling her with his warm, thick seed.

Slowly, their climaxes ebbed, but Diana's skin continued to tingle. She slid her legs off his shoulders and sat up. Lorne stood in front of her, his arms still around her waist, gazing deeply into her eyes. Their breath was ragged, both their faces etched with blissful smiles. He leaned forward and gave her a gentle kiss. Diana traced the line of his jaw with the tips of her fingers, holding his gaze, a small smile playing across her lips.

"So, I take it me faither gave us his blessin' then?" she asked.

His eyes sparkled. "Aye. He gave us his blessin'."

She pulled him into a tight embrace, her heart swelling and thumping hard in her breast. The joy in her heart made her feel like she was soaring amongst the clouds and she couldn't keep the smile off her face as she leaned forward and pressed her forehead to his chest. But even still, shrouded by happiness, there was that dark, whispering voice in the back of Diana's mind telling her that her joy was not permanent. That eventually, it would all come crashing down around her.

CHAPTER THIRTY-THREE

Munro rode into the yard and quickly dismounted, handing his reins off to one of the boys who rushed out of the stables to take his horse for him. The rest of his party rode into the yard after him, smiling and laughing after a successful hunt. And last came the wagon pulling their catch—two large bucks and a boar. There would be a feast in the great hall that night.

"Well done, me laird," somebody from the group called. "Very well done."

He walked from the yard and into the castle, bypassing the line of servants who welcomed him home with solemn and polite bows of the head. Making his way through the bowels of the castle, he marched to his study. He threw the door open and stepped inside, then slammed it closed behind him.

Munro poured himself a cup of wine and drank deeply. Not satisfied, he next turned and poured himself a cup of whisky and took a swallow. That was better. Grabbing the bottle, he brought it back to his desk and dropped into the chair behind it and took another swallow of before topping off his cup again.

Munro leaned back in his chair and blew out a loud breath. A hunt usually relaxed him. The fresh air and clean smell of the forest ordinarily soothed him. Being out on a hunt was where he could go to get away from court politics and all the annoyances that plagued him every single day. It was just he and the animal he was hunting. Man against beast.

Today though, he had not been able to relax. He had not been able to free his mind, nor enjoy the sunshine and fresh air. All the annoyances he sought to escape had followed him into the woods and he was unable to shut out the yammering voices of those he sought refuge from in the forest. His day in the woods had been ruined.

The door to his study opened and Graham slipped in, quiet as a whisper, then shut the door behind him. He glided across the room and perched on the edge of the chair in front of Munro's desk. The man had a sour look on his pasty face, which irritated Munro today more than it usually did. He drained his cup and poured another.

"Dae ye ken what ruins a good hunt faster than anythin'?" Munro asked.

"I've never been much of a hunter meself," Graham replied.

"Listenin' tae people whisperin'. Listenin' tae them spreading gossip and rumor," he said. "That ruins me mood every single time."

"Perhaps ye should think more carefully about who ye take on yer hunts, me laird?"

Munro regarded him coldly, his lips curled back over his teeth. "Is it true?"

"Is what true, me laird?"

"Dinnae play games with me, Graham. Ye ken what I'm talkin' about," he said. "Are these bleedin' rumors true or nae?"

The man's shoulders slumped and he sighed. "I'm afraid they're true."

With a snarl that echoed around the chamber, Munro hurled his cup across the room.

"So, she's marryin' him then," Munro said, his voice tight.

"It appears so, me laird."

Still stung over the loss of his men in the ill-fated attempt to abduct her, Munro's rage at both Diana and Lorne Davidson had only grown. His fixation on her had intensified, becoming an obsession. He wanted her. He was entitled to her. And it bothered him to no end that some other man believed he was going to have her.

"Our men cannae have died in vain. I willnae let that happen," Munro said.

"Me laird, if I may say somethin'…"

"Can I stop ye?"

"I think we've expended enough resources on this lass," Graham said. "She's chosen another, and I think—"

"NAE!"

Munro slammed his fist down on the table so hard, it shook everything sitting on top of it. Graham recoiled like he had just been struck, fear crossing his features.

"She is mine, Graham. Dae ye understand me?" Munro hissed, his voice low and threatening. "She belongs tae me."

"Aye, me laird. I understand ye feel this way—"

"Who is the laird here, Graham?"

The man cocked his head. "Well... ye are, me laird."

"Good. Then it's me who makes the decisions around here."

"Me laird, I just... I've put together a list of suitable matches—very comely women from some of the surroundin' clans—"

"I want Diana," Munro hisses. "I want nobody but her."

The older man sighed, his shoulders slumped in resignation. "Aye, me laird."

"Good," he said. "Now that that is settled, assemble the council so we can start discussin' options tae go and get me bride."

CHAPTER THIRTY-FOUR

Still hiding in the storeroom, Lorne and Diana giggled together as they got dressed and smoothed out their clothes. Even though they were getting married, there was no sense in announcing what they were doing to the world. Her father had given them permission to wed, but Lorne didn't think the man would approve of him bedding his daughter before their actual wedding day.

"How dae I look?" she asked.

"Ye're beautiful. An angel come tae earth."

She laughed and slapped his arm playfully. "Stop. Ye ken what I mean."

"Well, ye're dress is on straight. Ye've smoothed out all the wrinkles," he says. "I dinnae ken what ye're goin' tae dae about yer glowin' skin though."

Diana giggled and slapped him again. "Ye're unbelievable."

"Nae as unbelievable as ye."

Diana leaned forward and placed a gentle kiss on his lips. "Ye make me happy," she said. "Now, come. We need tae get out of here before somebody finds us. We're nae married yet and I dinnae think me faither would appreciate ye tastin' that fruit before ye've bought the bushel."

Lorne couldn't stop the laugh that burst from his mouth. Diana grinned and looked especially pleased with herself. But he knew she was right. Lorne crept to the door and slowly opened it, though just a crack. He peered into the corridor then turned back to Diana and nodded.

"'Tis clear," he said. "Come on, let's go."

They slipped out of the storeroom and walked briskly down the corridor. With Diana by his side, Lorne felt as if he was walking on air and he couldn't keep the smile off his face, nor his heart from fluttering. He had never felt so incredibly good as he did in that moment. A quiet laugh burst from his mouth, feeling like a besotted boy as he walked beside her.

"So now ye are goin' tae see Gavin?" she asked.

He nodded. "The healer said he's on the mend and they moved him back tae his bed chamber. I have tae speak with him about something and then I will find ye again," he said looking a bit worried, which seemed odd. "Have ye already told yer sister?"

Diana's cheeks flushed and she giggled, telling him all he needed to know. "I did tell her already," she admitted. "I was just so excited."

"I didnae even have yer faither's approval yet."

"I kent he'd give it tae ye."

"Oh, did ye?"

"Aye, I did," she chirped. "And she's very happy fer us, and even more excited because with us bein' wed, it means she'll be able tae marry Gavin."

Lorne tensed a bit and she felt that his smile was not entirely genuine as he spoke. "Aye. Yer sister and me cousin are—"

Lorne bit off his words when he realized what he'd just said. He quickly glanced at Diana, a bolt of fear shooting through him. At first, nothing seemed amiss. But then she stopped short and turned to him, a curious expression on her face. As he watched, her face blanched and her eyes widened. Her mouth fell open and she was silent for a moment.

She swallowed hard and seemed to find her voice. "Yer... cousin?"

"I—I..."

His words trailed off as his gaze fell to the stone floor beneath their feet. Her eyes narrow and her jaw sets, her lips a firm line across her face.

"Did ye say yer cousin?" she asked again.

"Did I say cousin? I—I—I meant tae say—"

"Dinnae lie tae me, Lorne."

Her tone was accusing, her face confused. Lorne racked his mind, searching for a way out of the mess he'd just created but came up with nothing. This was not how it was supposed to happen—but then, he had no idea how it was. He'd been so caught up in his feelings for Diana and the fact that they were to be wed that he had forgotten about the lie that had brought them there in the first place.

Lorne shook his head, not knowing what to do. He reached for Diana's hand, but she pulled hers away quickly then took a step back. His heart clenched with a pain so intense, it nearly crippled him. Lorne manage to keep his feet and held his hands up, taking a step toward Diana, knowing if she just gave him a chance to explain, she would understand. Maybe one day, it was something they would look back on and laugh about. Not anytime soon, but maybe one day.

As he moved closer to her though, Diana stepped back again, keeping a physical distance between them.

"Diana, please. Give me a chance tae explain," he said.

She fixed him with an icy glare. "Is Gavin yer braither? Truly yer braither?"

Lorne ran a hand through his hair. "We grew up like braithers."

"Dinnae play games with me, Lorne. Is Gavin yer braither by birth?"

He sighed and ran a hand over his face. He was not going to lie to Diana. Well... not any more than he already had. The guilt that gripped him about lying to her to begin with was gnawing at his soul and he'd be lying if he said there wasn't some small piece of him that felt a sense of relief that the truth was out there. He no longer had to pretend. But as he looked into Diana's eyes, he saw nothing but hurt and betrayal.

"Nay. He's me cousin," he said finally. "I wanted tae tell ye. I've wanted tae tell ye from the moment we set foot in yer castle. I never wanted tae lie tae ye—"

"And yet, ye did lie tae me," she said, her voice cold.

"'Twas never me intent," he said looking down at the floor.

He could not bring himself to look her in the eyes, too afraid was he of seeing the hurt, the anger.

"Then what was yer intent?" She asked.

"I never expected tae fall in love with ye, Diana. But now that I have—"

"'Tis all a lie." Her voice was brittle and furious.

"Nay," he said, shaking his head. "Me feelings arenae a lie—"

"How can I trust ye, Lorne? Ye lied tae me. Ye lied tae me family about who Gavin truly is," she said, her voice rising. "How can I trust a word that comes out of yer mouth?" She said, almost shouting.

"Diana—" He took another step forward, reaching for her again, but she stepped back, maintaining her distance from him.

"Dinnae," she said. "Dinnae touch me."

"Diana, I was only tryin' tae protect me cousin. He's in love with yer sister, but when he met her he didn't know he would ever see her again and told a white lie to look better in her eyes. He was desperate tae see her again. He's a part of our family and he is head of our household guard—"

"That daesnae excuse what ye've done. Ye lied tae me. Ye ken station is important in our world, Lorne. What were ye both thinking?"

"When I came here, it was tae help him, I wanted to see him happy. I never thought we would really court… but then I started having feelings fer ye and I begged him tae tell yer sister. He was planning tae, he just didnae ken how."

Tears streamed down her cheeks then, and Lorne ached to touch her. To pull her to him and hold her. To make her believe him and to find some way to make everything all right again. She shook her head and took another step back before turning and fleeing.

"Diana!"

He watched her go until she turned the corner and disappeared from view. His heart sank into his stomach, a pain in his heart that rivaled any cut of a blade he'd ever taken. He fell to his knees and buried his face in his hands, doing his best to stifle the scream that rose in his chest. His eyes stung as tears formed in them.

Lorne knew, as sure as he knew his own name, that he had lost the love of his life. That as he'd watched her disappear around the corner, he knew he had lost her forever. Diana would never forgive him for his lies.

She would never be his again.

CHAPTER THIRTY-FIVE

When she rounded the corridor and did not hear Lorne chasing behind her, Diana slowed to a walk. Her movements were quick and precise as she concentrated on keeping her feet moving—left, right, left right. Tears streamed down her face, and she felt like she couldn't breathe. The sense of betrayal she felt was like a fist of ice squeezing her heart.

She walked down the hall, trying to put as much distance between them as she could. She fled to her room, slamming the door behind her, then threw herself onto her bed. She buried her face in her pillow and let out all the sobs and screams in her body. She kept it up until her throat was raw, her breath was labored, and her head was pounding inside her skull.

Then, Diana sat up on her bed and stared at her bedchamber, feeling as if her entire world was crumbling into dust around her. Lorne had lied to her. He'd looked her in the eye and had lied to her.

And what of Beatrix? If Lorne was to be believed, this was all set in motion because Gavin fell in love with Beatrix and they believed her father would never let him court her sister if he'd known he was not the son of a laird.

But their lie wasn't sustainable. Eventually, it would have come out that Gavin was Lorne's cousin and not his brother. What was their plan? How did they hope to get away with this?

She sat on the edge of her bed, wiping her eyes with the back of her hand, her mind spinning as fast as her heart. She had truly fallen in love with Lorne, he made her feel ways she never thought possible or existed. Before Lorne, Diana had expected that she would eventually marry, of course, but her union would be loveless and joyless. A duty she had to perform.

But Lorne had changed all that. Her marriage was not going to be a duty, but a privilege, an honor. A marriage that would truly make her as happy as it made her feel fulfilled and complete.

That was all gone now though. Like a puff of smoke on a breeze, her chance at joy and at love was gone. Because of a stupid, careless lie.

Wiping her tears away again, Diana got to her feet and left her bedchamber. She made her way to Beatrix's door and knocked before pushing it open and stepping inside. She closed it behind her and found her sister sitting on the bench before her looking glass, fussing with her hair. She looked at Diana in the mirror and smiled, blissfully unaware that their worlds were coming down in flaming heaps around them.

Perhaps seeing her face, Beatrix turned on the bench and faced her. "Diana, what is it? Has somethin' happened?"

"Aye. Somethin's happened ye need tae ken about, sister."

"What is it?'

Diana crossed the room and grabbed a chair, pulling it over to where Beatrix was perched on the bench. She sat down and took her sister's hands in her own and squeezed them tight as she held her gaze firmly. She swallowed the lump in her throat and tried to quell the churning in her heart.

"Ye're scarin' me, Diana. What's goin' on then?"

"They lied. They've been lyin' tae us all along."

Beatrix shook her head, her face twisted with confusion. "Who's been lyin' tae us?" she asked.

"Gavin and Lorne," she said. "They lied tae us."

"About what?"

"Gavin is Lorne's cousin. Nae his braither," she said. "Gavin is nae a laird's son. He use it as an excuse tae court ye."

Beatrix pulled her hands away and sat back, a thousand emotions scrolling across her face. She stared at Diana and shook her head, staring at her with disbelief.

"Nay. It cannae be," she said. "Gavin wouldnae have lied tae me."

"He did, Beatrix. And Lorne went along with the lie."

"Diana, nay. It cannae be."

"Lorne admitted it tae me himself."

"What? When?"

"Just now," she replied. "He let it slip while we were talkin' and when I pressed him on it, he admitted the truth. Gavin isnae his braither."

"Nay. 'Tis nae true." Beatrix jumped to her feet, her eyes narrow, her jaw set, and that look of stubborn defiance on her face she got when she was digging in and set on something. "Why are ye daein' this, Diana?"

"What dae ye mean? Ye need tae ken the truth."

"Why cannae ye let me be happy?"

"Beatrix, I want ye tae be happy. This is why I am tellin' ye this."

Beatrix backed away from Diana the way she had backed away from Lorne in the corridor. She shook her head, her eyes filling with tears. Her sister's cheeks flushed and her lips trembled as the tears rolled down her soft, pale cheeks.

"Why are ye tryin' tae steal me happiness?" Beatrix asked, her voice quavering. "Ye've got Lorne and ye're happy. Why cannae I have that happiness too?"

"I want ye tae have that happiness, Beatrix. But he lied tae ye about who he is," Diana said. "And I dinnae have Lorne anymore. I willnae be with a man who can look me in the eye and lie tae me. And neither should ye."

"Get out."

"Beatrix—"

"Get out of me chambers!" she shouted, her voice shrill and saturated with agony. "Get out, Diana! Get out and leave me alone! Now!"

Her heart was heavy and sat in the pit of her belly, but Diana got to her feet. She looked to her sister, but Beatrix turned her back on Diana, folding her arms over her chest, and walked to the window, staring out at the lands beyond the castle. Diana took a step toward Beatrix but saw her body stiffen. Tears streaming down her cheeks, the already broken pieces of her heart shattering even more, Diana turned and left Beatrix's chambers.

She softly closed the door behind her and shuffled down the hallway, sobbing to herself as she went. She wandered the hallways of the castle alone, not knowing where to go. Not knowing what to do. She passed the servants in the hallways who looked at her curiously but steered clear of her, as if afraid her melancholy was contagious.

Never in her life had Diana felt so alone.

CHAPTER THIRTY-SIX

For a couple of days, Diana had done her best to avoid everybody. She snuck out of her bedchamber late at night to steal food from the kitchens then scurried back to her room to eat. Unable to sleep much, she roamed the halls in the small hours. She was heartbroken and constantly felt sick to her stomach. She had stopped crying, likely because she had spent all her tears and could not cry anymore. She felt lost, alone. She had not only lost the man she had come to love but had lost her sister as well. The pain was immeasurable.

Diana still found herself in a state of stunned disbelief. She could not believe that Lorne had done all that to protect his cousin's lie. She did not understand how they had expected to get away with it. Had Gavin lied to Beatrix simply because he was trying to bed her? He would hardly be the first man to deceive a woman to get her to open her legs.

But when it became clear Gavin and Beatrix's feelings were more than just lust, what was their plan? She had thought a lot about it and the only thing she could surmise was that once Lorne and she had wed, they'd hoped Beatrix would be free to marry whom she wanted and the fact that Gavin wasn't a laird's son would be moot. But that thought gave rise to another one—one even more painful than the rest: that Lorne had offered to marry her not because he wanted to, but because he was providing cover for his cousin.

Diana knew she should have gone to her parents the moment she found out about Lorne and Gavin's deception. But she'd hesitated, knowing that if Beatrix still believed she was lying, she would seize upon that as proof of Diana trying to steal her happiness away. She would eventually have to tell them. But she hoped that before she had to, Beatrix would come around to see the truth of it all.

A soft knock sounded at her door and Diana scowled. Lorne had come by a number of times, and she had rebuffed him every single time. On the few occasions he had tried to speak with her in the corridors, she had walked away without saying a word. She didn't want to see him or talk to him. The knock sounded on her door again.

"Go away!" she shouted.

The door opened anyway and Diana turned, her face twisted with rage, ready to give a tongue lashing to Lorne. The words died on her tongue when she saw it was her sister stepping in. Beatrix closed the door behind her and leaned against it, her face pale and drawn. Her eyes were red and puffy, and her cheeks were wet with tears.

"Ye spoke tae him, didnae ye?"

Her sister crossed the room quickly and threw herself into Diana's arms. She held her sister as she sobbed, gently stroking her hair. They sat in silence for several long minutes as Beatrix fought to rein in her emotions.

"What happened?" Diana asked softly.

She finally turned to face her and Diana's heart ached for her the devastation she saw in her little sister's eyes. Diana reached out and tucked a lock of Beatrix's hair behind her ear.

"I found a letter among Gavin's things—"

"Why were ye lookin' through his things?" Diana asked.

"I was tryin' tae prove ye wrong about him."

Diana felt a stitch in her heart and nodded. "I see. And what did ye find?"

"I found a letter from Lorne's faither—the laird of their clan. He referred tae Gavin as his nephew," she said. "I confronted Gavin about it, and he admitted it. Told me everythin'."

The pain in her voice tore at Diana's heart.

"I'm so sorry, Beatrix."

"I should have believed ye," Beatrix said, her voice soft as a whisper. "I'm sorry I didnae believe ye, Diana."

"Naethin' fer ye tae be sorry about. I understand."

She shook her head. "Ye were lookin' out fer me, like ye always dae," she said. "I ken we've had our differences, and we didnae always get along, but ye've always had me best interest at heart. I ken ye were always tryin' tae protect me."

Beatrix's words hit Diana right in the heart, making it swell with emotion. All her life, she had tried to look out for her little sister and it warmed her from the inside to know that Beatrix knew that.

"I love ye, Beatrix."

"Aye. I ken," she said. "I didnae always show it, or appreciate ye the way I should have, but I love ye Diana. And I'm grateful fer all ye've done fer me all me life."

Diana stroked her sister's hair and offered her a wan smile. It was hard to be truly happy with everything going on, but she was close to it knowing she and her sister finally had the closeness she had always longed for. Beatrix laid her head on Diana's shoulder.

"What did ye tell Gavin?" Diana finally asked.

"I told him he and Lorne had tae tell our parents what they'd done and let them decide what tae dae with them," she said. "I gave them a day tae dae it or I'd tell our parents meself."

"I'm proud of ye, Beatrix. I ken that couldnae have been easy fer ye."

She shook her head sadly. "Nay. 'Twas nae. But it had tae be done."

"Aye. It did."

CHAPTER THIRTY-SEVEN

Lorne stood with Gavin in the great hall, his hands clasped behind his back, his body rigid, his head held high. Though still not entirely healed from his wounding, Gavin stood as properly as he could. Laird Dunn and Lady Elayne sat in their chairs on the dais in front of them, their faces neutral, their gazes frosty. Lorne didn't know how much Diana and Beatrix had told them yet, but he could tell by the way they stared imperiously down at them that they knew something.

His stomach churned and he felt queasy as he stood before them, ready to confess to his lies. This was not how he'd wanted this story to end. But as he reflected on everything that happened, he knew there had never been any other way it could end.

"I understand ye have somethin' ye want tae tell us," Laird Dunn intoned.

"Aye, me laird," Lorne said. "More like somethin' we need tae confess."

Laird Dunn exchanged an uneasy look with his wife. Her face remained blank and expressionless, but there was a hardness in her eyes Lorne did not miss.

"What is it ye need tae confess then?" Dunn asked.

Lorne cleared his throat. "Laird Macgillivray, I wish tae confess tae ye that we, Gavin and I, arrived here under false pretenses."

Laird Dunn bristled as he leaned forward, his eyes narrowed, jaw clenched, anger flashing through his eyes as he stared at them. Lady Elayne put a hand on his arm to steady her husband.

"What are these false pretenses ye speak of, Maister Lorne?" she asked.

"Gavin is me cousin. Nae me braither."

Lorne exhaled and steadied his feet, bracing himself for the coming explosion. He fully expected Laird Dunn to come flying off the dais and beat him senseless. And if he did, Lorne would do nothing, for he deserved it. He'd gone along with the lie.

"Yer cousin," Laird Dunn says.

"Aye, me laird. Me cousin."

Laird Dunn got to his feet, his hands balled into fists. He took a step forward but Lady Elayne again, put a hand on his shoulder, restraining him. Dunn growled under his breath and took a step back. Elayne turned to them, her eyes icy.

"Why did ye lie in the first place?" she asked.

Lorne's gaze dropped to the floor as he pondered the question. She gave him a moment. He finally raised his head again and licked his lips.

"'Tis a complicated answer tae that question, me Lady," he said.

"Try tae explain."

Before Lorne could respond, Gavin took a step forward. "'Tis me fault, me lady—"

"Gavin—" Lorne hissed.

His cousin rounded on him. "Lorne, I cannae stand here and let ye take the blame fer somethin' I did. I'm the one who lied. Nae ye."

"I covered up yer lie. That makes me just as guilty as ye," he replied. "Let me speak," he then turned toward the dais again. "We met Beatrix at yer masked ball and me cousin was smitten with her. He wrote tae yer daughter after that. They fell in love. But he kent he would never be allowed tae court her because of who he is. Because he's nae of the laird's bloodline."

"So, then he convinced ye tae write tae me pretendin' ye wanted tae court me eldest daughter all so he could cozy up tae me youngest?" Dunn seethed.

Lorne lowered his gaze and nodded. "Aye, me laird. Instead of daein' the right thing, I allowed it tae happen," he said. "And because of that, because of who I am, I'll accept whatever punishment ye see fit tae dole out tae me. I only ask that ye let me cousin return home."

"Lorne—"

"Please, Gavin," he used his authoritative tone. "Let me handle this."

Gavin fell silent and lowered his gaze. Lorne turned back to the Laird and Lady, his teeth gritted, his body taut, waiting for their punishment.

"Ye asked fer our daughter's hand," Lady Elayne said. "Why would ye dae that if all this was just a fiction ye and yer cousin created."

"Because 'tis nae a fiction, me lady," Lorne said. "I mean, at first, aye, I was playin' along. I came here nae tae court Diana, but tae let Gavin court Beatrix. Somewhere along the way though, I fell in love with Diana. When I asked ye fer her hand, 'twas nae fiction. I asked fer her hand because I love her. Laird Dunn, Lady Elayne, I love yer daughter. 'Tis the only reason I'd dae that. I'd never dishonor her or ye by lyin' about that. I swear tae God."

The Laird and Lady turned to each other, some silent bit of communication passing between them. In that silence, he knew they were debating his fate. And Gavin's. Lorne was most concerned about what they would do if they knew he'd taken Diana's virtue. That he'd ruined her, as she had called it, for other potential matches. He was fairly certain she would not tell them for fear of what they would do to her. But he couldn't know that for sure and he shuddered. Luckily for Gavin, he did not have that additional worry on his shoulders.

Lorne's stomach churned and his mouth grew dry. Elayne and Dunn nodded to one another, their silent discussion over with each of them satisfied. Lorne swallowed hard but stood up straight with his shoulders back, his chin raised. He would accept his fate with dignity and courage.

Dunn stared daggers at him. "When ye say ye love our daughter, we believe ye," he said. "But that daesnae change the fact that ye lied. That ye deceived us."

"Nay," Lorne said. "It daesnae."

"And fer that, we are puttin' ye out of our home," Elayne said. "Ye will both leave our lands and return tae yer own."

"And of course, we will be writin' tae yer faither and lettin' him ken what ye've done here," Dunn said. "I'll let him deal with ye as he sees fit."

Lorne was surprised. He had expected much worse, perhaps a feud between clans, so he was grateful. He gave them a deep bow.

"That is very generous, me laird and me lady," he said. "I am grateful fer yer kindness. Ye have been naething but welcoming, warm and hospitable throughout, and believe me when I say it made all of this even harder tae bear."

"That is all yer own daein'. Now go," Dunn said, his booming voice echoing around the hall. "I want ye gone from me house within the hour."

Lorne and Gavin both bowed respectfully then turned and walked out of the hall. Lorne was still in disbelief of the pain of never seeing Diana again.

"Lorne, I'm sorry," Gavin said.

"Dinnae speak tae me right now."

Gavin fell silent as they made their way back to their chambers. As Lorne packed his bags, he felt his heart breaking, nearly crippling him. He sniffed loudly and tried to fight his emotions but couldn't stop the single tear from slipping from the corner of his eye.

CHAPTER THIRTY-EIGHT

Diana walked through the rear grounds of the castle as the sun slipped toward the horizon. The sky above was cast in fiery hues of red and orange and clouds the color of onyx gathered ominously to the east. Her parents had gone to her bedchamber a while ago to let her know that Lorne and Gavin would be leaving Castle Macgillivray. They'd asked if she wanted to see them off, but Diana had no desire to see Lorne Davidson ever again. As far as she was concerned, the sooner he was gone from their lands, the better.

Sending them away seemed a fitting punishment. Her parents had always been kind. Compassionate. And there was a piece of Diana that was glad her parents had avoided a war between clans. She was angry. Furious. But deep down, she still cared for him and would never wish hurt upon him.

It was frustrating and disconcerting and she wished she could stop the feelings she had for him, but she couldn't. Diana couldn't deny that she still loved Lorne.

I love him with every single piece of me shattered heart.

As bad as she felt for herself, she felt even worse for her sister. Even now, she was locked away in her bedchamber, sobbing her eyes out. Diana had tried to get her to take some air with her, but Beatrix had refused, wanting to be alone instead.

It would take her some time to recover. As it would take Diana time. She had never considered the idea she could be so heartbroken before and yet, as she walked along the path, moving deeper into the gardens, she couldn't deny her pain. She tried to swallow it down, knowing that when Beatrix emerged, she would need to be strong for her. And she would be.

Diana rounded a turn in the path and looked to the hidden doorway in the rear curtain wall she and Lorne had slipped through after their tryst at the loch. She ruthlessly stamped out the rush of warm feelings that welled up within her. She realized quickly that somebody had left it open.

"Och, someone was in a rush I guess," she muttered.

The doorway was hidden to keep anybody from slipping in and catching them unawares. It was there to give the family a chance to escape in the event they were overrun. Of course, everybody knew about the door, but the unspoken rule was that it was to remain locked at all times.

Diana wound her way down the path to lock the door. As she reached for it though, the door was yanked open and two men she'd never seen before reached through it and grabbed hold of her. She opened her mouth to scream but one of the men clamped his hand over her mouth, stifling her cries.

They dragged her through the door and out behind the castle. The man holding her cried out when she bit down on his hand hard enough that the taste of his blood filled her mouth. The second man rushed in and drove his fist into her side, driving the breath from her lungs before she could scream again for help. Diana staggered away, her hand pressed to her belly, her breath bursting from her mouth in a ragged wheezing sound.

"Stop muckin' about and grab her," the first man growled.

"She bit me bleedin' hand. Ye grab her," the second man spat.

Diana's mind flashed back to the lesson Lorne had given her in the yard when he was teaching her how to fight. She thought back, trying to remember what he'd showed her.

As the second man advanced on her, Diana balled her hands into fists and as he closed in, she raised her hand as if she was going to strike. He lunged for her, intending to swat her punch to the side. At the very last minute, she drove her foot upward, connecting with his groin. The man's eyes bugged out and he let out a sharp "oof" sound as he covered his injured crotch. She felt a momentary flush of triumph.

It was short lived though, when a pair of arms encircled her from behind, squeezing her like an iron band, quickly cutting off her air. Diana screeched but the other man, the one she didn't kick, lunged forward, driving his fist into her face. Her head snapped backward, and her mouth filled with the coppery taste of her own blood. Diana's vision wavered and she saw stars bursting in her eyes.

She staggered and her knees turned to water. If the man behind her hadn't been holding her up, she would have fallen. She struggled, but didn't have the strength to break the hold the man had on her. Instead, he bound her hands with rope, tying them tightly together then fixed a rag in her mouth and tied that too. Bound and gagged, the man scooped her up and threw her across the back of a horse that stood nearby.

The man jumped into the saddle behind her and held her down. "Come on, let's go."

CHAPTER THIRTY-NINE

"Are ye all right?" Gavin asked.

"Nay. I'm very far from all right," Lorne replied.

They rode slowly along the wide path that would lead them out of Macgillivray lands. With every mile they traveled, the further he got from Diana, and Lorne's heart grew heavier. Darker. The pain that gripped him was like an iron vice around him that was slowly squeezing the air from his lungs.

"I am sorry fer all of this, Lorne. I ken it's all me fault," he said. "I ken that I've caused this mess and I'll never be able tae tell ye just how bleedin' sorry I am fer it. If it is any consolation, I feel just as wretched as ye dae."

"I ken cousin. I've forgiven ye."

"I can tell by the way ye're lookin' at me that ye're mad."

"I'm nae lookin' at ye."

"Exactly."

Lorne clenched his jaw and kept his eyes fixed on the road ahead. He could feel Gavin's eyes on him. The truth was, Lorne had forgiven Gavin, but that didn't mean that he was not upset with the whole situation. The hard truth was that he was just as angry at himself as he was at his cousin. More so, perhaps, since he should have known better, given he had not yet fallen in love and lost his wits. Should have put a stop to the madness before it ever began. But he hadn't. And that was his fault.

Suddenly, the thundering of hooves drew his attention. He reined his horse to a stop and turned around to see a dozen men on horseback riding like mad down the road they were on.

"They're Macgillivray riders," Lorne muttered.

"Are they comin' after us?" Gavin asked.

"Nay. Laird Macgillivray promised tae let us go," he replied. "He's a man of honor. He wouldnae go back on his word."

As the men on horseback raced past, Lorne held up his hand, stopping one of them. He was a man Lorne knew. They had sparred together a few times while they'd been staying at Castle Macgillivray and were friendly.

"Noah, what is goin' on?" Lorne asked.

"I cannae say," he said.

"Come on, man. Why are Macgillivray soldiers movin' so fast?"

Noah hesitated, his face etched with indecision and concern. He finally blew out a breath and shook his head.

"'Tis the lady Diana," he said. "She's gone."

"Gone?"

"Taken, 'tis feared."

"By whom?"

"We dinnae ken," Noah said sternly. "Now, I need tae go. We're searchin' fer her."

The man wheeled his horse around and raced away, leaving Lorne and Gavin standing on the side of the road. His heart lurched at the thought of somebody taking Diana. He realized quickly who had taken her.

"We need tae get back tae the castle," Lorne said.

He spurred his horse and with Gavin by his side, they thundered down the road, streaking back down the road. It wasn't long before the castle came into view. Lorne spurred his horse faster and they rode beneath the sallyport in the curtain wall and into the yard, dismounting before he'd brought his mount to a full stop. He dashed up the steps and into the keep, running through the corridors until they came to the great hall where he assumed Diana's parents would be.

Lorne pushed through the doors so hard, they banged into the wall behind them with a loud crash. The air in the hall was heavy and saturated with currents of fear and grief. Laird Dunn and Lady Elayne stopped their nervous pacing and turned to them, eyes wide, faces etched with fear. Beatrix sat at a table, her arms wrapped around her midsection. Her cheeks were flushed, eyes red and puffy, tears glistening on her face.

Dunn stepped forward. "I banished ye from me lands."

"Aye. And we'll go," Lorne said. "As soon as we find Diana and bring her home safely."

The laird opened his mouth to argue, but Elayne put her hand on his arm and shook her head. "We're grateful fer any assistance ye can provide."

"'Twas Munro who took her," Lorne said.

"We cannae be sure," Dunn replied. "We're nae sure she was taken yet. She's been so upset about all this we fear she may have run."

"The man vowed to have her, whatever it took," Lorne said. "He's already tried once. Killed some of yer men in the effort—"

"I ken."

"Then what makes ye think he didnae try again?"

"What makes ye think what ye did tae her didnae make her run?"

Lorne lowered his gaze, stabbed by a needle of guilt. He had no way of knowing, not for sure. But everything in him was telling that wasn't her. In times of great turmoil, she would hunker down at home.

"We have an army bein' prepared, yet we're still nae sure attacking without proof is a good idea." Laird Dunn said. "If I send an army intae his lands, it'd be an act of bleedin' war."

"I'm ready tae fight, me laird. Tae lay down me life if I have tae, tae save her and bring her back where she belongs."

Before Dunn could say anything, one of his servants burst into the hall, a harried look on her face.

As she crossed the room, Lorne noticed that Gavin sat beside Beatrix, his arm around her shoulders comfortingly as he whispered to her. She leaned into him, her chest heaving, her shoulders shaking, apparently too distraught to remember she was angry with him. Lorne thought it was good. In times of distress, people needed to find comfort where they could.

"Me laird," she called while waving a piece of paper.

"What is it, lass?"

"A letter has just arrived fer ye. The messenger who brought it said it was urgent."

Dunn took the letter from her, a deep frown crossing his lips as he stared at the seal. His face darkened and anger flared in his eyes.

"'Tis Munro's seal," he said.

The laird broke the wax seal and read the letter, his face blanching with every word. He lowered the letter and turned to the others. "I believe this is all the proof needed. That bleedin' bastard aims tae wed me daughter—"

"Against her will," Elayne said through a choked sob. "She didnae like the man. Wanted naethin' tae dae with him."

"I'll dae whatever it takes tae bring her home," Dunn said. "I'll pay the man whatever he wants tae return her tae me."

"I will help ye. I will go with ye and make sure tae protect her with me life. I'll also send me faither a letter askin' fer men and coin—or whatever ye need," he said. "And then we march on Castle Munro and get her back."

Laird Dunn stood stone still, his face considering. Lorne watched as the man's eyes drifted to the letter in his hand and watched the anger flare brighter and hotter in his eyes. He clenched his jaw and raised his gaze to Lorne, giving him a firm nod.

"All right," he said. "We need tae prepare."

"I'll write me faither," Lorne said. "Send it with yer fastest rider."

"Aye."

"Gavin, ye're with me."

Gavin got to his feet and Beatrix stared at him with worry on her face knowing he was going into battle and may not return. The air was thick with the weight of their unspoken words. But Gavin turned to him and nodded, his face stern and ready.

"All right," Lorne said. "Let's go get Diana back."

CHAPTER FORTY

Diana's eyes fluttered, then opened slowly. Her mind was fuzzy, and she was having trouble holding onto a coherent thought. Her head and body ached and her throat was cracked and dry. She licked her lips and winced. Her bottom lip had been split in the struggle and stung sharply. She gave her head a little shake as images of what had happened flooded into her mind.

She'd been abducted!

Diana tried to stand but found that her hands had been bound to a chair. Frantic, her skin prickling and her heart racing, she saw she sat in the center of a large, empty chamber. A pair of windows were set high in the wall to her left. Golden rays of sunlight slanted in through the openings and motes of dust sparkled as they danced in the air.

"Hello?" she called. "Let me out of here!"

She thrashed against her bonds, struggling to break free, but they would not give. Desperation and fear bloomed in her heart squeezing tears from the corners of her eyes. Diana forced herself to calm down, to sit still and to think. She cast her mind back as she tried to understand the situation and figure out who had abducted her. It took her only a moment to land on the answer and when it did, she knew she was right.

"Munro," she whispered.

As if speaking his name had summoned him, the door to the chamber opened with a sharp squeal and Finley Munro stepped in. He walked to the center of the room and stared down at her imperiously. He said nothing at first, simply staring at her with a near crazed light in his eyes. Goosebumps prickled her skin, and she suppressed a shudder. She would not show him her fear.

"Good morning," he finally said. "I finally have ye."

"Ye were behind the attack in me faither's castle," she stated. "Ye sent that woman in tae abduct me before."

"Of course, I wanted ye. I willnae be denied those things I want, Diana."

"Ye need tae untie me right now," Diana demanded. "Ye need tae let me go."

The corner of his mouth quirked upward. "Dae I?"

"Me faither will kill ye fer this," she said. "But if ye let me go right now, I'll tell him tae spare yer life, Laird Munro."

He chuckled and clasped his hands behind his back as he started to pace the room. His lips pursed, Munro seemed to be deep in thought for a moment. He finally stopped pacing then turned and offered her a ghastly smile that sent a flood of ice through her veins.

"What dae ye imagine is happenin' here, lass?" he asked.

Diana sat up straight and lifted her chin defiantly. "Naethin' a noble man should be daein'."

His laugh was loud and genuine. Munro clapped his hands as if it was the funniest thing he'd ever heard. He slowly fell quiet, and a strange expression crossed his face that raised the hair on the back of her neck.

"Ye've got spirit, lass. I like that," he said. "And I look forward tae breakin' it."

"Let go of me," she hissed and thrashed in the chair.

"We're goin' tae be wed, ye and me," he said. "Ye belong tae me."

"I'd rather die first."

"Nae yet, but maybe after ye give me an heir. I may tire of ye by then," he said coldly. "Until then, ye are mine. Ye belong tae me and no one else."

"Ye may as well kill me now because I'll never be yers."

"Oh, but ye will," he countered. "Because once we're married, I'll have claim tae yer clan. Once I remove yer faither and take over his lands, I'll be the most powerful laird in all of Scotland. And when I am, me true ally, the King of England, will lavish me with riches and titles beyond anything I could have ever imagined. Scotland will be mine. And maybe, one day, England will be too. I havenae decided on that yet."

Diana stared at him, eyes wide, mouth agape. "Ye're bleedin' mad."

"Merely ambitious, lass," he said with a smirk. "But simple people who are content tae live small lives often mistake the two."

"Nay. I ken what ambition looks like," Diana growled. "And ye're nae ambitious. Ye're greedy. Ye're a small man. A bully who—"

The sharp crack filled her ears just before her face exploded with pain. And only as her head rocked to the side did she realize Munro had delivered a vicious backhand. He stood over her, glowering down at Diana with his lips curled back over his teeth in a feral sneer.

"Ye will be mine, we will be wed," he said. "And I will break that spirit of yers."

She spat a crimson glob at his feet. "Never."

An older man stepped into the room behind Munro. His eyes fell on Diana and a look of concern flashed across his face, but he tore his gaze away and cleared his throat.

"Me laird," the man said. "Laird Magillivray and Lorne Davidson, son of Laird Davidson, have arrived. They wish tae negotiate fer lady Diana's release."

"Send them away," Munro said coldly, never taking his eyes off her.

"Me laird—"

Munro's face brightened and a smile spread across his lips. "Nay. Wait," he said and turned to the other man. "Bring them here. I want them to see her. I want them tae ken that she is mine and that there is naught they can dae about it."

"Me laird—"

"Go, Graham. Bring them here."

The man gave him a respectful bow. "Aye, me laird."

Munro stood before Diana, his grin filled with malice as he stared at her. The way he did it made her uncomfortable and despite her vow to not show him her fear, Diana couldn't stop herself from shuddering. He remained silent for what felt like an eternity, and when she finally saw Lorne step into the room, followed by Gavin, and then her father, Diana wanted to cry out in relief. But the looks on their faces stayed her tongue. Their bodies were taut, their faces etched with worry, which only scared her more.

"Welcome tae me home," Munro said as he turned to them. "Me and me soon-tae-be wife welcome ye."

Her father stepped forward, casting a worried glance at her before turning to Munro. "I am here tae negotiate the release of me daughter."

"There will be nay release," Munro said. "But I will give ye prime seatin' at the weddin'. How daes that sound?"

"Laird Munro, ye need tae stop this foolishness," her father said. "Stop this before we dae somethin' that cannae be changed. Ye ken I have allies and ye ken yer clan will perish. Dinnae be a fool."

Munro stepped over to her father, glaring at him with pure fire in his eyes. "Is that a threat, Laird Macgillivray? Did ye actually come intae me home and threaten me?"

"'Tis a peace offer," Dunn said. "I'll give ye what ye want if ye let me daughter go."

"I dinnae think ye have enough tae satisfy me wants, Laird Macgillivray," he sneered. "Or, can I call ye Dunn, now that we're tae be kinfolk and all."

And then he punched her father in the jaw so hard, Diana heard a crack.

Lorne stepped forward putting Dunn behind him, his eyes fixed on Munro, burning with rage. "I'll give ye everythin' ye want," he said. "Just let her come home with us."

Munro turned to him, a wicked smile on his face. "Ye'd give up all that. Fer her?"

"Aye. I'd give up everythin' fer her."

It was a strange moment for Diana to feel touched, but she did all the same. Knowing that Lorne would sacrifice his life just to save hers sent a flood of warmth through her that made her heart swell until it felt too big for her chest. That he would give all up to save her made Diana realize Lorne's offer of marriage was not for Gavin. It was for her.

"'Tis a sweet gesture, but I think I'll have tae pass," Munro said dismissively. "Through her, I can have everythin' I want —which includes her. So, I'll give ye fools this one chance tae leave me home or I'll have ye tossed intae me dark cells."

Lorne's gaze lingered on her and she could see the love he carried for her. She could feel it. Then, at a glance from Lorne, Gavin produced a horn from his bag and blew deeply. The long, sonorous note filled the room and echoed down the hall. Munro stared at them, his mouth agape.

"What in the bleedin' hell are ye daein'?" he asked.

His question was answered a moment later by the sound of men shouting and clashing steel. Munro's advisor's eyes widened.

"They're nae here tae negotiate," he gasped. "They've brought an army tae free her."

"'Tis nae so. I came here tae make a good faith effort at negotiatin' with ye," Dunn said. "Ye proved that ye cannae bet trusted and ye have nay honor. So, now we fight."

As men fought in the halls outside the room, her father and Gavin drew their blades and joined in the fray. Lorne pulled his sword and launched himself at Munro, who barely had time to react, but managed to get his own blade out and deflect Lorne's thrust. Diana sat strapped to the chair in the midst of the battle. The sound of steel ringing and men screaming as they died rang in her ears. She thrashed at her bonds but could not break them.

Suddenly, Munro was at her side, and she felt the cold touch of steel on her neck. She gasped and he chortled and snarled "Come and get her, if ye want her so badly! But it'll be over me dead body!"

Lorne moved closer and when he had nearly approached them, Diana felt the tip of the sword pierce through her skin, and as she cried out in pain, she felt warm blood trickling down her neck.

Lorne stopped for an instant as if thinking what to do. She stared at him with begging eyes to please save her from that horrible man who wanted to marry her and make her his prisoner for life. Then she saw Gavin cornering Munro from the side and realized why Lorne had hesitated. Gavin lifted his finger to his lips as he looked at her. She only turned her eyes to follow, so as not to give herself away. Then he was behind her and he grabbed Munro with such speed, he startled him and dropped his blade.

Lorne drove his foot into Munro's chest, sending him flying backward. Her captor hit the wall with a loud "oomph," and nearly fell. Gavin quickly sliced through the ties on her wrists. Diana shook them off and ran to the side of the room, pressing her back against the wall as she watched Lorne engage with Munro. They battled fiercely, each of them sustaining minor wounds in the fight. And with each drop of Lorne's blood that spilled, Diana grew ever more terrified that the man who loved her—the man she loved—would perish in the fight.

She gasped as Munro moved in, his blade spinning dizzyingly, and clipped Lorne's forearm. Blood flowed from the wound, but Lorne didn't flinch. Instead, he spun to his left and lashed out with his sword, opening a deep wound along Munro's ribs that sent the man down on his knees. He pressed a hand to the wound, and it came away dripping with blood. Munro grimaced in pain.

"Stay down and I'll spare yer life," Lorne commanded.

But, of course, Munro didn't. Though weakened and wounded, he launched himself at Lorne with a vicious roar. Lorne easily sidestepped the clumsy advance, then spun and drove his blade through Munro's stomach. The blade erupted through his back and Diana watched as Munro's eyes bulged and blood spilled from his mouth. Lorne yanked the blade free of his body then used the toe of his boot to push him backward. Munro fell to the ground, hand pressed to his belly, his face quickly paling.

As she watched it all in horror, Diana turned to see a man advancing on her father. She screamed but Lorne was already there, parrying the man's thrust then running him through. The body fell with a wet thud and her father gave Lorne a grateful nod. Movement from the corner of her eye drew her attention and Diana screamed once again when she saw the wounded Munro moving toward, dagger in hand.

"If I cannae have ye, naebody will," he growled.

Lorne and her father were too far away and would not get to her before Munro struck. She opened her mouth and screamed as he raised the blade, the sun slanting in through the windows glinting off the blade. But seemingly out of nowhere, Gavin raced in and deflected the dagger thrust, then turned and drove his sword into Munro's chest, burying it to the hilt. Munro let out a weak gasp and Diana watched as the life left his eyes for good.

Gavin ripped his sword free and turned to her but before he could say anything though, Lorne was there, pulling her into his embrace. She melted into him and sobbed as he stroked her hair.

"'Tis all right now," he whispered. "Ye're safe. Everythin's goin' tae be all right."

She raised her head and looked him in the eye. His stormy blue gaze pierced her deeply and Diana felt her heart stutter drunkenly in her chest. Then, her father was wrapping her in a warm embrace as well. He told her how scared he had been, but that everything was fine, that she was safe and that all would be well.

As she hugged him, she watched Lorne and Gavin and Diana wondered if all truly would be well. How could it when the man who'd captured her heart had been ordered to leave?

CHAPTER FORTY-ONE

Lorne and Gavin were invited back to Castle Macgillivray to have their wounds tended to. As they passed beneath the sallyport and into the yard though, he paused when he spotted his father and a hundred of their fighting men. His father stepped forward and greeted Laird Macgillivray with a warrior's embrace. They shared a few quiet words together before turning to Lorne.

"Come," Laird Dunn said.

Lorne and Gavin exchanged glances but followed his father and Laird Dunn into the castle. They walked through the winding corridors until they came to the council room. The doors were opened by two of Dunn's men and they were ushered inside. Laird Dunn took his usual seat at the head of the table then offered his father the seat to his right. Lorne sat down beside his father and Gavin took the seat beside him.

"I arrived as quickly as I could," Lorne's father said. "I lament I couldnae be here sooner."

"I am grateful ye came at all, Laird Davidson."

"Tiernan, please."

"Very well. And ye may call me Dunn," he replied. "I am thankful ye didnae have tae be part of the fight. 'Twas over much quicker than I'd anticipated. Even so, I appreciate ye bein' willin' tae fight alongside me."

"Ye're welcome," Tiernan said. "When I got me son's letter, I feared the worst. I ken of Laird Munro and that he's an ambitious bastard. A snake is what I've been told."

"Would be an insult tae snakes tae compare them," Dunn said with a chuckle. "However, Munro is dead, thanks tae yer son."

Servants entered the room bearing trays with food and drink. Dunn directed them to spread it out on the table. As they tucked into their refreshment, Lorne caught his father's eye. His gaze was as cold and unyielding as ever, but he saw something different in them this time. Something unfamiliar. Something he could not quite place.

"Yer son acquitted himself quite well out there," Dunn said around a mouthful of food.

"Did he?" Tiernan asked.

"Aye. Had the right measure of Munro, kent what he would dae," he said, "and he put a plan in place tae beat him. He saved me daughter's life. As did his brai—his cousin."

Lorne turned to Dunn and the man tipped a wink to him. Lorne gave him a grateful nod, but was curious as to why he didn't take the opportunity to expose their deception. He assumed the man was simply thankful they had saved Diana's life and that that was his way of expressing it. Whatever it was that kept the man from telling his father what they'd done, Lorne was profoundly thankful to him for it.

Dunn took a drink of his wine and set his cup down. "The thing that impressed me the most about it was that before it came down tae fighin', yer son said he would give up everythin'—includin' his life—in exchange fer Diana's life."

Tiernan turned and gave Lorne a strange look. "Did he?"

Och, God. He will kill me himsel' if he kens I actually offered everything.

"Aye," Dunn said. "And 'twas a sincere offer, I reckon. That he would give up everythin' fer her... 'tis a sign of true love, I'd say."

"I'd say so," Tiernan agreed. "Would ye have gone through with it, son? Would ye have given up everythin', even yer birthright, fer her?"

"I would have," Lorne replied without hesitation. "Diana's life 'tis worth far more than I could ever possess in this world or the next."

His father nodded and put a hand on Lorne's shoulder, giving it a gentle squeeze. That strange look Lorne couldn't identify was back on his father's face and it was then that he realized what it was. Respect. For the first time he could recall, his father had looked at him with genuine affection and respect—the two things he had been chasing his entire life. His heart swelled within him, growing so big, he thought it might burst.

"Well done, son. I am proud of ye," Tiernan said. "Sacrificin' fer somebody other than yerself 'tis the mark of a man ready tae be a laird. 'Tis the mark of a good man."

"Thank ye, Faither," Lorne said, his voice thick with emotion.

Tiernan leaned over and put his arm around Lorne warmly. He melted into his father, savoring the moment. It was something he'd longed for, something he'd wanted all his life. To finally have his father show his affection and respect was almost as grand a prize as Diana's hand would have been. His father's embrace meant more to him than he could ever possibly express.

As they parted, his father clapped him on the shoulder. "I'm proud of ye," he said again.

"Thank ye, Faither," he replied. "But I couldnae have done anythin' without Gavin by me side. He delivered the killin' blow on Munro—"

"Because yer son was busy savin' me hide," Dunn said with a chuckle. "I fear I'm gettin' too old tae be ridin' intae battle anymore. I'm slowin' down."

"Ye looked plenty fit tae me," Lorne said.

Tiernan looked at Gavin and nodded. "Yer cousin has been by yer side from the first. He's always had yer back without question," he said. "'Tis why I am makin' him yer second. And when ye ascend tae me chair, he'll be yer chief advisor."

Gavin's face paled and his mouth fell open. "Uncle Tiernan, ye honor me."

"Ye honor me by the way ye've taken care of me son all these years without question or complaint," he said.

Lorne caught Gavin's eye and nodded. His cousin looked too stunned to react though. He slumped back in his chair with a look of wonder on his face. Being moved from household guard to chief advisor was quite the promotion and sent him up a number of rungs on the social ladder.

They spent the next couple of hours talking and reliving the assault on Munro's castle. His father was particularly interested in how Lorne and Gavin had acquitted themselves during the fight. The light of pride gleaming in his father's eyes made Lorne feel whole. He felt complete. And happy. Save for one thing.

The fact of the matter was he had deceived Diana. And though her father might have forgiven him and was willing to let them go without consequence, there really was nothing he could have done to Lorne that was even close to the pain of having lost the one woman he had ever truly loved.

Eventually, their meal wound down and it was time to go. Lorne reluctantly got to his feet, knowing that once he walked out the doors and rode off, he would never see her again. Gavin must have felt the same way because he too, trudged along behind Dunn and Tiernan who laughed and talked together like old friends. But when the doors to the hall were opened, Lorne paused and felt his heart lurch in his chest.

Diana and Beatrix waited in the corridor outside the hall. Beatrix rushed forward and threw herself into Gavin's arms. He swept her up and held her tight and Beatrix kissed him, drawing a scandalized expression from her father. Lorne was happy for him.

"It seems that me sister has forgiven yer cousin."

Lorne turned, surprised to see Diana standing beside him. His heart leapt into his throat and his belly churned. He ached with the desire to reach out and touch her, but he stayed his hand, knowing it would be unwelcome. But then

Diana turned her face up to him and a soft smile touched the corners of her lovely mouth. Her eyes glimmered and her expression softened. For the first time since their lie had been exposed, she didn't look angry with him.

Lorne cleared his throat. "Diana, I ken I lied tae ye and deceived ye. But can ye ever find it in yer heart tae forgive me?"

"I've already forgiven ye," she said.

"Ye have?"

She nodded. "In that room, when I thought Munro might kill me... when I saw what ye did fer me, it made me realize that ye didnae deceive me. I mean, ye did, but I understand why. After all, I, too, deceived ye at the beginning by pretendin' tae court ye tae help me sister. And then, when ye offered tae give everythin' up fer me, it made me see just how much ye loved me. How could I nae forgive ye?"

A river of relief rushed through Lorne's chest. To be forgiven by Diana was a feeling as close to the divine as he'd ever felt. It even overshadowed the respect his father had given him. He offered her a weak smile.

"Thank ye, Diana. I am grateful."

"Besides," she said with a shy smile. "It would nae dae fer me tae be angry with me husband on our weddin' day, now would it?"

A lump formed in Lorne's throat as he stared at her. "Husband? Daes that mean ye still want tae marry me?"

"Aye. I want tae marry ye."

Lorne swept her up and spun her around in the hallway. They laughed together like they'd gone mad then Diana pressed her mouth to his, kissing her as unabashedly as Beatrix had kissed Gavin. Lorne pulled his head back and looked her in the eye.

"I love ye, Diana. With all that I am," he said.

"And I love ye too."

Lorne hugged her tightly, pressing his face into her hair and breathed deeply. It was the best day of his life. And he knew, with Diana by his side, it was only the beginning.

EPILOGUE

One Week Later...

The celebration in the grand hall was in full swing. Musicians played, the corridors vibrated with music and laughter, and the smell of roasted meats and a plethora of different foods saturated the air. It was the biggest celebration Diana could ever recall her parents hosting. And for good reason. It wasn't every day their eldest daughter got officially engaged.

Her father and Lorne's had officially sealed the pact by signing their marriage contracts earlier in the day. Their alliance was now iron-clad and the only thing left was the official ceremony which would happen in a month.

Diana had spent the day with Lorne, feasting, drinking, dancing, laughing, and of course, loving. She never knew her heart could be so full and yet, whenever she was with him, she felt it growing even fuller.

In the week that had followed the events at Munro's castle, she and Lorne had been inseparable. They had talked through everything that had happened, they had opened up to each other and shared their hopes and fears, and their dreams for the future. And they had started talking about what their life would be like once they'd wed.

"Tae look at them, ye'd think our faithers have been friends since they were bairns," she said with a laugh.

Lorne nodded. "Aye. They get on well. 'Tis good tae see."

She took a sip of her wine and turned to him. "And how are things between the two of ye?" she asked. "Ye and yer faither."

Lorne took a drink from his glass and smiled. "Better than I ever thought they could be, tae be honest," he said. "Fer the first time in me life, I feel like he values me."

"He's got plenty of reason tae be proud of ye," she said. "He's got a good son."

"A good son with an even better wife."

"Aye. And dinnae ye forget that."

"How can I, when I've got ye here tae remind me?"

Diana laughed and leaned into him. Lorne pressed a kiss to the top of her head and slipped his arm around her waist. She had never felt so loved before in her life. More than that, she had never felt safer. She looked up at Lorne again and saw the playful smile on his lips.

"What is it?" she asked.

Instead of answering, he took her hand, and she squeaked as he pulled her out of the hall. They laughed together as they dashed through the labyrinth of corridors. Lorne led her to the old storeroom where the dried herbs still hung and they slipped inside. He locked the door behind him and turned to her with an impish grin.

Lorne stepped forward and slipped his hands around her waist. She turned her face up to him and he leaned down, pressing his mouth to hers. Lorne slipped his tongue past her teeth and rolled it around hers languidly. Diana melted into him. Their kiss deepened and she slid her hands up his chest, still marveling at the hard angles and planes of his body. As he ran his fingers through her hair, she whimpered, her body burning with need.

He pressed her back against the table and Diana gasped when she felt his rigid length against her belly. She felt herself get wet and she was overcome with the need to feel him inside of her. As if he was reading her thoughts, Lorne picked her up and set her down on the table. She parted her legs as he ran his hands up her thighs, pushing her dress up around her waist. She kissed his neck and ran her fingers through his hair, pulling and yanking on it, drawing a low, rumbling moan from him that resonated through her entire body.

"I need ye inside me," she gasped.

His mouth found hers and she forced her tongue against his. They devoured each other, their bodies burning, skin tingling as she ground herself against him. Lorne reached down and with clumsy fingers born of desperate need, fumbled with the laces of his breeches. He finally got them undone and Diana reached in and took hold of his rigid length. She squeezed and stroked it, swallowing his groans of pleasure.

Lorne's eyes burned with need as he stepped forward, pressing her down on the table. Diana wrapped her legs around his waist, locking her ankles behind her back, and nestled the head of his staff between the velvety folds of her warm, slick sex. He stared into her eyes as he stepped forward, the length of his rigid staff sliding easily inside of her. Diana gasped and smiled, relishing the feeling of Lorne filling her up so completely.

As he started to roll his hips, plunging himself into her core, Diana bit her bottom lip. Her body was alive with sensation, her skin tingling, goosebumps running up and down her body. She was so warm and slick that Lorne slid in and out of her with ease, driving himself deeper with every thrust. He slid his hands up her body, cupping her breasts through her gown then quickly unlaced her bodice, pulling it down to reveal them.

Diana gasped as Lorne leaned forward, taking her breast into his mouth. His tongue flickered upon her stiff nipple, and she yelped as he gave it a nip. As he licked and sucked on her breasts and kneaded them, she arched her back and yanked his hair. All the while, he plunged his staff into her flower, driving her mad with desire. Diana's head spun and a trembling laugh trickled from her lips as a million sensations wrapped themselves around her. She gave herself over to them, relishing the heat flowing through her veins.

Diana sat up and slipped her hand behind his neck, pulling him to her and kissed him. She clung to Lorne's hard, toned body as he drove himself into her, her lips burning against his. Lorne grunted as he sheathed himself inside of her, as deep as he could go, and held himself there. Diana gasped and her eyes grew wide as her head began to spin. Her vision wavered and she felt weightless. A moment later, a wave of sensation crashed down over her, and she cried out.

Diana dug her nails into Lorne's shoulders so hard, he gasped but smiled at her. She held on tightly as she writhed and thrashed against him as her climax washed over her in powerful waves that left her breathless. As she gave herself over to the sensations, Diana let out a long, breathy moan, her voice trembling as hard as her body. She threw her head back and laughed.

Lorne slipped his hand around and cupped her backside, pulling her closer to him. He slowed down, his strokes long and slow. Diana felt herself pulsing and growing tighter around his staff. Lorne's teeth were gritted and his shoulders tense as he continued sliding in and out of her wetness. The rapture in his eyes was unmistakable and the way his neck and cheeks had grown red, she knew he would not last much longer.

Diana leaned forward and felt him quiver as her full lips brushed his ears. She kissed his neck and bit the lobe.

"'Tis yer turn," she whispered. "I want tae feel ye release inside of me."

Lorne's rhythm faltered and he groaned. His entire body grew taut, drawing a satisfied smile across Diana's lips.

"Finish inside of me," she whispered again. "Let me feel ye."

Lorne threw his head back and cried out her name. He swelled, then twitched, and a moment later, he burst inside of her. Diana gasped and pressed her forehead to his chest as she clung to him and together, they trembled and writhed, riding the currents of ecstasy together.

Slowly, their breathing softened, and their hearts began to slow. But they remained in each other's arms, the air around them thick with their love and the scent of their sex. Lorne leaned forward and this time, it was Diana who shuddered at the feeling of his lips brushing her ear.

"I love ye," he whispered. "I love ye now and I'll love ye until the end of me days."

Diana turned her face up at him and smiled as she bit her bottom lip. "And I'll love ye a day longer than that."

Lorne wrapped her in his arms, and she leaned into him, pressing her ear to his chest. She closed her eyes and listened to the steady thump of his heart. It was beating in time with her own, fitting since their two hearts were now one.

EXTENDED EPILOGUE

One Month Later...

The sky was a clear field of azure above their heads and the sun cast its rays of warmth over them. Lorne smiled. The day couldn't have been more perfect if he'd crafted it himself. It had been a fight to get everybody to agree to hold the wedding outdoors. Most feared the volatile nature of Scotland's weather.

It was a roll of the dice and had taken some time and plenty of arm twisting, but Lorne had eventually managed to convince everybody that an outdoor wedding would be wonderful and it had worked out. For that, he breathed a small sigh of relief and said a silent word of thanks. He never would have lived it down otherwise.

He stood at the head of the aisle, Diana on his arm, and across from them, Gavin stood with Beatrix on his. Knowing they couldn't wait to be married, Lorne and Diana had decided to hold a dual wedding. It was unorthodox, but the way Lorne saw things, it was a day of joy for everybody.

Adding Gavin and Beatrix's nuptials to the day only spread more joy.

Laird Dunn and Lady Elayne stood on the dais before them, while Lorne's father stood beside them. They looked out over the gathering, smiles on their faces. Tiernan gave Lorne a knowing nod and a smile. The pride and unfettered joy he saw in his father's eyes made Lorne's heart swell.

After Diana's rescue, they had become close. They were developing a real relationship. It seemed odd, now that he was older, but he thought perhaps it was easier for his father to relate to him as a grown man than when he had been a child. Whatever the case, he was glad to have grown as close to his father as he had.

"Are ye ready?" Diana whispered. "Last chance tae back out."

"Maybe I should take it then."

She slapped his arm playfully and giggled. "Beast."

"Aye."

Lorne looked across the aisle to Gavin, who was puffed up and smiling. Moved up in position had done wonders for him, but not nearly as much as being with Beatrix had. In the weeks since they'd first come to Castle Macgillivray, Lorne had seen his cousin grow and change. Had seen him eschew some of his childish habits in favor of a more adult view of things. He had started to take things a bit more seriously.

He was still prone to bad jokes and there were times he didn't seem to take things all too seriously, but Gavin was growing into a man before his very eyes. More than that, he was growing into somebody Lorne knew he could count on as his chief advisor whenever they both assumed their roles once his father stepped down.

"Friends, thank ye fer comin' today," Laird Dunn intoned. "We come together for the most auspicious of reasons, to celebrate love and joy. 'Tis nae often faithers and maithers get tae celebrate the weddin' of nae just their oldest daughter, but their youngest one at the same time."

Laughter rippled through the crowd behind them. Lorne snuck a peek over his shoulder and saw people from his own lands and many he had only just started to get to know from Diana's. There were good people here in Clan Magillivray. They reminded him of the people back home. Hard working, honest, charitable, compassionate. The two clans seemed to share many of the same values and he knew that because of that, the alliance they'd forged would stand for generations.

Tiernan stepped forward. "I am very proud of me son and me nephew. Good men both. Honest. Devoted. Earnest. I am hard pressed tae name two better men," he said, his voice deep and resonant. "But now that I've had the chance tae meet and get tae ken the women who will be their wives, Diana and Beatrix, I cannae think of two better women for them. I dinnae need tae tell most of ye just how special these two women are. But what I admire most about them is their ability tae make both Lorne and Gavin better. I can see that they have inspired them tae grow, tae be more thoughtful, more compassionate. And I believe that is a testament tae how they were raised. Laird Dunn and Lady Elayne are a couple of the finest people I've gotten a chance tae ken."

Lorne listened to his father words, stunned at his eloquence and loquaciousness. Growing up, he had been hard pressed to get a full sentence out of his father. But hearing him made him realize there were layers to his father he had yet to discover.

"We come together, Lady Elayne, Laird Tiernan, and I, tae join our families. Tae join our clans. Tae build an alliance and a kinship we all hope will last forever," Dunn said. "And I cannae think of a better family tae unite with."

The gathered crowd behind them applauded and the buzz of conversation filled his ears. He held onto Diana's hand and gave it a gentle squeeze. Her smile was radiant, and she was ethereal in her wedding dress. Lorne looked at her and felt himself warm from the inside, his entire body flowing with emotion. Her dark eyes sparkled as she looked back at him.

"Are ye all right?" she whispered.

"I'm better than all right," he replied. "'Tis like a dream, tae be honest."

"If this is a dream, I dinnae want tae wake up."

"That makes two of us."

"Will our brides and grooms step forward," Dunn called.

"Here we go," Diana said. "Last chance tae run."

"I've never been so certain of somethin' in all me life."

She smiled. "Nor I."

As Dunn, Elayne, and Tiernan stepped to the side of the dais, the priest stepped forward, looking at them with a wide smile on his face. He had been Diana's family priest since they were young, and he knew them well. He'd been hearing their confessions all their lives.

"We are here, before ye all and in the eyes of the Lord and in the spirit of their love, tae join these two couples in Holy matrimony," the priest began. "I've always kent that I would one day have tae marry these two women away, but I never expected it tae be the both of them on the same day."

That got another laugh from the crowd and the priest gazed upon Diana and Beatrix affectionately. He gave Lorne a nod, then Gavin.

"Ye two are marryin' two of the finest, most upstandin' women I've ever kent," he said. "Be sure ye appreciate them, cherish them, from today tae the end of yer days. Can ye make that commitment today? Before all these witnesses and in the eyes of God?"

Lorne nodded. "Aye, faither."

"Aye faither," Gavin echoed.

"Very well," he said. "Dae we have the bridal cloths?"

Tiernan stepped forward and produced the cloth he and Lorne's mother had bound themselves together with so many years ago. The moment he saw it, Lorne felt a stitch in his heart. He raised his gaze to his father who stood before them, his eyes shimmering with unshed tears.

"Thank ye, Faither," Lorne whispered.

"Aye."

Their hands clasped together, Lorne gave Diana a smile as he raised them. Tiernan wound the cloth around their hands then stepped back. On the other side of the aisle, Dunn was doing the same with Gavin and Beatrix, using the same bride cloth he and Elayne had used. The two men smiled then stepped back to the dais and Elayne leaned against her husband, tears of joy spilling down her cheeks.

"In the eyes of the Lord and by all the witnesses here today, we join these two couples, Lorne Davidson and Diana

Magillivray, Gavin Davidson and Beatrix Magillivray, in the bonds of love and marriage from this day until yer last," the priest intoned, then with a proud smile, said, "yer union is recognized by God and is now sealed."

The crowed erupted in applause and cheers as Lorne pulled Diana to him and kissed her deeply, letting her feel the depth of his emotion. She returned his kiss with equal fervor. Eventually, they parted and stared into one another's eyes.

Lorne smiled. "From this day—"

"Until our last," she finished.

A SURPRISE!

Your love and support mean the world to me, and as a heartfelt thank-you, I have something special just for you...

The Highlander's Dark Obsession, the next fiery chapter in the *Kilted Kisses* series, is officially available for pre-order—and you're among the very first to know.

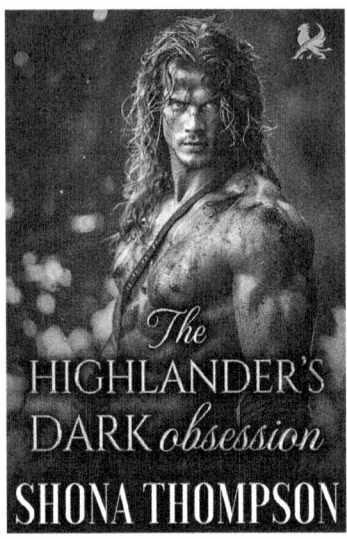

If you've been swept away by the brooding heroes and fiery heroines of the *Kilted Kisses* series, **Sorcha & Willelm** will own your heart—whether you're ready or not.

In ***The Highlander's Dark Obsession***, a stolen kiss becomes a dangerous game when a spirited Highland lass is taken in the night by the very man sworn to destroy her clan. What starts as a ruthless strategy turns into something far more dangerous: desire, obsession, and a battle of wills neither is prepared to lose.

All you need is to scan this QR code with your phone...

to be the first to dive in.

I can't wait for you to fall as hard for Sorcha & Willelm as I did.

—Shona

DO YOU WANT TO SEE HOW THINGS WILL UNFOLD?

If you enjoyed *Scot of Passion*, turn the page to dive into the first chapters of the next thrilling installment in the series, *Scot of Sin* , which will explore **Lavinia & Ian's** story.

Lavinia Shaw thought breaking Ian MacBean's heart was the only way to protect him. Six years later, he's back—colder, harder, and about to marry another. Trapped in his castle, she swears she won't let old feelings resurface. But every glance, every touch, reminds her of what they lost. And when danger closes in, she may lose him all over again—this time, forever.

∽

SCOT OF SIN

CHAPTER ONE

MacBean Castle, August 1717

Castle MacBean. Home.

How long had it been since he'd last been home? It seemed like a lifetime.

Ian felt his heart pounding in his chest just as hard as it had the day he'd stepped on the boat that would bear him to the Continent. Everything looked just as he remembered from his childhood, and yet, everything felt different.

He'd been gone so long. Years, ever since that fateful day when he'd left his home and refused to look back. Ever since… Ian shook his head and dismissed the old memories.

He didn't want to think about the circumstances surrounding his departure. He'd most likely never see the woman who had broken his heart again. Besides, he and his father were already discussing an alliance marriage to aid the clan after the poor harvest season.

He would wed a woman whose family could help his own, enjoy a comfortable, if not loving, marriage, and take over Clan MacBean as its laird. There was no need to remember old wounds. Far better to focus on the present and the future.

Ian rode closer, a small grin lifting his lips as he heard the bell from the upper guard tower begin to ring out. The cadence of the tolling was so familiar.

His parents must have ordered the watch to ring out when he arrived. Though they'd visited him a couple of times on the Continent, he'd seen little of them in the intervening years, and he'd missed them. Besides, a meeting in a tavern in France wasn't the same as being together at home.

The gates opened, welcoming him home. Ian saw the grins on the faces of the guards, slightly exasperated, confirming his guess that his mother had been bedeviling the poor lads every candle-mark since she had risen. He returned the smiles with one of his own, waving to old friends and new faces alike.

Devin, the stablehand, was waiting for him as he rode his horse to the doors, a grin on his weathered face. The old man had been his first teacher in riding, and his smile was proud as Ian dismounted. "I see ye've nae forgotten the lessons I taught ye, lad."

"Never, Master Devlin." He exchanged a strong handclasp with the stablemaster. That was all he had time for before two sets of arms wrapped around him in a tight embrace.

"Ian!" His mother Catreena's voice was breathless, her cheeks damp. She was smiling and crying at the same time, her eyes bright with joy at seeing him. "Och, Ian, 'tis been too long!"

"'Tis good tae see ye home, son." His father, Tad, clapped him on the shoulder.

"'Tis good tae have finally returned." Ian returned his mother's embrace, then his father's, his heart so full it felt near bursting. "Och, I've missed these old stones, more than ever I thought possible."

His mother Catreena slipped free of his arms with a smile, before tugging impatiently at his hand. "Yer timing's as good as it ever was. The evening meal is about tae be served, and the cook has made all yer favorite things. Including spiced honey cakes fer the sweet."

Ian laughed. "I'd never say nay tae a spiced honey cake, especially from our kitchens. There's nay one on the continent that could make them half as good."

The servants hurried down to collect his things while Ian followed his parents inside, to the worn, heavy oak table that sat at the top of the Great Hall. He caressed the sturdy wood as he settled into his old, familiar seat. The oak was worn smooth with countless meals and memories, and it fit his frame as if he'd only just risen from the table yesterday, rather than several years ago.

He watched the clansmen trickle in. Many where whiter than he recalled, with more wrinkles and scars. It was odd, somewhat disconcerting, to see the marks of time passed on faces of men, lads, and lasses that he'd known since his boyhood. Odd, and bittersweet.

The servants began to bring out the food, and Ian frowned, scanning the hall for a face he had been expecting to see. Once the servants had left, he leaned toward his father's chair. "Where is Thor? I dinnae see him."

His father made a wry expression. "Aye, ye dinnae, and he'll nae be thankin' us fer it, fer he wanted tae see ye when ye arrived home. But there was a small matter tae be dealt with on the border, and I couldnae send anyone else. He should be back on the morrow."

Ian nodded his understanding and sat back. He regretted that Thor wasn't there to greet him, but ever since his departure for the continent, his childhood friend had served as his father's second-in-command and war leader. If there was trouble on the borders of the clan, it was Thor's duty to go if the laird could not.

Not that Ian felt his father unable to fight. Laird Tad MacBean was still whole and hale as any man with his seasons could be. But his hair was fully silver, and he moved slower than he once had. He'd told Ian during his last visit to the continent that the healer had told him that his heart was not as strong as it once had been and that too much strain was not good for him. It was not a great concern, but something to be aware of.

That was why he'd bid Ian to return and claim the heirship and the duties of leadership until Tad could formally step down and pass the lairdship to his son. It was easier this way, rather than Ian coming to it suddenly, if his father was either killed in battle or struck down by some illness.

Better that Tad MacBean spend his elder years in peace and joy with his beloved wife, rather than saddled with the stresses and dangers of being the Laird of Clan MacBean. Besides, it would allow him to still be available to advise Ian and to sit as Elder in the Clan Council. The clan would not be entirely bereft of his leadership and wisdom.

Ian could only hope the rest of the clan would see it that way. After so long an absence, he was glad to be home, but he felt the differences keenly and he feared he would not be the only one.

"Ye're too somber, me son," Tad thumped him on the shoulder. "I ken ye have yer concerns, as do we all, but this is a time fer joy an' homecoming, nae moroseness." The older man smiled. "Enjoy the feast an' leave the thoughts for afterward."

"Ye're right, as ever." Ian brought a smile to his lips and toasted his father with the tankard of mead at his elbow. "Tae yer health, Faither, and the fortunes o' Clan MacBean. May we grow and prosper."

"May we grow and prosper."

All those within earshot raised their cups in response, then drank deep. Ian did as well, then turned his attention fully to his meal. After so long away, it would be poor showing and absolute folly not to do full justice to the work of the MacBean cooks and scullery staff.

After the feast, Ian joined his parents in one of the downstairs sitting rooms. A servant poured whisky for the men and strong hot tea for Ian's mother Catreena. Once they were all seated, Tad spoke. "There's been some happenin's since we sent the letter tae ye, and 'tis best ye were aware o' them."

"Have ye received any aid fer the crops an' the farmers?" Ian's glance drifted to the window. He'd ridden through MacBean lands for most of his journey since landing, and he'd seen the poor remnants of the fields, some of them still full of water from the rains that had washed away their crops.

"We've some. A neighborin' clan has a feud on the border, an' asked fer us tae care fer one o' their own lasses while the men see tae the fightin'. We've taken her as a guest here, an' she brought with her some much needed grain and gold from her kinfolk."

"That's a help, tae be sure. Is she…"

"She's nae the lass we were considerin' fer yer betrothal, nay. Unfortunately, the clan we hope tae forge an alliance marriage with couldnae be here taenight. 'Tis hoped they'll be able tae visit within a few days time." Catreena smiled warmly at Ian. "I hope with all me heart ye'll find the girl a pleasing match."

Ian shrugged noncommittally. So long as the lass wasn't a harridan, he suspected the marriage would be tolerable. But harridan or no, he would find a way to live with her, and do his duty by her clan and his. That was the way of alliance marriages, and he was no callow, naive youth to think otherwise.

He'd lost that innocence long ago. He no longer expected, or even hoped, to wed for love. At best, he supposed he might hope for a wife with whom he could hold a decent conversation, and who was pretty enough to make bedding her more of a pleasure than a duty.

"Daes the Council ken ye're lookin' fer a marriage alliance?" He hadn't thought to ask before.

"They dinnae. Nay more than they ken that I'm thinkin' o' steppin' down. I wanted ye here afore we spoke o' it tae the clan." Tad responded easily. "'Twill be easier."

"I cannae argue that." Ian nodded. He was actually relieved. He'd feared his father would want to step down immediately upon his return. The chance to relearn old haunts and reacquaint himself with the clan was a welcome one.

"I didnae think ye would. Likewise, we planned tae delay announcin' the betrothal and alliance until ye've met the lass and decided whether ye get on well taegether."

"Thank ye." Ian heaved a sigh of relief. "I'd hate tae have tae disappoint the Council."

A knock on the door interrupted his mother's words. A moment later, the door opened, and Ian just missed spilling his drink. Or shattering the glass.

For one moment, he could only stand there, staring at the woman who'd shattered his world six years before. Then he found his voice with a snarl. "What in the devil's name is she daein' in me home?"

CHAPTER TWO

*L*avinia Shaw winced and brushed back a tendril of auburn hair.

Och, I kent seeing him again was goin' tae be bad...

She'd tried to avoid meeting Ian that night. She'd known he was returning. Lady MacBean had told her days ago that her son was coming home. She'd pleaded a headache to avoid the welcoming feast, after she'd heard the bells toll for Ian's return, and she'd hoped he'd retire shortly after the meal.

Unfortunately, it seemed her hopes were in vain. And it was clear that six years had not dulled his anger even the slightest.

They hadn't dulled the ache in her heart either. She pushed the thought away, and focused her attention on the laird and lady of the castle, both of whom looked very surprised at their son's outburst.

As well they might. She had never told them about her relationship with Ian, or the events of that fateful day six years ago, and she very much doubted Ian had told them either.

She took a deep breath and forced herself to stay calm. "Forgive me, me laird, me lady. It appears that I've interrupted ye…"

"Dinnae be silly. We were just telling Ian that ye're staying with us as a guest." Catreena waved her forward and gestured her toward a seat. "Please. Come in. Sit down a moment."

Faced with a direct request, there was little she could do. Lavinia crossed the room and sank into the chair Lady Catreena had indicated, acutely aware of the burning glare leveled at her back with every step.

Catreena poured her some tea, and Lavinia took it with both hands, glad for something to keep her occupied and ensure that no one could see how her hands were beginning to shake.

Oh, but it was hard to see Ian again. And to see him glaring at her with such intense dislike, at least for a moment, until his expression smoothed over into one of cold indifference.

"I didnae expect tae see ye, Lady Shaw." Ian's voice was icy, the sullenness of it stabbing like knives.

Lavinia shook her head, and tried to offer what conciliation she could. "Aye, I realize that. And I didnae intend tae intrude on yer homecoming…"

A cool, challenging smile curved one corner of Ian's mouth, and an eyebrow rose in what might almost be considered a mocking expression. "What brings ye here, if it wasnae to welcome me home after so many years?" The words were quiet but forceful, with no sign of yielding. It was all Lavinia could do not to flinch.

"Ian." Laird MacBean's voice was quiet, but stern, and Ian subsided with another sullen glance. "Lavinia is here under the protection o' the clan, an' whatever is goin' on now, yer maither and I would have ye treat her as a welcome guest." The laird's expression softened slightly. "I ken children grow apart, but ye were friends when ye were younger. I recall ye rather enjoyed yer time together."

Inwardly, Lavinia winced, knowing the reminder of their childhood closeness would be unwelcome, even if Laird MacBean had no understanding of why.

Instead of arguing with his father's words, however, Ian turned to him with a question. "An' why can her own clan nae protect her? We've surely enemies enough o' our own."

"Clan Shaw is besieged by Clan Comyn. Laird Comyn once demanded me maither's hand in marriage, an she refused him tae wed me faither. Now he attacks us. Me parents feared I'd be tak'n and used as a hostage against me faither, so they asked yer kin tae shelter me."

She'd told the story more than once, but it got no easier with the telling. Speaking the words made her mouth sour, as if she'd swallowed bile.

Bard Comyn, her mother's old suitor. Why he refused to accept her mother's rejection, she didn't know. No more did she know why he'd chosen to attack her clan now… though her mother feared thatit was Laird Comyn's intent to take either mother or daughter, or mayhap both, by force. It was as if a demon's madness and obsession had overtaken him.

That was why her parents had sent her away. A bitter rival might be reasoned with, but if bitterness had become madness, and desire had turned to obsession, then there was no speech on earth that would protect her.

"I see." It was just as well she'd not hoped Ian might soften toward her, because his scowl remained deep as it had before. "So we're tae be yer shield against yer maither's jilted lover. I suppose I shouldnae be surprised, seein'..."

"Ian." This time, it was Lady Catreena's voice that cut through his words. "Why are ye in such a mood?"

Ian's lip curled. Then he drained the rest of his drink and rose from his seat. "Ye'll forgive me, Maither, Faither, but I'm more wearied than I thought from the long ride. I think 'tis best I seek my rest fer now, as I am nae the best company at the moment."

Catreena and Tad's features both softened. "O' course." Catreena rose and embraced her son. "I should have realized. We've prepared yer rooms already, an' set one o' the men-at-arms tae serve ye. Camlin is his name."

Ian grunted. "Camlin... I dinnae ken him."

"He's a young lad, just finished his training as a page, and nae yet ready tae be considered a warrior, or trained as a messenger. But he's quick and quiet and does his work well. I think he'll suit ye fine," Tad smiled.

"I'll trust yer word on it," Ian bowed.

Catreena, however, was frowning at Lavinia. "Ye look pale, Lavinia. Dae ye still have the headache from afore?"

Och, nay, she cannae be thinking...

Lavina forced herself to smile slightly. "'Tis mostly gone, thanks tae Arabella's tonics, but I willnae deny feelin' a little wearied and worn still."

"Then mayhap ye should get some more rest. Yer room is nae far from the one we've prepared fer Ian, so perhaps he can walk with ye, in case ye start tae feel faint again?" Catreena smiled. "'Twill give me some peace o' mind, kenning someone's with ye."

Lavinia bit the inside of her cheek to keep from groaning aloud. She understood that Lady MacBean was only trying to restore peace between them, but the older lady couldn't know what had happened between herself and Ian.

She hadn't wanted to shatter his heart any more than she'd wanted to break her own. But she'd known then that Ian was in danger so long as he stayed, and that he'd never leave unless she went with him. And that, she was certain, wouldn't have been permitted. Not then, with his clan's future so uncertain. So she'd done what had to be done, to keep Ian safe, never mind the cost to both of them. She'd broken his heart and sent him away.

She knew Ian was unlikely to forgive her, let alone forget what she'd done, any time soon. She understood his anger. Even so, the thought of trying to make peace with someone who clearly had no desire to do the same…

She didn't want to. Ian was already giving her an angry glare, as if he thought she'd planned the whole thing. Still, what else could she do? She couldn't pretend she was fine, not after suggesting the opposite. There was nothing she really needed to speak to Laird and Lady MacBean about. There was no real reason for her to stay, and no way she could avoid Ian's company without causing offense.

With a sigh that she hoped none of the others in the room could see, Lavinia forced her mouth into a demure smile and nodded. "As ye will." She opened the door and inclined her head to Ian with as much grace as she could muster. "If ye'll come with me…"

"I ken the way tae me own quarters." Ian brushed past her, mouth set in a scowl black as a thundercloud.

Lavinia took a deep breath and followed him, hoping against hope as she fell into step beside him.

I ken 'tis me fault we parted badly... but even so, if we must share the same building fer who kens how long, surely there must be some way tae make things civil between us at least.

The words echoed in her mind like a prayer, but listen though she might, no answer was forthcoming. Ian's scowl altered not a whit as he strode along the corridor beside her.

It seemed that if peace was to come, it would have to be Lavinia's doing - but she had not the slightest idea of how to go about it, nor how to mend the breach caused so long before.

CHAPTER THREE

Ian scowled at the corridor walls as he made his way toward the family wing. He'd hoped to find some respite from Lavinia Shaw's presence in leaving, but of course it couldn't be that simple. Of course, his mother would choose to have him 'escort' her to her rooms, as if Lavinia was even ill. She looked healthy enough, so far as Ian was concerned.

And I dinnae care either way. It shouldnae matter tae me if she's well or nae.

He knew that in truth, sick or not, his mother wanted them to resolve whatever had happened between them.

Ian forced himself to look away, and focused his attention on the hall, trying to see what might have changed while he was gone. If he couldn't send Lavinia away, then at least he could keep his eyes on the path in front of him, and try to ignore her presence.

Not that Lavinia made it easy. Despite his best efforts, he

couldn't help but notice certain things as she strode along beside him.

She wore her auburn hair longer than he recalled it, braided back in a simple but elegant style. The years had matured her figure, adding subtle curves and changing the lines from those of a young lass to those of a lady. She was also more graceful than he recalled - her steps quick and light.

Beautiful and graceful, with more assurance than she'd had six years before. Lavinia had grown into the beauty her younger years had promised, and it made his heart clench and heat tingle through his veins. His chest ached, the memories of sweet, long summer days and gentle, teasing kisses hovering like ghosts around him.

Ian bit his lip and willed the ghosts away, trying once more to focus on the walls around him. He tried to look for new tapestries, new artwork, even new cracks or patchwork in the stones - anything to avoid looking at the woman walking along beside him.

It worked, until they ascended to the upper floor of the castle. "I heard ye were in France. What was it like, over on the Continent?"

The question startled him so much he nearly lost his footing. Ian glared at her. "'Twas nae home."

He'd hoped to put her off with his brusque manner, but Lavinia was just as stubborn as he remembered. "How were the French wines? I have nae had them often."

Yes he had. Not that he'd cared. He'd never liked wine much in any case, and after her... "Prefer ale."

"Och." Her voice was soft. "What o'... did ye compete in tournaments? Or were ye committed tae other things?"

Ian grunted. He wasn't about to tell her that he'd spent six seasons on the front, throwing his rage at the French until his father had come to see him and gently reminded him that he'd been sent to France to protect his life, not endanger it. Nor was he going to tell her how many tournaments he'd won, or lasses he'd bedded in an attempt to forget her.

Lavinia didn't need to know about his life since they'd parted. By her own word, it was none of her concern.

"Did ye travel then? We used tae speak o' travelin' when we were younger. Ye always said…"

"I kent what I said. Dinnae need ye remindin' me." Ian snarled the words.

"Ye neednae be rude. I'm only tryin' tae make conversation." He could hear the spark of frustration in her voice, and a part of him revelled in it.

"I dinnae want conversation." They turned the corner into the family wing, and Ian made his way toward the door that had been his ever since he'd been moved from the nursery chambers as a wee lad.

"I'll bid ye good night then." Lavinia stepped past him, down the hall to another chamber nearby.

Ian grunted in reply. He knew what courtesy would have demanded, but he was in no mood for courtesy, no matter what his parents had said. They might convince him to tolerate Lavinia's presence, but nothing would make him do so gracefully or with any more than the absolute minimum of acceptance.

He was about to enter his chambers when he heard Lavinia mutter under her breath. "Send a boor abroad an' he's still as surly as a scorned bastard, it seems."

Enough was enough. Ian spun around on his heel. "What was that?"

Lavinia flushed, her cheeks burning as she realized Ian had heard her. She hadn't even really meant to speak aloud, but his behavior had been so grating...

She knew she had hurt him. She didn't expect forgiveness and pleasantness after what had passed between them. But surely it was not too much to expect some common courtesy!

Anger, she could accept. But rudeness, worse than any barbarian lout might be expected to display, that she would not tolerate, not even from Ian MacBean.

Still, she hadn't intended for him to hear the words she'd spoken in a fit of pique.

Ian was staring at her, an eyebrow raised in challenge, daring her to say the words to his face. Once, she might have. But now, she was a guest in his home, and in any case, it was hardly appropriate to behave like a harridan after complaining about Ian's rudeness.

The proper thing would be to apologize, but she couldn't bring herself to do that either. It wasn't as if he didn't deserve a sharp word or two, behind his back or not.

She was still trying to think of a proper response when Ian smirked, tipped his head in a gesture of 'now I've got ye' that she knew all too well, and turned to enter his quarters.

Two could play at that game. Lavinia tossed her head, opened the door in front of her, and stalked inside, shutting it firmly behind her.

She promptly tripped over a bucket, and clattered into something that felt like a broom or a mop handle. "Ow!" She stumbled a few more paces forward, then caught herself on some shelves. The scent of heather and lavender met her nose, even as her fingertips encountered soft linens.

Och, nay. Lavinia winced, mortified at the realization that, in the heat of the moment, she'd chosen the wrong door and walked herself, very neatly and energetically, into the storage room that housed the extra linens and cleaning supplies for the family wing.

Now she was standing in the dark, toes aching, shin throbbing, and utterly embarrassed at her own mistake. She couldn't believe she'd allowed herself to become so flustered, and by Ian MacBean of all people.

I really should have simply repeated me words tae his face, and had it out with him. 'Twould surely have been less humiliating than this.

With a sigh, Lavinia turned and grasped for the door handle. At the very least, she could take some small comfort in the knowledge that Ian had already gone into his rooms. She wouldn't have to endure the additional embarrassment of having him catch her exiting the linen closet and seeking her own rooms. It was a small mercy.

She twisted the handle and pushed the door. The handle turned freely enough, but the door remained in place, even when she shoved at it, then tugged at it with all her strength.

She shoved at it again, but it didn't budge. It was only then that she recalled her maid had mentioned this closet in passing a few days ago... something about the door having warped, or the wood swelling with age, and needing to have the village carpenter up to look at it.

Whatever the cause, her predicament was the same. No matter how she tried to force it, the door remained fastened in place, as surely as if it had been nailed shut. Lavinia pushed and tugged for several minutes, until she was breathless, then slumped against the wall with a sigh of frustration.

I didnae think the day could get any worse after seein' Ian again after years, but it seems the gods and gremlins are determined tae have a fair good laugh at me expense taeday.

'Tis truly been a wretched day. I wish I'd stayed abed!

But wishing she'd stayed in her bed where it was safe wouldn't get her out of the closet. She considered trying to pry the door open with a broom handle, but there wasn't enough light to see what she was doing. Besides, she couldn't hold the handle down and attempt to shove the door with a handle... she didn't have enough hands.

Lavinia wrenched at the door, then set a shoulder to it and shoved with all her might. It didn't yield so much as an inch. She felt along the edges, for any gap that she might wedge something in - if she could find anything to use as a wedge - but there was nothing. The wood was swollen with age and the dampness of the season, and there were no gaps that her fingers could detect. At least, there were none big enough for her to use for her purposes, and nothing, when she explored the closet by feel, that was suitable for use as a tool.

Clean linens, a broom and a bucket. There were candles, but no spark-tools with which to light them.

She was stuck, until a maid or someone passing by the door heard her and helped her escape.

She was just considering whether she might create a makeshift pallet of the clean linens when she heard footsteps.

Lavinia bolted for the door and began hammering on it. "In here! Whoever ye are... in here! The door is jammed shut, an' I cannae get out! Please... open the door! I dinnae wish tae be stuck in here all night! Please!"

She heard the footsteps stop. Heard a shuffling sound as whoever was in the corridor returned to the door. She sighed with relief.

Then the person on the other side of the door spoke, and any sense of relief she felt was wiped away at the sound of the last voice in the world she wanted to hear. "Who's there?"

Lavinia groaned under her breath. "'Tis me, Lavinia..."

The voice on the other side of the door was none other than Ian's.

Ian stared at the door. He'd only left his rooms with the intention of seeking out another bottle of mead to enjoy in the privacy of his chambers when he'd heard the woman shouting from the other side of the heavy oak door.

The heavy oak door that, if memory served him, he'd last seen Lavinia standing in front of.

It was curiosity more than anything else that prompted him to walk over. "Who's there?"

Silence. Then a low sound, that might or might not have been words, followed by a plaintive "Please, can ye open the door? 'Tis stuck."

The voice was most definitely Lavinia's. Ian smirked to himself. "Aye. I can. But what are ye doin' in there?"

A pause. Then, "I wanted some extra candles, but the door shut behind me, and it willnae open."

He sighed. "Give me a moment." He grasped the handle, turned, and pulled hard.

The door barely budged. Ian blinked. He'd been sure Lavinia was exaggerating her predicament to force him to speak to her. He pulled again, with a little more force.

The door remained in place. Ian scowled at it. "Are ye sure it isnae locked?"

Indignation and frustration were clear in Lavina's voice when she responded. "O' course I'm certain! This closet cannae be locked from the inside."

It was a valid point, but the truth did little to ease Ian's annoyance. He growled under his breath, then turned his attention to the door. It was old, and it appeared that either it had become crooked in its frame, or the wood had swelled to render it difficult to move.

He tugged at it again, this time pulling until his muscles were strained with the effort, and still it didn't budge. He stopped, panting for breath. "How in the devil's name did ye get in there to begin with?"

The door was thick, but not thick enough to muffle Lavinia's huff of exasperation. "I dinnae ken! I suppose it must nae have been fully closed, and I didnae notice."

Ian was tempted to make some sort of remark, but decided against it. Instead, he studied the door more closely.

He might have to break it down, if he couldn't get it open. Ian groaned. His first night home, and he might have to take an axe to a door – or take it off the hinges. He wasn't sure which was worse, the idea of damaging the door or admitting that he hadn't the strength to force it open by conventional means.

After a moment, he decided to try once more. If he failed, he'd seek out someone to assist him, but for now... one more attempt.

He grabbed the door, braced himself, then wrenched hard, jerking backward the way he would if he'd accidentally stuck his hand in a fire. There was a moment of resistance, an ache in his shoulder... and the door came free, opening so suddenly he staggered and almost fell on his arse.

Lavinia emerged from the room, candle in hand and hair disheveled, just as he recovered his footing.

Ian smirked as he took hold of the door and offered her a small bow. "Shall I hold the door to ensure ye dinnae get trapped again, Miss Shaw?"

Lavinia heard the mocking note in his voice, as he'd intended her to. Her expression darkened further, anger washing across her features as her hands tightened on the candles.

Good. Be angry with me. 'Tis only fair ye feel some o' the frustration and fury I once felt toward ye. Besides, if I must be around ye, I'd rather ye nae be tryin' tae be friends with me again. I walked that road with ye once, and I'll nae be walkin' it again.

DO YOU WANT TO READ MORE?

To read more, scan this QR code with your phone!

ABOUT THE AUTHOR

Shona Thompson is an American based author of Historical Scottish Romance. She spent her student years in the majestic city of Edinburgh, where she fell in love with the history, the legends and the people of Scotland.

Her own Highlander husband was the one who inspired her and awoke her passion of writing. He became her muse, and all her love stories are dedicated to him.

Note from Shona

I'm always happy to communicate with my readers. So if you want to stay up to date with my newest releases and win little treats, please subscribe to my newsletter, and you will always be the first to know about my newest Scottish novel.

To subscribe to my newsletter, scan this QR code with your phone!

Thank you.

Your friend,

Shona ⚔

~

      If you want to keep in touch...

      You can follow me on Social Media.

Printed in Dunstable, United Kingdom